For Gwen

Robert Kerr

LASZLO

AUSTIN MACAULEY PUBLISHERS™

LONDON • CAMBRIDGE • NEW YORK • SHARJAH

A CIP catalogue record for this title is available from the British Library.

ISBN 9781528995894 (Paperback)
ISBN 9781528995900 (ePub e-book)

www.austinmacauley.com

First Published (2020)
Austin Macauley Publishers Ltd
25 Canada Square
Canary Wharf
London
E14 5LQ

Chapter One

I've been working in these undertakers since I left school. I was sixteen then, and I'm thirty now. That's all my adult life; working full time at H Partridge & Sons Funeral Directors. My best years so far, and I've been surrounded by stiffs. In truth, the perks of the job far outweigh the negative aspects, which is why, I suppose, I haven't got off my arse and found another job. It's quiet here, which suits me. I play my music while I work and I live pretty stress free. And I get to work with Henry Partridge and his son Nicholas Partridge. There is another son, William Partridge, but he didn't like the smell of embalming fluid so he fucked off somewhere else. I've heard them mention his name but they don't discuss him with me. I'm not sure how much either of them likes me, but we get on, and they know I do a good job. Some days I don't get much conversation out of them at all, but they mainly talk about the undertaking business, so I don't feel like I'm missing out. Henry and Nicholas were old when I started working here, but are ancient now. They're so old that they look the same age. When I started, Henry was grey and stooped, and he's the same now. Though he does have more hair growing out of his ears now; two thickets growing in tandem. The extra weight can't help the stoop. Nicholas is taller, not because he doesn't stoop, but he keeps his back straight nonetheless. Both have eyes like hawks when it comes to money. They monitor the contents of all bottles, boxes and cans. They scrutinise every penny going out, and hoard all the pennies coming in. I get paid what I should, and they treat me kindly, but I've never been invited to a family do. I only met Henry's wife once before she died, and then again after she arrived here. I've met Nicholas's wife many times, she comes in here from time to time. She's ancient too, so I try to be sweet to her, but she's enormously annoying. If I see her, I duck out the backyard to the shed, but sometimes she sneaks up on me. I don't know how, she moves really slowly and can barely see. But she'll trap me in a conversation and there's no escape. Everything I try, she ignores. She just keeps talking. Curtains, Mrs Riley's gout, flans, her grandson Simon, the latest daytime quiz show, washing machine tablets, Mrs Pearson's new prosthetic eye, the list is actually endless. As long as I get to the shed, I'm all right. The garden is about ten metres across and eight metres long, and there isn't a blade of grass in it. It's brown and dry with bits of gravel lying around. It's not a place to entertain friends; it's just used for storage. There are a few different coloured waste bins and some discarded items under a tarpaulin. I can't remember what they are. The other end of the garden is where I'm interested in; there's a beautiful apple tree in the right corner, and next to it, in the left corner is my shed. It was going to be pulled down and scrapped, but I persuaded the Partridges to let me have it. I have decorated it with style. There is an armchair, a bin and a table upon which I have placed an ashtray.

I'm walking through the building, heading to my office after having lunch in the kitchen. 'Laszlo,' I hear the strained voice of Henry behind me.

'Yes Henry,' I turn around and see he's enjoying a stoop as usual. He's almost side-on and I look at the thicket growing out of his left ear. The hair is so dense in there, it's a wonder any sound can get in, but Henry can hear a sparrow cough from half a mile away. He has one of those old men hairstyles. It recedes past his crown and down the back of the head, past the top of his ears; it keeps going, until it stops with an inch to spare. He has an unbroken line of hair arching up and over his ears; it's like a beard on the back of his head. I have been tempted to draw a face above it; it would freak people out. But he'd need to be asleep, and as old as he is, he doesn't have afternoon naps. I'd have to break into his house at night, and that's just silly. What if he wakes up and I'm in his bedroom? What the fuck could I possibly say? The only plausible explanation would be to tell him that I was going to draw a face on the back of his head; and I'd have the pen in my hand as proof. I'd get the sack, but he wouldn't think I was a pervert. I decided against it.

'There is a new arrival at Saint Catherine's. Are you able to collect it?'

I have a mate who works at the morgue, Con, and sometimes it's better if we chat where there are less people around. There aren't many visitors to the morgue, and the residents don't mind our conversations. 'No problem Henry, I'll collect it. I'll head over there straight away.'

'Marvellous, I'll fetch the paperwork.' He shuffles off in the direction of the office.

Aubrey is the official driver for the Partridges, but he's two hundred thousand years old as well, so he only works part time. He's been with the Partridges longer than I have, used to be full time, but as age has had its wicked way with him I've taken over day-to-day driving duties. Aubrey takes care of formal occasions, taking the wheel for funerals while I'm passenger and pallbearer. Traditionally the driver can be a bearer too, and Aubrey used to be, but he gave it up some time ago. He's as fit as a fiddler's elbow, unlike most men his age who would struggle to lift a tin of soup above their heads, but lugging coffins around is a stretch. And he still drives well; he's only required to go at twenty miles per hour, but I'd be happy to accompany him if he had a job delivering furniture to Inverness.

I'd best head to the office, reduce the amount of floor Henry has to cover in giving me the paperwork. There are stacks of papers on the desk, and one loose sheet. He picks it up and extends his arm towards me as I enter the room. He hasn't even managed to raise his arm much higher than waist height, so I reach over and take it from him. I give him a great, big smile, 'See you later Henry,' and I'm out of there. The hearse is parked in the front yard, which is tastefully decorated with trees and various types of shrubbery. The area has five visitors' car parking spaces, but the main area in front of the building is reserved for the hearse. I jump in and key the ignition; a tune blasts out of the speakers, mid-song. I have a habit of forgetting to turn the music off when I park, so I sit here boogieing to "Foggy Road" by Burning Spear. Aubrey hates it when I do that, says it scares the shit out of him sometimes. He's a quality guy Aubrey, I like his company; he tells me some good old stories. Not just about funerals, though he does have some funny stories there, but about his life. He's put himself about a bit in his time, and remembered to live his life. I enjoy the days he works.

I started work here as an apprentice, which meant I got to do all the shit jobs, and they got to pay me next to fuck all. I did that for six months, and then they tried to get me to sign up for another six-month apprenticeship. I refused. I told them I wanted a full time, permanent contract. I said I'd accept the going rate, which I thought was pretty decent of me. During those six months, I'd kept my nose clean, arrived on time every day, and worked really hard. They gave me the contract, and I've been here ever since. Fourteen fucking years, be careful what you ask for. I wouldn't mind a bit of adventure in my life, everything's so pedestrian. Slower than pedestrian! At work people don't move, or walk incredibly slowly. When visitors arrive to view their deceased, they too walk unhurriedly. You rarely see someone striding through the building. Maybe the grieving find it more respectful to walk below average walking speed, maybe their legs are sapped of energy through supporting sobbing relatives who look ready to topple over. Well, gentlemen, you'd better regain some of that leg strength by the time we're carrying the fucking coffin.

After my apprenticeship finished, I was employed at Partridges as a funeral services operative. I've always been Aubrey's passenger on funeral days, and we used to be bearers together. We have a good laugh, but whenever families are around we've always been fantastically good at hitting the required level of respect and empathy. Aubrey would bring the stiffs to the prep room, and the Partridges were responsible for the embalming and preparation of the body. At first, my role was preparing the coffins; fitting and lining them. After a while Henry allowed me to dress the

8

'Yeah, why not.' He heads over to the bench near the fire escape to fetch his bag. I look around the room, there's one empty table and two occupied. The tenants are hidden under sheets. There are twelve chambers at the end of the room, all with their steel doors closed and their chrome plated latches clasped firmly shut. There's plenty of equipment covering various surfaces, yet there is a serene sense of emptiness.

Con's back and unzipping his bag. 'As requested,' he says, flashing me one his smiles. 'Half an ounce of super lemon haze, and a Q of Lebanese hash.' He hands me the two items, both wrapped extremely tightly in cling film.

'I see you're still keeping the cling film business buoyant.' I can smell it through the layers of film; smells good. I hand him the correct amount of money and he puts it straight into his pocket. He's never counted it in front of me, but you can bet he counts it as soon as I'm out the room. Just to make sure. If I'd underpaid him the first time we made a deal, he wouldn't have trusted me after that. I have no desire other than to keep him sweet; he always has good stuff. I put the two parcels in my pocket.

'Are you going to Anton's party on Saturday?' I know why he's asking me, he's after a bit more business. 'Do you need anything for the party?' He flashes me another smile.

'A couple of grams of charlie should be fine for me,' I tell him and watch him smile as he registers more money coming my way. I don't normally do coke. It's too expensive and it doesn't do much. All it does for me is make me drink more, talk to people I don't want to talk to. I only buy it so that I drink more. Usually, if I have a skinful, and a few biftas, I feel quite tired. But with a few sniffs of coke, I'll be going all fucking night. And you never know, Rosie might be there. I met Rosie last Saturday down The Wooden [...]. She was with Ingle, he was acting like they were [...], but that's not what I heard. Just friends from work to me, and I'm taking that as a signal. That fucking [...] kept trying to talk to me all night, and I couldn't get [...] Rosie for long. Of course, when we did find the [...] to chat, Ingle was quick to interrupt too. I want to

bodies. I'd been asking for ages and he finally relented. It's nothing sexual, I don't find dead bodies erotic. At the time I wanted more interesting duties, but underneath that, I wanted to be involved in the process of making them look peaceful to their loved ones.

I'd been working for the Partridges about two years when I got an itch to try something different. I spoke to them about it, and they said they'd be sad to see me go. I didn't think they'd miss my personality, but they would miss my work. I don't know why I did it, but I suggested being trained up as an embalmer. They were resistant at first, and I was about to take it personally, but then I realised it would cost money. Tight old fuckers. We agreed to pay half each towards the two-year course I took, and for the membership to the British Institute of Embalmers. I'm good at it, and I enjoy it. It helps the Partridges out as it eases their workload and allows them more time to devote to stocktaking and adding up numbers. No two stiffs are the same, they all present their own challenges. I delight in making these lifeless shapes look recognisable. I can't restore them to their former vibrant selves. I can't get them dancing around the Chapel for one final fandango, but I can make their loved ones' experience less traumatic. Fucking well done me.

A few years later, I suggested to the Partridges that I study a Diploma in Funeral Services. I could then be a member of the British Institute of Funeral Directors, and would be eligible to become a partner in the business. They were adamant that it was a poor idea, and became a little anxious whenever I brought it up. They would change the subject as quick as they could, but oddly would talk about things I'd never heard them speak of before—the paintings of Frank Bassoon, tiger moths, Brazilian gold mines. Then they would stampede out of the room at half a mile an hour. I brought it up every now and then for about six months. I had no intention of doing the Diploma, but I had a fun six months.

I swing the vehicle out of the premises and head in the direction of the morgue. I've done this route so many times. I prefer heading out on Winchester Road, which leads out of town towards the hills. I avoid driving through town this way, and I get to see a bit of greenery as I drive past Gravely Woods and the fields that extend beyond it towards Howard Manor. I cruise all the way there, it wouldn't be good for the hearse to be seen speeding. Ambulances can tear around town, but a hearse? It's a bit late by then. Besides, Henry and Nicholas know it takes as long as it takes to fetch a new arrival from its current location to our prep room. I keep the windows up in town when I'm listening to music; I don't think Mrs Pearson would appreciate me driving past her blasting out tunes. Now that I'm driving along the outskirts of town, I've got the windows down and the wind in my face.

When I first worked here, I'd go easy with the undertaker talk when I was chatting to a woman down the pub. I tended to get a few funny looks, and the usual questions: 'Isn't it depressing', 'Isn't it weird touching dead bodies'. I decided to put that conversation off until she'd got to know me a bit. The idea being that she wouldn't find me creepy working with dead bodies if she liked me. I slow down as I reach a junction and turn left onto Steeple Street, and hit the button for the windows to slide up. Saint Catherine's Hospital is on the other side of Oakley, but there's little traffic at this time of day. I wouldn't bring the subject up, but if she asked what I did for a living, I informed the lucky woman that I was a pastry chef, or a plumber, or a postman. After a few dates, when it was clear we liked each other, I'd confess. She would invariably tell me that I was silly for thinking she'd mind me working with dead bodies. She'd ask the usual questions, but wouldn't want to talk about it for long. We'd see each other for a while, until it suited us to part. I'm not a player, I just haven't settled down yet. I drive past Oakley Park and the row of shops selling all manner of things to eat, and take the turning that leads to the hospital. I did have a few things thrown at me though; shoes, hands, bottles. I've been told I'm a dirty liar, but it was only ever meant to be a temporary fib. I remember one woman was keen for me to have a look at her dishwasher; what was I supposed to do? I don't know anything about dishwashers. That's when I realised how ridiculous my

behaviour was; what a stupid situation to put myself in. I promised myself I'd tell the truth from then on, and I have, and that was a long time ago. Here's Saint Catherine's, the morgue is behind the West Wing. I slow to five miles per hour and glide around the front of the enormous glass fronted hospital towards the morgue. It's not like I told any woman I was a doctor or a lawyer; that would have just been bullshitting. I kept my professional untruth within my income bracket: bank clerk, dental nurse and taxidermist. No, not taxidermist, that wouldn't have worked. I also kept it slightly boring, so she wouldn't ask too many questions, like estate agent or recruitment consultant. Imagine if I'd said I was personal doctor for that singer, Tiffany Walnut? That would have invited a barrage of questions. I pull into a parking space outside the morgue and kill the tunes, then cut the engine. Fucking great time to remember to kill the music, I forget again the next time Aubrey drives the car.

I'm walking down the main corridor in the hospital towards the office and the morgue. I see Doug in the corridor and give him a wave, which he returns. Doug's a morgue attendant, he's been here years. He still walks to work every day. I get on fine with him, but I'm here to see Con, so I head into the morgue. Con's a few years older than me and has been a morgue attendant for some time. He's gone from one job to another, not really enjoying them. One of those jobs was a hospital porter, and that's when he decided to train up to be a morgue attendant, and he's been doing it ever since; I can relate to that. He came to Saint Catherine's a few years ago, after Bradley. I like Con, we get on well, but he can be also a bit of a dick sometimes, but he has a heart fantastic. I see him at the far side of the morgue and shout, 'Hey Con.' He looks up and smiles. 'Hey Laz,' he calls back. Con is short, but he has endless energy and moves with ease. He has a tangle of black hair that he thinks makes him irresistible. We exchange pleasantries and he asks me if know if Rosie's going to the party but I'm not going to ask Ingle. He'll definitely try and put the kibosh on any romance developing between me and the beautiful Rosie. 'Are you going?' I ask him as he's putting his bag back.

'Definitely.' He'll be high and looking for company, and looking to sell more bifta and coke too.

'We're meeting in The Talented Crow at eight, and heading to the party from there.'

'Who else is going?'

'The usual crowd, Eddie, Dalton, Lucy, Ingle—' He cuts me off; he knows who the usual crowd are. I invited Con out for drinks with my mates a few times when he arrived in Stumpton, and he's been hanging around with us on and off since.

'Is Miriam going?' he asks, not attempting to hide his lust. 'She was all over you down The Wooden Octopus last weekend, and you didn't make a move. What's wrong with you Laz?'

'I'm not interested in Miriam. She gives me the creeps, just wants to talk about dead bodies all the time. I have a feeling that if we fucked, she'd want me on my back, remaining perfectly still with my eyes open, staring beyond her into space.' He's laughing, but I'm being quite serious. 'Who was she anyway?'

'A friend of Binky's from work apparently. Well, if you're not man enough to give Miriam what she wants, then I shall be only too happy to provide that service for her.' He gives another smile, but this one's a bit pervy.

'You're welcome.' I give him a sarcy smile in return. Con has a favourite fib he tells to women to deflect from the whole touching dead bodies thing that some people seem to have a problem with. He says he's an ornithologist, specialising in the conservation of barn owls. He's researched the species and knows fucking loads about them. Last weekend, he told this to Miriam and she wasn't interested; she found out where I worked and was all over me. Con was fucked off, and he tried desperately telling her he works in the morgue, but she wouldn't believe him. You're just trying to get in my

13

knickers, she accused him. Nothing wrong with that, she was trying to get into mine.

'Just convince her you work here and she'll be all over you like a flannelette nightie. I'll have a word with her if she's there,' I tell him, and he smiles his appreciation. 'Remember not to blink, it will put her off. Anyway…' I pull the paperwork from my pocket and hand it to him.

He reads the name, 'Mr Joseph Figg, you're going to like this one, come and have a look.' I follow him over to the autopsy table and he pulls back the sheet covering the stiff. 'This is Joseph Figg, or Big Joe, as he was affectionately known.'

You're not wrong there Con, this guy is a bruiser. He looks in his fifties, and he's a big bastard. It looks like he used to carry a little extra weight, but that's not why they call him Big Joe. He looks about six feet six and is a monster of a man. He has what looks like two bullet holes—one in his chest, the other in his stomach. 'Who is he? What happened? Are those bullet holes?'

'Yes indeed.' He's loving this, it's like he's a gossiper who has someone's secret and now he's going to reveal it. 'Do you know the Figg family from across the river?' I shake my head, so he carries on. 'They run the south side of the city.'

'What? Gangsters?'

'Yeah, you never heard of them?' he asks almost mockingly. The implication is that he's somehow cooler than I am. He doesn't wait for me to shake my head again. 'It looks like this guy paid the price.' He can see my expression of non-comprehension, and like any proud gossiper, he continues with delight. 'There's been some trouble between the Figgs and the Dancers recently. I take it you don't know who the Dancers are.' I don't have time to answer again. 'They run the north side.'

'How do you know all this?'

'It's been in the papers for several months. I see you're still maintaining your usual ignorance of current affairs.'

I don't read the papers. Henry and Nicholas have several delivered each day; I don't know how they find the time to bodies. I'd been asking for ages and he finally relented. It's nothing sexual, I don't find dead bodies erotic. At the time I wanted more interesting duties, but underneath that, I wanted to be involved in the process of making them look peaceful to their loved ones.

I'd been working for the Partridges about two years when I got an itch to try something different. I spoke to them about it, and they said they'd be sad to see me go. I didn't think they'd miss my personality, but they would miss my work. I don't know why I did it, but I suggested being trained up as an embalmer. They were resistant at first, and I was about to take it personally, but then I realised it would cost money. Tight old fuckers. We agreed to pay half each towards the two-year course I took, and for the membership to the British Institute of Embalmers. I'm good at it, and I enjoy it. It helps the Partridges out as it eases their workload and allows them more time to devote to stocktaking and adding up numbers. No two stiffs are the same, they all present their own challenges. I delight in making these lifeless shapes look recognisable. I can't restore them to their former vibrant selves. I can't get them dancing around the Chapel for one final fandango, but I can make their loved ones' experience less traumatic. Fucking well done me.

A few years later, I suggested to the Partridges that I study a Diploma in Funeral Services. I could then be a member of the British Institute of Funeral Directors, and would be eligible to become a partner in the business. They were adamant that it was a poor idea, and became a little anxious whenever I brought it up. They would change the subject as quick as they could, but oddly would talk about things I'd never heard them speak of before—the paintings of Frank Bassoon, tiger moths, Brazilian gold mines. Then they would stampede out of the room at half a mile an hour. I brought it up every now and then for about six months. I had no intention of doing the Diploma, but I had a fun six months.

I swing the vehicle out of the premises and head in the direction of the morgue. I've done this route so many times. I prefer heading out on Winchester Road, which leads out of town towards the hills. I avoid driving through town this way, and I get to see a bit of greenery as I drive past Gravely Woods and the fields that extend beyond it towards Howard Manor. I cruise all the way there, it wouldn't be good for the hearse to be seen speeding. Ambulances can tear around town, but a hearse? It's a bit late by then. Besides, Henry and Nicholas know it takes as long as it takes to fetch a new arrival from its current location to our prep room. I keep the windows up in town when I'm listening to music; I don't think Mrs Pearson would appreciate me driving past her blasting out tunes. Now that I'm driving along the outskirts of town, I've got the windows down and the wind in my face.

When I first worked here, I'd go easy with the undertaker talk when I was chatting to a woman down the pub. I tended to get a few funny looks, and the usual questions: 'Isn't it depressing', 'Isn't it weird touching dead bodies'. I decided to put that conversation off until she'd got to know me a bit. The idea being that she wouldn't find me creepy working with dead bodies if she liked me. I slow down as I reach a junction and turn left onto Steeple Street, and hit the button for the windows to slide up. Saint Catherine's Hospital is on the other side of Oakley, but there's little traffic at this time of day. I wouldn't bring the subject up, but if she asked what I did for a living, I informed the lucky woman that I was a pastry chef, or a plumber, or a postman. After a few dates, when it was clear we liked each other, I'd confess. She would invariably tell me that I was silly for thinking she'd mind me working with dead bodies. She'd ask the usual questions, but wouldn't want to talk about it for long. We'd see each other for a while, until it suited us to part. I'm not a player, I just haven't settled down yet. I drive past Oakley Park and the row of shops selling all manner of things to eat, and take the turning that leads to the hospital. I did have a few things thrown at me though; shoes, hands, bottles. I've been told I'm a dirty liar, but it was only ever meant to be a temporary fib. I remember one woman was keen for me to have a look at her dishwasher; what was I supposed to do? I don't know anything about dishwashers. That's when I realised how ridiculous my behaviour was; what a stupid situation to put myself in. I promised myself I'd tell the truth from then on, and I have, and that was a long time ago. Here's Saint Catherine's, the morgue is behind the West Wing. I slow to five miles per hour and glide around the front of the enormous glass fronted hospital towards the morgue. It's not like I told any woman I was a doctor or a lawyer; that would have just been bullshitting. I kept my professional untruth within my income bracket: bank clerk, dental nurse and taxidermist. No, not taxidermist, that wouldn't have worked. I also kept it slightly boring, so she wouldn't ask too many questions, like estate agent or recruitment consultant. Imagine if I'd said I was the personal doctor for that singer, Tiffany Walnut? That would have invited a barrage of questions. I pull into a parking space outside the morgue and kill the tunes, then cut the engine. Fucking great time to remember to kill the music, I bet I'll forget again the next time Aubrey drives the car.

I'm walking down the main corridor in the building, towards the office and the morgue. I see Doug in the office and give him a wave, which he returns. Doug's the senior morgue attendant, he's been here years. He still wears a tie to work every day. I get on fine with him, but I'm here to see Con, so I head into the morgue. Con's a few years older than me and has been a morgue attendant for some years. He'd gone from one job to another, not really enjoying any of them. One of those jobs was a hospital porter, and it was then that he decided to train up to be a morgue attendant. He's been doing it ever since; I can relate to that. He took the job at Saint Catherine's a few years ago, after he moved here from Bradley. I like Con, we get on well and have a laugh. He's also a bit of a dick sometimes, but he thinks he's permanently fantastic. I see him at the far side of the room, so I give him a shout, 'Hey Con.' He looks up and gives me a friendly smile, 'Hey Laz,' he calls back. Con is about five feet ten; he's lean but he has endless energy and moves about with effortless ease. He has a tangle of black curly hair on his head, which he thinks makes him irresistible to women. We exchange pleasantries and he asks me if I want the stuff now.

11

'Yeah, why not.' He heads over to the bench near the fire escape to fetch his bag. I look around the room, there's one empty table and two occupied. The tenants are hidden under sheets. There are twelve chambers at the end of the room, all with their steel doors closed and their chrome plated latches clasped firmly shut. There's plenty of equipment covering various surfaces, yet there is a serene sense of emptiness.

Con's back and unzipping his bag. 'As requested,' he says, flashing me one his smiles. 'Half an ounce of super lemon haze, and a Q of Lebanese hash.' He hands me the two items, both wrapped extremely tightly in cling film.

'I see you're still keeping the cling film business buoyant.' I can smell it through the layers of film; smells good. I hand him the correct amount of money and he puts it straight into his pocket. He's never counted it in front of me, but you can bet he counts it as soon as I'm out the room. Just to make sure. If I'd underpaid him the first time we made a deal, he wouldn't have trusted me after that. I have no desire other than to keep him sweet; he always has good stuff. I put the two parcels in my pocket.

'Are you going to Anton's party on Saturday?' I know why he's asking me, he's after a bit more business. 'Do you need anything for the party?' He flashes me another smile.

'A couple of grams of charlie should be fine for me,' I tell him and watch him smile as he registers more money coming his way. I don't normally do coke. It's too expensive and it doesn't do much. All it does for me is make me drink more, and talk to people I don't want to talk to. I only buy it so that I can drink more. Usually, if I have a skinful, and a few biftas, I can feel quite tired. But with a few sniffs of coke, I'll be drinking all fucking night. And you never know, Rosie might be there. I met Rosie last Saturday down The Wooden Octopus. She was with Ingle, he was acting like they were together, but that's not what I heard. Just friends from work she told me, and I'm taking that as a signal. That fucking Miriam kept trying to talk to me all night, and I couldn't get talking to Rosie for long. Of course, when we did find the opportunity to chat, Ingle was quick to interrupt too. I want to

know if Rosie's going to the party but I'm not going to ask Ingle. He'll definitely try and put the kibosh on any romance developing between me and the beautiful Rosie. 'Are you going?' I ask him as he's putting his bag back.

'Definitely.' He'll be high and looking for company, and looking to sell more bifta and coke too.

'We're meeting in The Talented Crow at eight, and heading to the party from there.'

'Who else is going?'

'The usual crowd, Eddie, Dalton, Lucy, Ingle—' He cuts me off; he knows who the usual crowd are. I invited Con out for drinks with my mates a few times when he arrived in Stumpton, and he's been hanging around with us on and off since.

'Is Miriam going?' he asks, not attempting to hide his lust. 'She was all over you down The Wooden Octopus last weekend, and you didn't make a move. What's wrong with you Laz?'

'I'm not interested in Miriam. She gives me the creeps, just wants to talk about dead bodies all the time. I have a feeling that if we fucked, she'd want me on my back, remaining perfectly still with my eyes open, staring beyond her into space.' He's laughing, but I'm being quite serious. 'Who was she anyway?'

'A friend of Binky's from work apparently. Well, if you're not man enough to give Miriam what she wants, then I shall be only too happy to provide that service for her.' He gives another smile, but this one's a bit pervy.

'You're welcome.' I give him a sarcy smile in return. Con has a favourite fib he tells to women to deflect from the whole touching dead bodies thing that some people seem to have a problem with. He says he's an ornithologist, specialising in the conservation of barn owls. He's researched the species and knows fucking loads about them. Last weekend, he told this to Miriam and she wasn't interested; she found out where I worked and was all over me. Con was fucked off, and he tried desperately telling her he works in the morgue, but she wouldn't believe him. You're just trying to get in my

knickers, she accused him. Nothing wrong with that, she was trying to get into mine.

'Just convince her you work here and she'll be all over you like a flannelette nightie. I'll have a word with her if she's there,' I tell him, and he smiles his appreciation. 'Remember not to blink, it will put her off. Anyway…' I pull the paperwork from my pocket and hand it to him.

He reads the name, 'Mr Joseph Figg, you're going to like this one, come and have a look.' I follow him over to the autopsy table and he pulls back the sheet covering the stiff. 'This is Joseph Figg, or Big Joe, as he was affectionately known.'

You're not wrong there Con, this guy is a bruiser. He looks in his fifties, and he's a big bastard. It looks like he used to carry a little extra weight, but that's not why they call him Big Joe. He looks about six feet six and is a monster of a man. He has what looks like two bullet holes—one in his chest, the other in his stomach. 'Who is he? What happened? Are those bullet holes?'

'Yes indeed.' He's loving this, it's like he's a gossiper who has someone's secret and now he's going to reveal it. 'Do you know the Figg family from across the river?' I shake my head, so he carries on. 'They run the south side of the city.'

'What? Gangsters?'

'Yeah, you never heard of them?' he asks almost mockingly. The implication is that he's somehow cooler than I am. He doesn't wait for me to shake my head again. 'It looks like this guy paid the price.' He can see my expression of non-comprehension, and like any proud gossiper, he continues with delight. 'There's been some trouble between the Figgs and the Dancers recently. I take it you don't know who the Dancers are.' I don't have time to answer again. 'They run the north side.'

'How do you know all this?'

'It's been in the papers for several months. I see you're still maintaining your usual ignorance of current affairs.'

I don't read the papers. Henry and Nicholas have several delivered each day; I don't know how they find the time to

14

read them. Maybe I'll have a look through the old news when I get back. Nicholas stockpiles old newspapers in a box near the back door to the garden. I get the pleasure of putting them in the recycling bin.

I'm looking at the scars on his torso; the autopsy Y incisions run from his shoulders, meet at his sternum, and travel in unison to his pubic region. The incisions have been sewn back together with obvious care. 'Is this Doug's handy work, or did you do this,' I point at the stitches. I already know this is Doug's work; there is a beautiful symmetry to his stitching, and there is an equal gap between each stitch. Con's telling me that Doug wanted to do this one himself, and took his time over it. While he's chatting away, I look over the body. He has meaty fingers, but the skin is withering, like sausages left out on the counter. His nails stick out of his fingers like slate. There are ridges along the nails, like the slate had deposited over time.

Con slaps the body on the shoulder, which snaps me out of my thoughts, 'Maybe that's why Dougie's done such a great job. This guy,' he slaps the guy's shoulder again, 'Was the head of the family, the boss, the guvnor. I don't think Dougie wants the Figg family after him, accusing him of butchering the old man.' He's looking at me with an edge of seriousness, but I know he's fucking with me. He pretends to be hesitant, then says, 'The same goes for you Laz. You better do a fantastically good job of preparing the body for viewing or you might find your kneecaps hammered into a different shape.' He raises his eyebrows in mock fear.

'Fuck off Con,' I say casually, 'I'll have this guy looking like the Big Joe they all remember.' I don't want to listen to any more of his jokes about what a beating I'll get if I fuck this up. 'Help me get this brute in the back of the hearse will you. Have you got the paperwork?' He hands me some papers from the desk; I scan through the report—gunshot wounds, blood loss, catastrophic injury, usual damage from smoking and drinking, no other signs of foul play. 'Do you have a pen?' At the bottom of the form are two instructions— "print name" and "sign name". Henry is clear that he wants all printed names legible, we can scribble any signature we like, but all those that handle the stiff must be identifiable. I print my name, Laszlo Slippers, and scribble my signature next to it. I hand the paper and pen to Con, he neatly writes Conway Nest, and scribbles besides that. 'Come on, let's get him on his way, Henry will be worried about our new arrival.'

'New arrival,' he laughs the words into existence, 'You sound like Hank and Nicky.'

I do an impression of Henry, by stooping and imitating an old man's voice. The imitation sounds nothing like Henry, but that will do for Con, he nearly pisses himself laughing while clapping me on the back. After we've loaded the immensity of Big Joe into the hearse, I remind him, eight o'clock in The Talented Crow on Saturday. I drive back the way I came, back to the undertakers, with another stiff for the coffers. Henry and Nicholas don't like it when I refer to the business as an undertakers, they prefer Funeral Directors. I do it for fun to wind them up, but I try not to take the piss.

Chapter Two

I pull into the front yard and see we have some visitors. Two expensive-looking cars are parked in the visitors' spaces. I don't know much about cars, but I know I couldn't afford either of those two. I drive around the front of the building and pull in next to the side entrance. I cut the engine, get out and open the hearse rear door. I lower the ramp on the hearse deck over the bumper, and pull the removal trolley out of the vehicle. There's a bit of weight on Big Joe, so I give one big tug on the trolley and its legs drop down to the ground. For one horrible second the trolley rocked under Big Joe's bulk and I thought it was going to keel over. That would have been great, Big Joe crashing to the ground; I'm not sure I'd be able to lift him back up on my own. And I don't think Henry or Nicholas would be much help either. Better get him inside quick. I wheel him down to the prep room and straight into the fridge. I'll get the paperwork to Henry, then crack on with this brute.

I approach the office and I can hear voices; Nicholas and an unidentified male voice. The door is open and I peer in from a tight angle to remain undetected. I'm spotted immediately and the conversation stops; four people are looking at me. One of them is Nicholas, looks like he'll be directing this funeral. Between us there are two men and a woman sitting down. The men look like younger versions of Big Joe, big buggers, both in their thirties; must be his sons. The woman unfortunately also looks like Big Joe, must be his daughter. She's maybe late twenties, and has a big man's face. She has her hair long in an attempt to look more feminine; it's an expensive cut, but it makes her look like she's in drag. 'This is Laszlo,' Nicholas informs the gathering, 'He's going to be preparing Mr Figg.' They all stare at me; nobody says anything, including me. 'These are Mr Figg's children—' he was about to introduce the Figgs, but one of the men stands up and walks towards me. It reminds me of the statue of Talos coming to life in "Jason and the Argonauts". I hold my hand out and he engulfs it with his huge ham-sized paw, and squeezes until the ends of my fingers start to bulb. IT'S FUCKING EXCRUTIATING. STOP IT. FUCKING STOP IT. I resist the urge to scream in his face, and manage a strained, 'I am sorry for your loss. I will take good care of your father.'

He's still gripping my poor hand, and looks down at me and growls, 'You'd better take good care of him. I don't want you fuckin' up.'

With that, Nicholas jumps in, 'Laszlo's work is of the highest quality, and all our clients have been highly satisfied with his work.' Big Joe Junior releases my hand. Apart from my purple fingertips, it's gone a sort of dull yellow colour where the blood has been squeezed out of it back up my arm, and my fingers have changed shape where my finger knuckles have been kneaded into each other. I let my arm hang down, and like a butterfly emerging from its cocoon that unfolds its wings and lets them take shape by filling the constructions with liquid, I let the blood flow down into my hand pushing my fingers back to their original shape. I must remember to thank Nicholas for helping me out there.

Junior's looking me up and down, and not even trying to be subtle about it. I think that's the point, he's letting me know I'm in his sight. 'I'm Tyrone Figg,' and with a sweep of his thick arm, he indicates the other two seated. 'This is my brother Tommy, and my sister Frannie.' I nod and say hello to the two, but I don't venture any more handshakes, so I stay where I am. Frannie Figg? I think of telling them there's a spoonerism there, but I decide against it.

'I assure you I will produce my best work,' he's about to say something, fuck that, I get the idea, I don't want to stand here listening to more of it. I carry on quick, 'Have you brought any clothing with you?' I could stand here all afternoon saying all the right things in a perfectly professional manner, but this guy isn't interested in any of that. I have a feeling they have prior experience of death, and judicious platitudes are not required. Let's get to the point and we can all get on with our days. Nicholas is trying to indicate something to me, but the frame of Tyrone gets in the way and he's obliterated from view. Tyrone reaches for an item I hadn't seen. It's a black garment bag, one of those expensive types. There won't be just a suit in there, there's room for the entire ensemble, shoes included. He hands it to me, but there's not enough room for both of our hands on the handle. Am I supposed to grab it from underneath? Why doesn't he put it on the floor? I try and take it as best I can, shitting myself that I'll drop it. I take a look at the fistful of sausages gripping the handle, the family sausages. I think of taking a quick look at Frannie's hands, see if she's inherited the Figg fingers. I decide against it.

'Thank you,' I say to Tyrone when I have the bag under control. 'If you would excuse me, I should start preparations immediately. I'm sure you have matters to discuss with Mr Partridge.' I nod to the three Figgs in turn, and get the fuck out of there. Big Joe's got his last date coming up, and I'm going to make him look his best. Well, not exactly his best, the "dead look" only works if you're a goth, and I don't think the Figgs will be happy if I back-comb the remainder of Big Joe's hair. I walk to the prep room and put the garment bag on the table, unzip it, and roll it out flat. I unzip the inner compartments and open them up, there's a nice-looking suit; I feel the fabric, it feels expensive. I pick up one of the shoes; size fourteen. You could club someone to death with it. I put it back down; that might very well have happened. I'm lost in thought when I hear someone approaching. It's Nicholas. Evidently, they didn't have further matters to discuss.

'Laszlo, the Figgs would like to view Mr Figg tomorrow morning. Are you able to prepare the body today?'

It's already mid-afternoon, so I'll have to work late to get the job done. I can see Nicholas is keen for me to do it, and I know why. I don't think it would be wise to upset the Figgs.

19

'I won't leave until I've done the best job I can, and he'll be ready for viewings tomorrow.'

'Marvellous! Thank you, Laszlo. Make sure you take the time back.' We don't have flexitime here. I work regular hours most of the time. But if I have to work over, I always get those hours back some other day. Some days, if it's quiet, I come and go as I please.

'Nicholas, thank you for sticking up for me back there,' I say genuinely, and hand him the paperwork. He recognises my sincerity with a nod and takes the papers.

'I meant it, you always produce marvellous work. How is your hand?' I like Nicholas, but I've always got on better with Henry. Nicholas has always been a bit aloof with me, but occasionally there are these pockets where he appears to like me.

I hold my hand up, flex my fingers a few times, and give him a big smile. 'Fine. That was odd. He wants me to do a good job on his old man, so he squashes my hand.' I give Nicholas a puzzled look, and he raises his eyebrows in agreement.

'I'll leave you to lock up,' he says, and shuffles off in the direction he came from. Right, first things first. The shed. I look up to see Nicholas hasn't even made it to the doorway yet, so I head out the side entrance, past the hearse and through the gate to the back garden. Decisions, decisions, what's it to be. Lebanese hash, or super lemon haze? Lebanese hash is the winner. I knock myself up a bifta, and sit back to spark it up. I inhale, it's smooth, and strong. Nice one Con. I'm sitting in my beat-up armchair enjoying the effects of the hash, thinking how stagnant my life is becoming, I need some excitement. I finish the bifta and nub it out. I'm feeling suitably stoned so let's get to work.

I stand deep in thought, scrolling through my music collection, trying to decide what to listen to. All these decisions suddenly! I go for "Led Zeppelin II". I press play and the sound of Jimmy Page's guitar fills the room. I'm immediately boogieing. I retrieve Big Joe from the fridge, and get my equipment ready, without breaking boogie. I gently massage his hands and limbs, to mitigate the rigor mortis. I wash his body with a disinfectant spray and wash his hair. I'm having intermittent boogies now; this work requires concentration and a steady hand. I set his face with cotton wool in his nose and mouth, sew his mouth closed, and fix eye-caps under his lids to keep them closed too. The Figgs have been kind enough to put a photo of Big Joe in his garment bag; interesting to note that they thought of doing that. I set his features to look like his image. I'm pleased with my work, he looks natural. I make an incision under his armpit and locate the brachial artery. Henry and Nicholas insist the brachial artery is used. I set up the pump and allow embalming fluid to flow through the body, replacing blood that is draining out. This takes a bit longer than usual, due to the volume of blood Big Joe used to carry around with him. I've been working in silence for a while, so I put on "Goats Head Soup" by The Stones. Keith starts us off, and I'm doing my Mick dance in no time. When the arterial embalming has finished, I suture the incision and use my trocar for cavity embalming. When I finish, I plug the holes and give him another wipe down. Now I just have to get him dressed. With a big guy like him, it may be difficult to make his clothes look like they fit, I may have a struggle getting him into them. I may have to cut his clothing to be able to adjust them correctly. I have a feeling the Figgs might cut me if they see I've carved up Big Joe's finest suit. No, I can use a few props, wedges and slings to keep him in suitable positions for dressing. There is sufficient flexibility in him now, but this is going to take some time to get it perfect. After an hour or so of lifting, sliding and straightening, I get him into his best bib and tucker.

For the final part of the process, I attend to the visible parts of his body. But, first things first. I head over to the shed for a top up, and get another bifta on the burn. I like it in here, the chair is comfortable and I'm getting nicely stoned. I take a drag, and empty a few previous nubs from the ashtray into the bin, to remind myself what a great setup I've got here. I've got everything I need. I have been meaning to put a few pictures on the walls, but I only ever remember when I'm sitting in this chair. I head back to the prep room and select some new tunes. I go for Augustus Pablo "East of the River Nile", an instrumental album. This is a different procedure; I need a different vibe. He looks a little rosy in colour but that will fade, so I get my powders and makeup and set about recreating his natural complexion. This too takes longer than usual, due to the size of his face and hands. Maybe, I should use a paint roller. I comb the filaments of his hair in the style he sported in the photo, and make a few small adjustments to the facial settings. I have Big Joe looking like he's taking a peaceful nap after a wedding. I look down at the shape of my knees through my trousers. I reckon you're safe boys, I tell them. I have knobbly knees, but I've never thought that a problem. I never thought I needed to find a solution, but if I did, I wouldn't propose hitting them with a hammer.

Now I've finished, I clean all the equipment and put everything away, including Big Joe. I turn the lights off, lock up, and head out. It's not too late, I've only worked a few hours over, so I could go to the pub. But it's best I just head home, we have the Wimbush funeral tomorrow morning, and I learned a long time ago that funerals with a hangover are truly awful experiences. Having said that, I do sometimes, overconfidently, think it will be okay this time, but I always regret it the next day. It's about a twenty minutes' walk to my flat, ten minutes longer if I stop off at Mohan's. I decide to take the detour and head down Orchard Lane towards Mohan Indian Cuisine, for the best *tarka daal* this side of the Punjab.

*****

I arrive at work early, but of course I'm the last to arrive. I have a key for the side door and enter through that entrance. I walk past the dressing room where I keep my funeral clothes, and turn the corner. I see Henry at the end of the corridor, near the office, and he signals for me to come over. He's managed to shuffle into the office as I approach him, and he turns and takes my right hand in both of his. 'Marvellous work on Mr Figg, Laszlo, marvellous.'

'Yes indeed,' comes the voice from behind me, Nicholas has entered the office. 'That is potentially your best work, Laszlo, a tremendous job.' There's no sarcasm in his voice, it sounds like he means it.

'Maybe some of the best work produced at Partridges,' Henry adds. He is also being sincere, but I notice Nicholas shift uncomfortably at that remark.

Henry is still holding my hand, I think he's forgotten he's got a hold of it, he's just grinning at me. 'Thank you both for saying that,' I give them a smile, 'I should get ready for the Wimbush funeral,' I say and indicate the door with the thumb of my spare hand. Henry releases me and I head to the dressing room. Fuck, praise indeed from the Partridges, I feel somewhat elated that they admired my work. I enter the dressing room and see Aubrey putting on his shoes. 'Hey Aubrey, how are things?'

'Good Laszlo,' he ambles over to me and puts his hand on my arm, 'I saw your work on Mr Figg, and I have to say that is splendid work. As good as Henry or Nicholas.' He gives my arm a squeeze before letting go. I give him a smile, and he opens the door and walks out. My clothes are hanging up, freshly returned from the laundry after I slipped in the mud at the cemetery after the last funeral. Aubrey could barely stop laughing on the drive back. Also, I didn't want to get the interior of the hearse muddy, so I had to take my clothes off and put them in a bag. I was down to my boxer shorts and socks for the drive back. I get myself suitably attired, and have a thought that makes me smile; Aubrey's bus pass.

Aubrey gets the bus to work, he doesn't live far away, but he's got his free bus pass so he uses it. He usually leaves his pass on the table, I look over and I see it's in its usual spot. I open his bus pass holder; Aubrey Wisp, the card reads, and his photo is hilarious. It looks like the wind caught his hair before the photo was taken and he didn't realise. He looks like an old lady having her hair done at the salon. I am laughing so much that I have to hold onto the table for support. Aubrey walks in and sees me looking at his pass, so I stifle my laugh until he closes the door behind him. He shuts the door and my laugh continues by bursting out of my mouth. 'Are you ever going to stop finding that picture amusing?' he asks me.

'No,' I tell him. It's all I can manage to say. It's not just that his hair entertains me, it's also that the assistant in the travel card office didn't mention it to him when they took his photo. They must have assumed he sported his hair like that on purpose. He takes it out of my hand and throws it back onto the table with mock disgust, but he only leaves it lying around so I see it. He knows how much it tickles me. 'Come on Gladys,' I say to him and we both stand here laughing. I open the door and we head down the corridor, 'I'll catch you up Aubrey, I'll meet you at the hearse.'

About fifteen minutes later, I'm out the back gate and walking towards the vehicle. Aubrey's already in the driving seat, so I get in. There's a waft of old man in the car, it's not Aubrey's fault, his personal hygiene and laundry are meticulously attended to. It's just nature. Strangely, I find the smell comforting. I tell myself it's because that's Aubrey's smell and I love the guy, but in truth, I know it's because I'm going to smell like that before long, and if I can convince myself it's acceptable, others can too. I cough and it's a good one. It came from deep and it felt like it shifted something.

'Have you just had a joint?' He's looking at me and I'm about to answer, when he beats me to it, 'No need to answer that question, I could smell it when you coughed. Make sure you know what you're doing Laszlo, its nine o'clock in the morning.' There's no reproach in his voice, I like to think I look out for him too. I never have a bifta when I drive. I know I'd only be going at twenty miles per hour, but there's no way I'd jeopardise my job or the reputation of the Partridges. But on match days, Aubrey drives, so I usually have a bifta or two during the proceedings.

'You know me, Aubrey, I'll be fine.' I offer to make him some more hash cakes and he's well up for it. Aubrey's laughing, proper laughing. I join in, I can't help it. We're both nearly pissing ourselves and I don't know why. It doesn't matter why, I'm laughing with Aubrey. He's trying to talk, but can't get the words out.

'Do you remember...when...' he's holding onto the steering wheel, '...when...when we ate some hash cakes in the park...while those oldies were playing bowls,' and he dissolves into a laughing meltdown. He always calls old people oldies, even though some of them are younger than him. We'd eaten some hash cakes in the park and some oldies started playing bowls near us. We were quite high, and it was a bit trippy, and we found everything funny. We were laughing so much that the bowlers got stroppy and asked us to leave. We tried to explain, but that only made matters worse, so we headed off to The Traveller's Chin for a few drinks. We kept cracking up there too, and got quite a few looks of annoyance. Suddenly he stops laughing, quite abruptly, and he's looking out the hearse windscreen. It's Nicholas, looking stern. He approaches Aubrey's window, which he duly lowers. 'Sorry Nicholas,' Aubrey says, and I echo it.

'Gentlemen, please, such behaviour is not acceptable. The Wimbushes are all ready to leave; if you would be good enough to start the procession to Saint Michael's.' I can tell he's thinking about saying more, but we're looking sufficiently guilty for him to opt out. I reckon Aubrey saved me there; if I was on my own, Nicholas would have carried on. I might cop it in the neck later though.

Aubrey starts the car and "Cigaro" by System of a Down comes blasting out of the speakers. I start to rock in my seat, but Aubrey looks horrified. 'Sorry Aubrey,' I venture, 'I was listening to that on the way back from the morgue yesterday.' He's already turned the tunes off, and sits regaining his composure. He doesn't say anything, he smoothly swings the hearse around the building, across the yard, and slowly pulls out onto the road. He's a beautiful driver, Aubrey; I want him to drive me to my funeral. The procession of Wimbushes follows us to Saint Michael's. Aubrey tells me about the time he and Joyce Catheter ate some of my hash cakes and things got romantic. He doesn't offer any of the details, and I don't ask, but I sit here looking at him with renewed admiration. This was only late last year. He's silent, but I feel he hasn't finished. 'Tenderness will touch you at various times in your life Laszlo; you just need to be alert to its presence. Don't let these moments pass you by.' He drives a little further before continuing, 'But be careful, moments come, moments go. Don't get attached to them, they'll take you away from where you are.' We sit in silence, both of us in thought. He has a hard exterior, that's something I've invested in too, but he sees the beauty in life as well. I hope I do.

We arrive at Saint Michael's and pull in by the entrance. Aubrey and I get out and attend to the rear door and the removal trolley. When the coffin of the deceased Wimbush is ready, the pallbearers step up, and off they go. I put the trolley and the ramp away, while remaining stoically cheerless. The sombre crowd file into the darkness of the church and disappear. On this occasion they didn't need me as a pallbearer. Often I'm requested to bear, because most people realise the coffin will be heavy. So I fill a vacant space. They're right, you can ache pretty quickly. I hope the offspring of Big Joe are numerous enough that my assistance is not required. Lifting one of Big Joe's legs was hard enough work. I reckon Frannie will volunteer.

Aubrey and I chat outside while the service is conducted. Neither of us likes all that religious shit, but we're always visible when the mourners are around.

'Come on, let's wait by the door,' and he slowly walks in that direction. We wait by the front door for the service to finish. We've had plenty of discussions about religion, and we're in agreement. Neither of us believes in a god, we see death every day, and we know it's coming. It doesn't scare either of us, it makes us remember to live our lives in a positive way. If you accept there is no God, you have to find your own happiness and your own purpose. And that's a kick up the arse we're both grateful for. The service finishes and the pallbearers are led to the grave site. When the congregation have found their positions, Aubrey and I retreat to a spot that is close enough to be on hand for any emergency, but far enough away that we can talk without being heard. We stand solemnly looking at the crying attendees, and sneaking a look at the woman with the short black skirt, and fantastic legs.

'That's hardly funeral attire, is it?' Aubrey asks.

'Do you want me to find her some trousers?' We're talking to each other but looking straight ahead. It's like we're in a prison camp, passing on information. On this occasion, I know we're looking in the same direction.

'You stay where you are, thank you.'

'You see that woman over there,' I indicate the direction I'm looking in with a brief nod of my head, 'Poor woman hasn't stopped sobbing since she left the church.'

'She was no doubt crying throughout the service too.' He sighs, and I echo it.

I lean in a little closer to him and whisper, 'I fear she might become slightly amphibious with her relentless crying.'

Aubrey lets out a slight snort, and expertly brings a hanky to his face. Brilliant. Whether anyone looks over in our direction, I don't know, because I rise to the occasion and put a comforting arm around his shoulder and lead him away from the proceedings.

Chapter Three

We arrive back at work and Aubrey parks the hearse at the side of the building. I follow him through the side door and we head towards the dressing room, when I see Nicholas waving his arm at me. I start in his direction and he continues waving, so I think he's keen to talk to me. He's smiling, so hopefully he won't carry on about our laughing fit earlier. 'The Figgs are here,' he informs me, and he looks in a good mood. 'They are very pleased with the presentation of Mr Figg, and they would like a word with you.'

He starts to walk in the direction of the office, but I don't move. 'Do I have to?' I ask him, but follow him anyway. We enter the office and I see Tyrone and Tommy, and a new Figg. This bruiser is younger, maybe late teens. They all stand up as we enter and Tyrone steps forward. He holds out his hand, but I'm frozen, I don't want to go through that again. Considering I don't have any choice, I give him my hand to do whatever he wants with. He gives me a regular handshake, it's a bit squeezy but I think that's just his way.

'You did excellent work on my dad, he looks very peaceful. Thank you.' And with that, he let's go of my hand. Phew, he doesn't want to hurt me. Now, don't say anything that will make him change his mind.

I nod appreciatively, 'Thank you, only the best is acceptable for Mr Figg.' I nod respectfully. Tommy steps forward and shakes my hand and says how grateful he is for my work. I'm introduced to Marco, Tyrone's son. He shakes my hand and tells me the same thing; I want to get out of here, this is Nicholas's job. To be fair, sometimes grieving relatives ask to speak to me, or for a message to be passed on. So it's not unusual, but the Figgs scare me, and I want to get to my shed. The conversation turns to viewing arrangements. Big Joe is in the Chapel of Rest in an open coffin, and apparently there are going to be quite a few family and friends visiting today. Nicholas is taking sole charge of the viewings, and it sounds like he's going to be busy. I'm still standing here like a pudding, I haven't spoken for several minutes. I discreetly point at my stomach, and Nicholas gets the message. He makes my excuses for me, and there are more thanks, nods and forced smiles.

I set off for the dressing room to get changed and to grab my bag and head for the shed. I see some newspapers piled up in their box and decide to take them with me. I throw my bag and the box in the shed, and have a quick look for Aubrey. I open the gate and see him with the bonnet of the hearse up, peering into the inner workings; I'll catch up with him later. Back in the shed, I eat my lunch. Some couscous and a box of crackers, I need to go shopping. I knock up a bifta and have a look through these old newspapers. The top one is The Stumpton Echo, there's a picture of the local councillor standing on a building site, wearing a hard hat. I don't even bother reading the headline. A lot of people I've encountered speak in headlines; they read the headline but not the article, then go around quoting the headline as their point of view. I find that as headlines are designed to catch the reader's attention, they are often not representative of the full article. They are also not representative of the truth, as it's just one person's view of the topic. So we get hordes of people spouting off about the latest news stories, when they know nothing about them; and arguing with people who know more. One option to fight the sea of shitty opinions we're bombarded with, is to immerse oneself in the flow and consult multiple sources of information. Find out the truth, about all the latest bits of news. Get up seriously close, and sniff the bumhole of current affairs. I find the thought unappealing because it sounds time consuming, unrewarding, and a bit stinky.

I flick through the next few pages and I'm reminded why I don't read the paper. Man finds woodlouse in a bag of frozen peas, Mr Scoops ice cream van catches fire, nurse abseils off hospital roof dressed as a pancake, burst water main floods Carpetland. This is what people call the news. And a host of horrible adverts, showing photographs of unappetising food that make me want to puke. I give up and try the next paper, The Stumpton Courier. More of the same bollocks in this one too, though there is a story about some parents' fury over crows attacking school children in the playground, so I stop to read that article before carrying on. I try The Chronicle and flick through it. I stop when I see Big Joe's face staring back at me. He's a lot younger, with much more hair; must be a stock photo they have of him. The headline reads, "Crime Boss Killed as Gangland War Continues", and the caption under his photo informs me, "Joseph Figg, known as Big Joe, died from multiple gunshot wounds yesterday". The article tells of a war between the Figgs and the Dancers; the situation has been escalating over recent months, with sabotage and retaliation mentioned. I flick through more papers, Con was right, it's been in the news for a while. The papers aren't in date order, so the story is unfolding to me in a peculiar order, but I get the idea. The Stumpton Bugle has photos of some of the Dancers too, getting into a car, walking out of the courthouse, various mug shots. The people in the photos all have varying degrees of ginger hair. The mug shots show Kenny Dancer, Colin Dancer and Desmond Dancer, and they all look menacing under their orange thatches. The papers only go back a few weeks, so I'm not getting the whole story. I head out to chat with Aubrey, see what he knows about it.

Aubrey has an air pressure gauge attached to one of the hearse's tyres, and he's monitoring the reading closely. It's great that Aubrey still takes an active role in duties around here. There was a time when I couldn't name more than a handful of parts under the bonnet, and I certainly didn't know how they worked. Over the years, Aubrey has taught me the basics of auto maintenance and repair, but he's better at it, and he enjoys doing it. 'What are you up to Laszlo?' he asks when he sees me approaching.

'Just having a spot of lunch and doing some reading.' He detaches the gauge, happy with the reading, and returns it to its box. Evidently, this was the last tyre to be tested. 'What do you know about the Figgs and the Dancers?'

He's thoughtful for a few moments, and when he looks at me there's a cheeky look on his face. 'I don't know much about the Dancers,' he smiles, 'But I used to date one of the Figgs many moons ago.' He gives me a few moments to digest that nugget then carries on, 'Maureen. Maureen Figg, such a beautiful woman. She got married some years later and changed her name to Turnip. She's still alive.'

Did he just say all of that? I wasn't expecting that. But I shouldn't be too surprised; Aubrey's still a man about town. She's still alive as well. Stumpton must have the highest average age of any city in the country. We've probably got more centenarians than Japan. 'Who is she?'

'The man you prepared, Joseph, she's his aunty. I remember Joseph as a boy.'

'Were the Figgs gangsters then too?' I sound impressed, and he hears it.

'No, no...' he says shaking his head. 'Joseph built up the crime empire, the family weren't trouble back then. We dated for a while, but it didn't work out. I see her around occasionally and sometimes we have a chat.'

'Keeping your options open, are you?' I ask him, and he gives me a quick smile, then looks quite serious.

For the rest of the afternoon, I take care of my duties and hang out with Aubrey. The place has been a hive of activity all afternoon with visitors coming and going, but it is peacefully quiet now. I find Nicholas in the office and he looks exhausted. 'Long day?' I enquire. He nods his head ever so slightly, poor man's knackered. 'I can lock up tonight, you get yourself home Nicholas.'

'Thank you, I think I will. I have agreed that the Figgs may continue with viewings tomorrow, so I will appreciate some rest this evening. Remember to put Mr Figg in the fridge, Laszlo. Enjoy your weekend, see you Monday morning.'

'Hope it goes smoothly, see you next week.' I give him a wave and leave the office. Right, what's the plan? It's Friday and it's five o'clock. I'll put Big Joe in the fridge, lock up, and hit the pub. I opt to say goodbye to Aubrey first. He's coming out of the dressing room, with his coat on. 'What are you up to tonight, Aubrey?'

'I'm going to have a quiet night in. I have a bottle of single malt whisky, and I will have a few sips whilst listening to Muddy Waters and Skip James.' Aubrey has great taste in music. When I've been round his place, we listen to all the old Blues players—Robert Johnson, Sonny Boy Williamson, Howlin' Wolf, Deaf Willie Peterson.

'Sounds good, I'll let you know when I've done some hash cakes.' He gives me a smile and starts towards the front door.

'Take it easy this weekend, Laszlo,' he says as I'm walking off to lock up the side and back doors.

'I'll try,' I shout back, but neither of us believes that.

Henry left early today and I see Nicholas's car leaving as I turn off the reception lights and lock the front door. I walk to the Chapel to fetch Big Joe and see his casket is still open. The Figgs have opted for a half-couch, so only the upper portion of his body is visible. I'm about to lower the open half, when I notice the lining and the cloth covering the closed half have been disturbed. I open the closed half to straighten everything out; I do not want to give the Figgs any reason to dislike me. I adjust the lining and see his leg has moved position too. I lift his leg to straighten it and see a package tucked under there. I pull it out and it's a cloth bag with a drawstring at the top. I untie the string and peer inside. Holy fuck! I look away. I think my heart has stopped. I have another look, I'm greeted with the same view. I stick my mitt in and pull out a handful of diamonds. It's dim in the Chapel, but they shine with an unstoppable radiance. Judging by the size and weight of the contents of the bag, I would suggest there are about another six or seven handfuls in there. Fuck! What do I do? Well, that's an easy question, put the bag back, or the Figgs will hurt me in ways that would terrify a seasoned masochist. Right, good decision, put the bag back. I'm in a bit of a daze, my heart undulates between beating faster than a hummingbird's wings and not beating at all. I close the casket and wheel Big Joe to the fridge without conscious thought; I'm in the fridge before I realise what's happening. I think about having another look at the diamonds, but I have a strong feeling that's risky, I should just lock up and get the fuck out of here.

In the dressing room, I put my jacket on and grab my bag. I suddenly feel a sensation of something pressing into my thigh; I look down and something is bulging in my trouser pocket. What's that, I don't remember putting anything in my pocket? I pull out the drawstring bag. How the fuck did that get there? I remember putting it back under Big Joe's leg. Well, I think I remember. I obviously didn't. Shit, what do I do now? I stuff the drawstring bag into my bag, turn off the lights, and lock up. I'm walking home a lot faster than usual. What am I doing? I'm going to get myself killed. I can always put it back. But I'm still walking home. When exactly do I plan on putting it back? I'll think it through tonight, make sense of it all. I can always put it back first thing in the morning before any Figgs arrive for a viewing and notice it's missing.

I get home and walk into the sun laden living room. I draw one of the curtains, casting half the room into shade. I sit motionless on the sofa for some time. I keep thinking there's going to be a knock on my door at any moment, and I'll hear Tyrone Figg telling me he knows I'm in here. Eventually, I take the bag out and have another look at the diamonds. I have no idea how much they could be worth, and I have no idea what to do with them. How do I sell them? Wait a minute, sell them? I'm moving quite quickly with my devious thoughts, while simultaneously shitting myself. This is the most fucked up thing I've ever done. I try and think of a good place to hide them, so I can organise my thoughts. I find myself in the kitchen, looking around. I'm opening cupboards and drawers, and closing them again without really looking. Now I'm back in the living room, I grab one of the sofa cushions, unzip it

33

and thrust the bag inside. I zip it back up and throw it on the sofa. I stand there breathing erratically, trying to keep calm, when my phone goes off and I let out an involuntary yelp. My heart is back, whacking itself against my chest. I look at my phone; relief. It's just a message from Eddie, he's down The Bloated Sailor with Stopher—do I want to join them? Too fucking right I do; something to calm my nerves.

I'm moving quickly through town, I need a fucking drink. I head down Osprey Grove so I can cut through the little square leading to The Bloated Sailor. I walk past the local supermarket on the corner and the alleyway behind it. There's a poor wretch of an alky sitting on her duvet by the bins. I see her there sometimes when I pass this way. She's probably about forty, but she looks ninety. I don't suppose sitting by the bins helps much. I turn away and head for the pub; what can I do to help? I enter the boozer and I'm greeted with the warmth of congenial chatter, laughter, stale beer and body odour. I see Eddie and Stopher at a window table and give them an invisible pint signal. They indicate they already have drinks, so I head straight for the bar. The bar is empty and the barman asks what I want. I order an ale, Croaky Toad, it's 5.5%, and it tastes pretty good. The barman brings my pint and says something. Numbers. I'm not really listening; I'm wondering if Rosie will be out tonight. I dig around in my pocket and give the guy a scuba diver. He brings me back some change and I stuff it in my pocket while taking a swig of my pint. 'Cheers,' I say distractedly, and join the guys.

I sit down and listen to their conversation; they're talking about crocodiles hunting wildebeest in the rivers of Africa. 'Have you seen lions lying around in the daytime?' Stopher asks. Eddie and I both nod, and I take another few swigs of my pint. 'Have you noticed all the flies buzzing around the lions' faces?' We both nod again, I take a few swigs. 'That would piss me off.' We both look at him a bit puzzled. 'If I was a lion, that is.'

'You're not a lion,' Eddie's busy informing him.

Stopher is a good bloke but he'd let me sit here all fucking night listening to his inane conversations, so I decide to put

34

an end to it. 'You know what I'd do if I was a lion?' I ask them, and they both look at me. 'I'd put a spider on my face, that would keep the fucking flies away.'

Eddie gives me a good laugh, and I join in. Stopher starts saying, 'Actually, that wouldn't work, because—' but I notice my glass is nearly empty, so I cut him off.

'Do you want a pint?' Stopher forgets I've interrupted him and asks for one of those gassy lagers. Eddie goes for a stronger lager, and tells me he'll knock up a bifta while I'm at the bar. I'm at the bar and I can see him doing it, he doesn't even go to the toilets to do it. I bring the drinks back, and all three of us go outside to smoke the bifta. We stand outside the window by our table to keep an eye on our drinks. This goes on for a while; inside for drinks, outside for biftas, but I'm drifting in and out of the conversation. I'm thinking of the diamonds, the Figgs, my knees, and trying to distract myself by thinking about Rosie. I'm not sure how many pints I've had, I'm not sure I've drank this quickly without the assistance of coke. I see Ingle at the bar talking to some bloke. 'There's Ingle,' I tell the guys and point at the bar. Ingle turns to point at us and finds all three of us looking over. He bounds over and sits down.

'Hey guys, what's up?' This is Ingle, Ingle Fwet. Some of the guys call him Fwetty, but I don't like him that much so I stick with Ingle. I can feel myself getting pissed. 'I'm with a friend of mine, Teek. He's coming to join us,' he says.

'Teek?' I ask.

'Yeah, Teek. He's a mate from work.' Ingle has started a new job recently and he's been hanging out with his new workmates a lot. That's fine by me. But there's one of his workmates I'm more interested in than Teek. He joins us, bringing two drinks, and we all say hi. Everyone's engaged in general pub talk, but I want to ask about Rosie. There's no way, even in my semi-pissed state, I'm going to let Ingle know I'm interested in Rosie. Hopefully Ingle will mention her. She's fucking hot, so he's bound to, but I don't know how much more of his company I'll be able to tolerate.

Eddie, the hero, asks, 'Who was that woman you were with down The Wooden Octopus last Saturday?'

Ingle jumps at the opportunity, 'Oh, yeah, that was Rosie,' he's trying to sound casual, but he's desperate to tell us. Cunt. 'We work in the same department.'

'Have you banged her yet?' Stopher asks, another perfect question.

'No, not yet, but I intend to,' he says self-admiringly.

Not if I have anything to do with it Fwetty, you fuknut. Stopher and Teak are laughing and congratulating Ingle, but Eddie is giving Ingle an ironic cheer. At this I burst into laughter, but Ingle is so self-occupied, he thinks I'm laughing with him. I feel like slapping his face apart.

'Is she coming to Anton's party tomorrow night?' Eddie majestically asks. I must remember to buy him a pint for all his excellent work. Wait! Unless he's interested in Rosie too. Shit! More competition. I need to find out Eddie's intentions, but I don't want to enquire while Ingle's listening. I need to talk to Eddie alone. I could follow him to the toilet, but the guys will want to know why we went to the toilet together; they'd think they were missing out on a line. Although I have been to the toilet about six times already, so it wouldn't be too suspicious.

Ingle's grin is so encompassing, it's pushing his eyes together. Evidently Rosie will be going to the party. I've zoned out of the conversation, lost in thoughts of whether Rosie will find me attractive after the Figgs have punched my face into a new shape. It might be a better shape, but I doubt it. I tune back in to the conversation to hear Ingle claiming that trousers were invented in China. I feel like telling him he's a monumental prick, but in my pissed state it might sound a bit provocative.

'No they weren't, you fuck-weasel,' Teak informs Ingle, 'The Greeks got there first.'

I close my eyes for a few seconds and contemplate the next ten minutes listening to a drunken conversation about trousers. I plan on alleviating the frustration by inventing a ridiculous point of view and sticking to it determinedly. If I have to get quite animated, I will. Eddie finds it hilarious when I do this, and invariably joins in with fictitious facts to support my position. I'm preparing such a tale when Ingle turns to Teak and asks him, 'Fuck-weasel? What's one of them?'

'Well somebody would have done it. It's the human race we're talking about here,' Teak states, as if he's stating the obvious.

'Are you suggesting people fuck weasels?' Ingle asks with disbelief, but then his face expands from a knot into a wider appreciation that it's probably true.

'Pass the weasel, it might be a game,' Teak says, taunting Ingle with the image.

'That's disgusting,' Ingle says, shaking his head at his pint.

Teak sees Ingle's discomfort and adds, 'At the end of the game there'd be a grotesquely swollen weasel lying on the sofa,' and smilingly waits for Ingle's reaction.

I don't bother waiting for it, I'm not sure I can take more of this. I lift my glass and throw the remainder of my pint in my mouth, swallow it with one painful gulp, and slam my glass on the table. 'I'm out of here,' I announce, 'I'll see you tomorrow at Anton's.' I stand up and wobble a little, but I make it look casual. Stopher, Ingle and Teak remain seated whilst we exchange farewells, but Eddie gets to his feet and says he's off too. See you tomorrow at the party, blah blah, and we're heading out the pub towards the square. 'I'm feeling quite fucked,' I inform Eddie, who just laughs.

I met Eddie about ten years ago. I was cutting through the park when I walked past four lads, who decided to act tough with me. I tried my best to placate the situation but they started shoving me, and I shoved one of them back. A fight broke out and I was doing quite well at first; I landed a few good punches. But then I had all four of them throwing fists at me, and it was starting to get a little overwhelming. I took a fair few hits to my head and face, and I was swinging away still making some solid connections, when I heard a noise. It was someone bellowing and roaring, and the lads stopped hitting me. I saw this bloke, who must have seen the fight and wanted to help out, shouting, swearing, acting crazy, running at them with his fists flying around. The four lads backed off, they clearly didn't like their chances when it was four against two. Especially when one of us was making loud animal noises at them. They retreated, shouting things that explained how tough they were. Didn't look tough to me, backing off like that. I stood there with my face puffy and bleeding, saying thanks to this bloke I just met. That was Eddie. I recognised him from some of the boozers around Oakley and West Bandage, and he said he knew my face too. He's a year or so younger than me, and it turned out he was shagging a woman I used to go out with. I suggested a pint to say thanks, and that's exactly what we did. We hit the nearest boozer, I got the drinks in, and washed my face in a grotty sink in an equally grotty shithouse. We stayed for a few drinks and he and I have been friends since.

'You were knocking back pints like it's your last day on Earth. Something on your mind Laz?' He's still smiling, but I know there's concern there too.

'Yeah, I think so,' I tell him, and nearly stumble off the pavement. There's a voice, but it sounds horrible and I don't know where it came from. It's the alky still sitting by the bins; she's speaking to us, but I can't make out what she's saying. Her voice is so raspy, I wince. It feels like she's tearing her throat to speak.

She rasps on, but not before coughing. Her body heaves, her eyes bulge, and the sound is like gravel being rubbed against sandpaper. '…hod…paft…tamba…' she's pointing at us now, like she knows us, or she has something important to say. '…hunst…pik…towel…' The fucked-up thing is, I think I know what she's talking about. I reach into my pocket, find a few coins and they fall onto her duvet.

'I think she likes you,' Eddie tells me, and he's holding onto me as he's laughing. To be fair, I think she does like me. She seems keen on telling me something, and she's getting up, sort of, and heading in my direction. I start to back off, but

Eddie's still holding me and as he's fucked too, we collide and nearly fall over.

'Aay…suk…yacok…fura…botla…sors,' she says as she nears us.

'I think she's telling you she'll suck your cock for bottle of booze,' Eddie dutifully informs me. I really don't want that to happen, my dick will smell of cigarettes. Besides, I'd have to provide the moisture for her withered dry mouth, and I don't want that to happen either.

I dig into my pocket and pull out a scuba diver. I put it into her hand and tell her I hope she has a good night. I wish I could help, but I don't know what else I can do. She needs a friend, a non-alky friend, but I've just got mixed up with gangsters, so I don't think I'm the kind of friend she needs. Eddie's pulling my arm, and we sort of run and stumble into the square. As we're alone and having a laugh, I feel brave and ask him about Rosie.

'No, I'm not interested in Rosie,' he says, and looks me in the eyes and smiles. There's no bullshit coming off him, he's a truthful guy. I want to know more, so I stay silent, and let him say what he wants. 'I saw the way you were with her last Saturday in The Wooden Octopus.' He's leaving a dramatic pause before carrying on, and to check for my reaction. I don't give him one, still playing it cool. He smiles and says, 'And she had eyes for you too, Laz. That was clear to see. You should go for it. Fuck Ingle.'

I laugh involuntarily, it bursts out. 'Yeah, I will.' I'm grinning now, but I assume it doesn't look as wanky as Ingle's grin. We walk through West Bandage and Eddie's turning down Toad Avenue is coming up, so we initiate goodnights. I take this opportunity to tell him that I bought us a gram of coke each from Con. He tells me that he'll pay me tomorrow, but I drunkenly tell him it's my treat. Quality guy Eddie, and he doesn't tolerate fools.

My walk home should have taken me about a further ten minutes, but it was twenty per cent walking, twenty per cent stumbling and sixty per cent between the two. So some of that zig-zagging delayed my return, but at least I didn't fall over again. I'm here at my front door, and I fumble my key into the keyhole in comparatively few attempts. I shut the door behind me and the reason I got so hammered tonight is refreshed and cloaks me. It's all over me, suffocating me; what the fuck have I done. I should check the diamonds, but I'm not moving towards the sofa. I'm sort of hoping that I've become confused; that I didn't take the bag, it's still under Big Joe's leg. That would be easier. I head into the living room and step towards the sofa. I attempt to sit down, but my legs are reluctant to retain their usual solidity, and I collapse. I reach my hand around the sofa cushion, and the lumpy bag is definitely there. I don't want to look at them, it will make the certainty that I'm going to be beaten unrecognisable more concrete. I look at my phone, it's not even eleven o'clock yet. I appear to be drinking myself into an early night. I'm hungry, so I stumble around the kitchen looking for something edible. I find some tofu in the fridge, I toast some rye bread; and with startling simplicity I have a toasted tofu sandwich. Delicious. There's time for a nightcap, so my plan is to have a whisky and a bifta, and think about what to do with the diamonds. I knock up a bifta and knock back a few whiskies. Fuck knows what I've been thinking about, but I forgot to think about what to do with the diamonds. Whatever I was thinking about was more important than saving a catastrophic beating, but not important enough to remember. I need to lie down, I'm spinning out. I'll think about it as I get ready for bed.

Chapter Four

I have a sense that I'm regaining consciousness, then I remember I'm human, my name is Laszlo Slippers, and I'm waking up from a heavy night's boozing. My head hurts, and each new thought creates a pulse of pain through my noggin. Try not to think, just act on impulse. More sleep. That's what's needed. My phone alerts me to a new message, and a fresh spear of pain travels through my poor brain. I see the diamonds sparkle in the cerebral darkness my hangover is maintaining, and I freeze in position, listening for any sounds. I hold my breath when I hear something, but the sudden silence makes me think I was hearing my own breathing. I start breathing again; yep, there it is. What have I done? What the fuck am I going to do? Viewings start at one o'clock today; how much time do I have to figure out what to do? And put the bag back if that's my conclusion?

I reach for my phone, bring it close to my face and look at it through the merest of cracks. I can make out its 09:07, and I have a message from Con. I'll read that in a bit, I need to rest now. I don't recall getting into bed last night. I must have managed to get here and collapsed into it. That last bifta didn't ease me into a good night's sleep, it catapulted me into unconsciousness. I'm drifting back to sleep when my phone goes off again. I have a look; it's 09:51, how did that happen? I must have had a sneaky doze. Nice one. It's another message from Con; I suppose I should see what he wants. He wants to meet up this morning, and he's suggesting a pint. With one eye squeezed shut and the other squinting, I send a message back, 'That's the worst idea imaginable, I have a hangover the size of Belgium'. I put my phone back on the bedside table, get into a comfortable position, and my phone sounds again.

I have a feeling that my desired state of horizontal immobilisation is not going to be allowed by others. I reluctantly reach for my phone, promising I'll turn it to silent after I find out what the fuck this cunt wants. It's Con again, 'Hair of the dog best meds'. He could have thought about using a comma in there; it's one extra touch on his phone. My head is throbbing, my body hurts, my throat feels like carpet, but I'm again distracted with another message, 'Kings legs 11:30?' It's Con again. The Kings Legs is a boozer not far from here, so I've got an hour and a half to feel human again. I can do it. 'Ok', I send him. I'll have a coffee in the pub.

I drag myself out of bed and into an upright position. I don't like it, I feel unsteady. My bowels feel quite troubled too. I think the combination of a belly full of ale and whisky, and the stress I've been under since taking the diamonds are giving me bad guts. I should evacuate, it's not healthy to be carrying that stuff around with me. I sort myself out, and while washing my hands I look at my face in the bathroom mirror. It feels a little looser than usual this morning, so I try lifting my face back into position. I try various angles but nothing works; my face is insistent that the laws of gravity will be strictly adhered to. Give it the morning, a shower and several coffees, and my skin will tighten up a few notches. I head to the living room and stand staring at the sofa. I brace myself, then relax sufficiently to unzip the sofa cushion. I pull the bag out, untie it, and pour the contents onto the coffee table. They make satisfying soft clinks as they topple onto each other, and slide off each other onto the table. For a while, I watch them sparkle in the strained light coming from the bathroom. I need a clear head to decide what to do, so I scoop the diamonds back into their bag. I shower, dress, turn on the coffee machine and throw some rye bread in the toaster. I remember I need some more hash if I'm going to make hash cakes, so I send Con a message. I'm eating my toast and drinking my coffee when Con replies, 'No problemo'. What time is it? My phone tells me 11:08. Shit, I'll have to leave in a bit. I know I should return the diamonds or I'm going to get myself into a giant shit-heap of trouble. What if Tyrone squeezes my body the way he did my hand? My head would bulb and pop. But this opportunity will never present itself again. I wanted more excitement in my life, and now I've got it. Maybe this is a bit too much excitement though, a severe beating doesn't sound particularly exciting. I'll meet with Con first, I'll still have time to return the bag before viewings. I stash the bag back in the sofa cushion, and tidy up a few things just to distract myself.

I walk into The Kings Legs and see Con at the bar. He asks me what I want when he sees me approach. I should have a coffee shouldn't I? 'Pint of Guinness please.' The barman hears me and attends to the pint, and brings Con his lager.

'Had a heavy night last night did you?' He asks me, grinning. He can see I'm in pain. 'Where did you get to?'

'I went to The Bloated Sailor with Eddie and Stopher, and got very pissed. And I feel like shit today.' The barman names a price, and Con pays up. He brings Con his change, and fetches my pint. 'Cheers,' I say and we pick up our pints and head to a table in the corner around the side of the bar.

'Sounds good,' he says, and starts rifling through his jacket pocket.

'Well, it was until Ingle turned up. What did you do last night?' I see Con's face wrinkle when I say Ingle's name.

'Ingle spends most of the day up his own arse, he must like the smell up there,' he reaches his hand out towards me under the edge of the table. I reach my hand out and he drops some objects into it. 'I went to The Wooden Octopus, was hoping to bump into Binky and Miriam.'

I withdraw my hand to my lap, out of sight of the barman, and I see two wraps of coke neatly folded, and a lump of hash. 'Did you?'

'No, they weren't there. There were a few people out, so I stayed for a few drinks, but I didn't see Miriam.'

'I can't pay you for this right now,' I tell him, as I'm putting the packages into my pocket, 'But I can give you the cash later at the party.'

'Yeah, no problemo, Laz. That's fine.' He takes another swig of his pint, and I realise I haven't touched mine yet. I

43

take a swig and my body responds by shuddering. It's as if it's telling me that more alcohol is not what it wants right now. Well, bad luck body, because here comes another swig. Another shudder, and I feel a bit cold. 'About the party,' Con is asking, 'Will Miriam be going?'

'How the fuck would I know?'

'Well you're good friends with Binky; you could ask her if they're going tonight.'

'You know Binky too, you can ask her.' I see a moment of frustration cross his face, and decide that I should probably help him. 'Is this the only reason you wanted to meet me this morning?' I see a look of recognition in his face, but he doesn't say anything. I take a swig of my pint and realise I'm half way down, it's slipping down a treat now. This was one of the best ideas imaginable. 'You could have messaged me,' I inform him.

'Yeah, and you'd have told me to fuck off.'

'And what makes you think I won't tell you to fuck off in person?' He's looking a bit pissed off with me now. 'If I tell you that Miriam is not going to the party, does that mean you won't go too?' I don't wait for him to answer, 'No, you'll go to the party anyway, so just go and see who's there.' I can see he's getting more annoyed, so I end this and say, 'All right, I'll message Binky this afternoon and let you know. Okay?'

Apparently, that is okay, because he's immediately smiling and looking happy. 'Cheers Laz, I'd appreciate that. Do you want another pint?'

'Same again, thanks,' I tell him, and he's off to the bar with a spring in his step.

He comes back with the drinks, still smiling. Right now he's in a good mood and happy with me, I try my luck. 'Con, you know lots of people; do you know a fence?'

He looks pleased at this question, he likes to think of himself as a man with connections. He must have a few, he doesn't grow his own marijuana and coca plants, but I don't know what other contacts he has. 'What is it, car stereos?' he asks, and laughs.

'Yeah, something like that.'

'You surprise me Laz, I didn't think you'd be into handling hot goods.' The implication is that he's tougher and more streetwise than I am.

I don't want to ignite his curiosity too much, I think telling him about the diamonds would be a bad move at this stage. 'It's not for me, it's for a mate.' That will do for now.

'Who?' he asks, his curiosity ignited.

'No one you know,' I say as if the whole matter is of little importance to me.

'Fair enough,' he says and smiles, and there's nothing pissy in his tone. He tells me he'll ask around, to see who's available. So that's that done, he'll let me know. We chat for a while about some interesting topics. He's a good bloke when he's not being a giant pillock.

My phone starts ringing, I take a look and see its Nicholas calling. Fuck. Nicholas doesn't call me over the weekend. My face slackens. I was just regaining some tension. Shit, fuck, shit. This must be something to do with the Figgs and the diamonds. Fuck. I have to take the call. 'Hello Nicholas,' I say, and sit here listening to him, while staring at my pint. After a while I say, 'Okay Nicholas, I'll get there as soon as I can.' Apparently, viewings started at noon today to accommodate the abundance of mourners, and the Figgs are furious because something valuable belonging to Big Joe has gone missing. And they want to talk to all staff. Nicholas sounded quite nervous. He's never been in this situation before, of course. What have I done? The Partridges don't deserve this. I can see Con has noticed the change in my demeanour but I don't want any questions about it. 'I have to go Con. I'll see you later at Anton's.' I take another few gulps of my pint, and get up to leave.

'I'll have a nose around for a fence for you. I'll let you know what I find out later. Don't forget to ask Binky.' He smiles, but I just give him a solemn nod, and leave the pub.

I can go straight to work, or go via my place. If I collect the diamonds, I could sneak them into the coffin, and ask what all the fuss was about. They'd know it was me that took the bag, but they'd be thankful they got their diamonds back, so

45

they'd leave me alone. Right? I could walk straight up to Tyrone and hand him the bag, and say I found it in the shrubbery. Is this what he's looking for? He'd know it was me that took the bag, but he'd be thankful blah blah. Right? Fuck, what have I done? I walk down Avenue Lane towards the new budget pub on the High Street, The Poached Egg. From there, one direction leads home, the other to work. I'll come up with a plan on the way. There are a few pedestrians about, taking up too much space as usual, and a few cars on the move. I avoid collision with anything moving and see an opportunity to cross the road. I hear a car approaching behind me, so I hop onto the pavement and carry on down the turning off the main road. I'm still weighing up my options when I'm aware of my surroundings. They're familiar, everything is in its place; but something doesn't feel right. I look to see The Poached Egg coming up, I can't see it, but something definitely feels wrong. Fuck, I've gone past it. I walked straight past the junction of decision, and took the road to work. I need to stop doing this. When decisions are being made regarding these diamonds, something is making them without my collaboration. It's me. I'm finding ways to distract my rational thinking and reasoning abilities, so my risk-taking side is getting its way. Well as I'm walking to work, I may as well get on with it. Maybe I'll get away with it, and keep the diamonds. I might as well see how far I can go before a fierce beating is imminent. At that point, I'll tell them I can get the diamonds back for them, and everyone's happy. Right?

I really need a wazz; those pints have washed through my system. I might get pounced on as soon as I walk through the Partridge's door, and my bladder's already burning. I need to find a convenient place. I turn and walk towards the library, there are pissers there. I cut through the arcade leading to Barrington Square, from here I can see the fountain in front of the library. The library is obscured from view by a gallery of beautiful towering poplar trees, but as I cross the square, the library reveals itself. It was built in 1804 as a personal residence for the Lord Mayor, Edward Janice. The toilets are on the ground floor, that's all I give a fuck about. I know where all the best pissers are in town. I'm not interested in using a filthy public toilet, that's a bit splashy underfoot. I prefer a certain level of cleanliness, and the library toilets usually attain that requirement.

After I've jet washed the toilet, which also provided a cleaning service, I head straight for work. I slow down as I approach the driveway, and peer around. There are some expensive cars in the visitors' spaces, I can't remember if I've seen them before, but they must be Figg cars. I tread softly past the front of the building and enter by the side door. I walk through the dimly lit building, past the dressing room, and tentatively look around the corner to the corridor leading to the interior. I see Henry at the far end moving towards the office at the speed of a sand dune. Fuck, Henry's here too; this isn't good. I need a quick debriefing before I tackle the Figgs. They're likely to be in the Chapel, the office or the reception area. I'll try the dressing room. As I open the door, I see the light is off. I flick the light switch and scan the room. What was I hoping to find? Nicholas sitting here in the dark? Actually, that's not such a bad idea; maybe I could do that. No, there's only one thing for it; I need to go to the office. Give some support to Henry and Nicholas. I walk with purpose towards the office, clearing my throat as I go. I hear voices as I approach, that's definitely Tyrone Figg. I could sneak up and listen in to the conversation, but I don't want to get caught doing that so I walk straight through the doorway. I see Nicholas and Henry standing by the desk, and Tyrone, Marco, Tommy and an unidentified associate standing between me and the desk. I don't think the new brute is a Figg, he doesn't share any resemblance. He's an ugly bugger though, I think he's taken a few knocks, his face looks like a bag of potatoes. I stand motionless as everyone is looking at me, and I'm about to speak when Tyrone, Marco, Tommy and Potato all move and gesture towards me. They look furious.

Tyrone speaks first, 'Did you go into my dad's coffin last night? Did you take somethin' that belongs to my dad?' It looks like he's about to grab me, so I back out one step.

'No,' is all I manage to get out, because Tyrone is glaring at me, he's fuming. He moves towards me, and the other three join in. I can't see Henry or Nicholas anymore.

'You didn't touch the coffin. Is that what you're sayin'?' He's closed in on me, there's no point continuing to back out, I can't do a runner. He puts his hand on my shoulder, in a mock friendly way. But his face isn't friendly, and I'm nearly shitting myself.

I'm scared that when I speak, my voice will be shaky, and I'll be given the title of Guilty immediately. 'Mr Figg's coffin was half open after the visits, so I closed the open half, and wheeled the coffin to the refrigeration unit.' Thank fuck for that, my voice held up. If anything, I sounded quite in control. Where is that coming from? I haven't taken my eyes off Tyrone's yet, showing him I'm not worried, I have nothing to hide. I hope that's the message he's getting. He might think I want a fight. I look across, into the eyes of the other three, to show I'm sincere. I still haven't seen Henry or Nicholas re-emerge. They're standing behind a wall of Figg meat, towering above them. Nicholas will be staring right at their backs, but Henry's stoop means he'll be staring at buttocks. I assume they're trying to peer through the cracks that come and go between the men as the four shift position. That's what I'm hoping anyway, because I'm trying to spot them through those sporadic cracks. I might need a bit of support here. 'I can assure you I did not take anything from the body of Mr Figg,' I look back at Tyrone when I say this. I'm hoping that by phrasing it that way, it will sound like I'm thinking of jewellery, a watch or something valuable in a pocket. If I'd said—I can assure you I did not take anything from the coffin—I might sound like their guy. The four of them are quite agitated and all appear ready to say something, so I carry on quickly. 'What item is missing? If I know what I'm looking for, I may be able to help.' Fuck me. I'm not wavering under this immense threat.

'Gentlemen, gentlemen, please,' Henry says as his arm appears between Tommy and Potato. He's attempting to squeeze between the two, and they recognise his fragility and move apart to allow him to pass. 'Let us be seated and discuss the matter with Laszlo one step at a time.' He indicates the seats, 'Please, be seated. Laszlo, fetch two more chairs please.'

'Yes, Henry. I'll be right back.' I turn to leave and Tyrone steps across my line of vision.

'Don't run off now,' he says to me. He doesn't snarl it at me, it's nicely monotone, and it's full of menace.

I walk to the store room with my heart pounding. There are a few chairs inside the entrance, so I stand for a moment trying to compose myself, organise my thoughts, and come up with a lifesaving story. It wasn't me. Stick with that, and I'll be all right. Play the rest by ear. I take the chairs into the office and see there is one empty chair next to Henry and Nicholas, and two people standing on this side of the desk. I put the chairs on the floor and head slowly to the empty chair on the other side of the room. The side of the room that doesn't have an exit. From there, my exit will be behind four angry bison. I think I can see steam coming off them. I take my seat and ask Tyrone what's happened.

'What's happened…' he repeats, and glares at me with such a ferocity I fear his eyeballs will pop out of their sockets. I assume I'd hear a popping sound. I'll be disappointed if not. I can see them swinging around on their stalks as he moves his head from side to side in a panic, knocking into each other like conkers. '…is that a valuable item belonging to my dad was with 'im when we left 'ere yesterday, and when we arrived today, it's missing. Are you still saying that you don't know anything about it?' He sits there staring again. That's it, he's done talking. Now he wants answers.

'I did not take anything from Mr Figg's body, I assure you. I care about my work and about the reputation of H Partridge and Sons Funeral Directors. I would never jeopardise that by stealing something from a body, and certainly not from such a respected family as the Figgs.' Shit, have I gone overboard there, they might think I'm trying too hard. I'm looking serious, and sticking with it as I think it might be working. The four bison have calmed a little, as confusion is drifting into the mix. Much to my advantage. Maybe if I keep the confusion supplied, it might take their minds off me.

'I have explained to Tyrone...' I see Nicholas wince a little when he said "Tyrone". Nicholas had it explained to him during their first meeting that Tyrone did not want to be addressed as Mr Figg. Nicholas should call him Tyrone. This is something that makes Nicholas feel uncomfortable, but for obvious reasons, he goes along with it. '...that your service is impeccable, with no incidence of theft, or any other illegal activity,' he says looking at me, but is really repeating it for our guests. He's looking a bit nervous, but he's keeping it together well.

'So where's the goods?' Marco asks the room, and the other three shift in their seats and make unnecessary and unprepared vocalisations to deflect our attention from Marco's words. I hear a few hmm's, erm's, coughs and throat clearings.

'What Marco means to say is, where's my dad's property? How has it gone missin'?' Tyrone is just about keeping a lid on his rage, but it's evident for us all to see. He's used to directing all conversations he has, but Nicholas is refusing to let go of control. He knows that would be disastrous.

'The alarm system shows no activity throughout the night, and since I unlocked the doors this morning, the only visitors have been for Mr Figg.' Nicholas is resolute, 'We treat the dead with the respect they earned while they were alive. We treat all our dead with honour and dignity, we do not steal from the dead.' Good show Nicholas, that was very impressive. He's looking very serious, and I sense that the Figgs, and Potato feel they are reaching a dead end with Nicholas.

'What about you Lazarus, are you sure you don't steal from the dead?' Tyrone asks me, trying to peel the skin off my face with his eyes.

I'm about to ease into my "it wasn't me" plan, when Tommy says, 'Maybe you found something, but you didn't know where it came from. So you're looking after it 'til you know who it belongs to.' He's trying to remain calm, but he too could pop at any moment. He's also offering me a way out. This might be my last chance to back out of this. They can't know it was me, he's just fishing, but it's a good tactic. Maybe they wouldn't beat the shit out of me if I returned the diamonds, they might only tell me to fuck off. That is a very good option.

'Yeah, that's very considerate of you,' Potato joins in. His face looked like it was having a fight with itself when he spoke. I'm reminded of what's at stake here. I do not want to end up looking like him. And I might. Even if I return the diamonds, they might still set about redesigning the bone structure of my face. I cannot collaborate with them; I won't know how it will end. My only choices are, return the diamonds anonymously, and stay the fuck out of it, say I found the bag in a rip in the coffin lining or keep the diamonds. What's that? Three options, that's pretty good.

'I haven't found anything, but I'm happy to help look for it,' I say to Tommy because it's too difficult to look at Potato without staring. I'm hoping I appear to be concerned and helpful, but I might look like I'm shitting myself. If they spot that, I'm in trouble.

Nicholas averts attention from me by announcing to the room, 'After all visitors had left the building, the only people remaining were Laszlo, Aubrey and I. Aubrey left soon after, I left shortly after him, and Laszlo kindly locked up.' All eyes are looking at him, thank you Nicholas, I needed a break. 'Only my staff were present other than those viewing Mr Figg, and I trust my staff unreservedly.'

The four bison are mainly exchanging looks between each other, but shoot the odd glare in my direction. Thankfully, Henry and Nicholas are exempt from the intimidation routine. I'm trying to avoid direct eye contact with the four, but I can see in my peripheral vision that Tyrone has locked on to me. I behave attentive to what Henry and Nicholas are doing, which is simply sitting there, but I make it look like I'm interested in it. I think he's still looking at me, so I check by looking over at him. Yep, there he is, staring right at me. The other three are saying things to each other that I can't make out, as I'm drifting in and out of various states that include: shitting myself, being hungover, thinking things are going well, the effects of lunchtime drinking, trying not to sweat or look nervous. Maybe I should offer some advice, they wouldn't be expecting that.

I've become momentarily lost in thought when I hear Tyrone say, 'And there was no one else 'ere yesterday?' in quite an unpleasant tone. I look at him expecting the usual glare, but he's looking at Nicholas. Then to me, back to Nicholas, back to me. This time he focuses a weird-looking stare on me.

Before I know what I'm doing, I say, 'Well, there was the bloke I saw leaving before I locked up.' Like four eagles opportunistically foraging, but then suddenly catch sight of prey, they lock eyes on me. I can hear their talons scrapping on the chairs.

'Who was that?' Tyrone wants to know.

What the fuck am I doing? What bloke? What do I say next? 'I don't know who he was, I thought he was one of your party that stayed late.' Keep talking Laszlo, keep talking. Don't give them time to think and interrupt. 'I was about to lock up the front doors when I saw a man walking quickly through the reception. I called to him, but he didn't answer. By the time I reached reception, he had left the building. I checked the front yard before locking the front doors, and saw a car driving off.' I let that hang in the air, and nervously wait to see who bites first. Everyone's looking at me; even Henry and Nicholas are craning their necks in my direction.

'What did he look like?' Tommy says in a calm and measured way, with flared nostrils and animal eyes.

What am I doing? What am I doing? What do I say? I'm going to get myself killed. 'I didn't see his face because he was walking away from me towards the front door'. Good, good, that's good. That gets me out of describing someone's face. My voice was steady too, but I reckon I need to carry on; they're still staring at me expecting more. 'He was wearing black trousers and a black coat…' they're still staring, why doesn't one of them have a break, '…and had ginger hair.' Shit, where the fuck did that come from.

The four bison swivel in their seats, shooting glances at each other in quick succession. Marco and Potato simultaneously exclaim, 'Dancers!' in two variations of anger mixed with pride in their powers of deduction. Tyrone is fully focussed in thought and calmly leaves the room without speaking. The other three follow him. Tommy stops and apologises to Henry and Nicholas for the inconvenience, then looks at me and nods. I don't know what that nod means, maybe he's saying "thanks for the info", so I nod back. What have I done? Where will this end? How far will I take it? I'm in too deep already.

'Will today's schedule of viewings continue as arranged?' Nicholas asks. I can hear the hope in his voice, the hope that the upsetting events of the day so far will bring an end to the viewings. As he asks, the exiting Figgs can be heard at the front door talking to new visitors. Tommy confirms the news and joins the new Figgs in the reception. Nicholas stands, straightens his clothing, sighs and leaves the office to greet the new visitors. Henry and I remain silent as he exits, it's been a strange and stressful encounter, and we're all a little shaken. Poor Nicholas has to conduct an afternoon of viewings now.

I break the silence and ask, 'Is there anything else you need from me Henry?'

'Doesn't look like it Laszlo,' he says with a smile. 'Thank you for coming in today at short notice, you were apparently very helpful.' He looks weary today, I assume he's been forced away from his usual Saturday routine, and he's probably keen to get back to it.

'No problem, glad I could help.' Did I? Who did I help? I didn't help Henry and Nicholas. I didn't help the Figgs. Or the Dancers. And I'm not sure I've helped myself either. 'See you on Monday, enjoy the rest of your weekend.' I give him a smile and head out of the office.

'You too, Laszlo.'

I head in the direction of the side entrance and see the door to the dressing room is open, and the light is on. I thought I closed up when I left. I have a nose in as I pass and see Aubrey sitting there. 'Hey Aubrey, what are you doing here?' I feel my mood getting better already.

'Waiting for you,' he says with a serious expression, and the smile drops off my face. When you've had as many conversations that Aubrey and I have had, you instinctively detect the other's mood. This one's serious. 'Why do you think I'm here?' he asks, but ploughs on, not waiting for a response. 'I'm here because the Figgs want to speak to all staff about a missing item.' Shit, I didn't think they'd drag Aubrey into it too. I should have known. I didn't think, I haven't been thinking clearly lately.

'Yeah, of course,' I say, too distracted to hide my surprise. He's looking at me in a friendly, reassuring way, but there's no mistake he's serious. There have only been a handful of times he's found it necessary to talk seriously with me. He gives his opinion on the matter, but only after offering a full critique of the situation and the options. But he does that in small ways regularly, and that's another reason I like him. He's honest, so even if I don't like confronting an issue, I know he means well by bringing it up. He wouldn't bother telling me if he didn't care. Besides, each time he was proven to be right. 'Did the Figgs speak to you too?'

'Yes,' he says immediately. 'They are missing something valuable, and they want it back. They are a dangerous family, and not people you want to make your enemies.' He's beginning to look his age, and I'm tempted to suggest it's because he's worried.

'What are you worried about Aubrey?' I ask, hoping to sound unconcerned about the plight of the missing Figg item.

'Do you know anything about it?' The directness of his question startles me momentarily, and I stand here looking like a bad actor. He's not messing about wasting time, he wants to know. I refuse to lie to Aubrey, but I can't tell him. What do I say? He sees my discomfort and helps me out by saying, 'Whoever took the item will likely be identified, and

I would not want to be that person.' He stands looking at me, with no movement at all. He wants that truth to land before he carries on. I know he hasn't finished. After a suitable pause he resumes, 'If they are careful, and know what to do with the item…then potentially they may escape the Figg's attention. But it is a dangerous game to play.' He maintains the same facial expression while speaking, and it's making me aware how massively fucked I might be. 'Is there anything you want to talk to me about Laszlo?' He knows. How does he know? What makes him think it could be me? I've never done anything like this before. He knows me, that's how. When we've talked over the years, I've told him the main occurrences that shaped my life before we met, and he knows my life since. So he knows me better than most. And I have been jabbering on about needing a change in my life.

'Yes…but not right now.' I look at him for recognition, and he nods slowly.

'Anytime you want to talk, Laszlo, you know where I am.'

He's not a pushy person, there's another reason I like him. 'I know.' I appreciate Aubrey's concern and offer of support, and while I usually look for excuses to chat to him, right now, I need to get home; the weight of what I've done is nearly crushing me. 'I'll speak to you soon.' I turn and walk out the dressing room without looking back.

The walk home consists of me wrestling with thoughts and decisions, but not getting as far as making any decisions. Why did I say my imaginary bloke had ginger hair? Well, obviously I know why, I needed a deflection. A big one, a plausible one and one straight away. So now the Figgs think the Dancers took the diamonds, and there will undoubtedly be some type of revenge. I've started a gang war! No, I haven't, that was already happening, it's been in the papers for months. But I've just made it worse, I've sent the Figgs after the Dancers. I've escalated a gang war! Actually, that is true. Maybe there could have been a truce in the war, it might even have been close, and I've just knackered it. No, wait, the Dancers are apparently responsible for the murder of Big Joe; the Figgs were bound to retaliate sometime soon. Surely? If

I've escalated the conflict, it's probably by a few days or so, nothing either side aren't prepared for. So I probably shouldn't feel responsible for the next murder, should I? It was probably going to happen next week anyway. I squeeze my eyes closed for a few seconds, it doesn't matter how much I try to excuse what I've done, I simply don't believe myself. I'm nearly home, walking past the small park on the corner of Horsefly Road, and the enormity of what I've done still weighs down on me. I'm walking so heavily, I feel like I'm shaving the bottom of my feet as I walk. I'm disappearing into the path, leaving a trail of shavings behind me. Loud voices bring me to my senses. I'm standing across from the park, a football game is underway and shouting from the players snaps my attention. It's the middle of the afternoon, and dark clouds are gathering overhead. They're moving quite swiftly, seemingly bumping into each other, exchanging matter before heading off in different directions. Their dark swirls look menacing. People are busy with their day off, walking in various directions, no one paying any attention to anyone else. I carry on walking home, even though I can't feel my legs.

I make it home, and lean against the front door as it's shutting. I feel the soft click behind me and stand here breathing for some time. In the main room, the sunlight pouring in through the windows has warmed the flat but I'm feeling a bit cold. I sit on the sofa and retrieve the diamonds. I scoop out a handful and let the little rocks trickle through my fingers, back into the bag. I do this several times, then put the bag down and fetch a pint glass from the kitchen. I pour the gems into the glass and rotate it, letting it catch the rays of sunlight entering the window, heading for the opposite wall. The rocks sparkle and appear to dance as I rotate the glass. They also look like lots of miniature lighthouse beams warning me of impending danger. I rest the glass on the table and consider again how much of a giant idiot I've been. I'm definitely going to be horrifically beaten, and there's a strong possibility it'll prompt my death. But there is a small chance I'll stay alive and make a lot of money. What's my next move? Maybe I should talk to Aubrey about it? First, I'm hungry. I turn the oven on to two hundred degrees and fetch some of the vegetable pakora I'd made a few days ago from the fridge. I get what's left of the couscous and eat that while the pakora are warming up. I message Binky asking if she and Miriam are going to the party tonight. I knock up a bifta, pour myself a good measure of whisky and rescue the pakora from a certain burning. I'd forgotten they were in there. Binky messages back with "yeh both going" followed by an emoji winking at me. "Not me, Con's interested. See you later", I send back. I message the good news to Con; good luck to him. My plan is, finish eating, smoke, drink, and relax for the remainder of the afternoon, putting serious thought into my options. A rushed decision will be lucky if it's a good decision. A dash to get to the decision will result in consequences that I don't foresee, because I didn't give myself enough time to consider their possible existence. I'll deliberate my best options, because my life may depend on it.

Chapter Five

I wake up. I'm lying on the sofa, in quite an uncomfortable position. I pull my arm out from under me, and wince when I straighten it out and flex it. The Sun's fucked off and so has my optimism. It's the party tonight, and I'm not sure I'm in the mood for going. I reach for my phone and see its 19:37, and I have several messages. I ignore all except Eddie's, "Talented crow at 8, see you there Laz". What time was that message sent? Several hours ago! How long have I been asleep for? It doesn't matter. I should go to the party, it will take my mind off the formidable beating I'll be receiving, and Rosie might be there. I message Eddie confirmation, while taking the pint glass of rocks into the kitchen and eating the rest of the pakora from the fridge. I can't be arsed warming these ones up, and they taste good cold. In an attempt to wake up my enthusiasm, I have a shower and put on fresh clothes. I feel a bit better, but all my thoughts are tinged with worry. I have a feeling it's showing on my face too. I get ready to leave and check I have everything: phone, money, keys, tin, lighter, coke. Check.

I walk into The Talented Crow. It's still light, but the dark clouds from earlier have settled and form an impenetrable barrier to the Sun's restorative powers. I enter the pub and see it's already quite busy. I can't see Eddie so I walk through the pub to the other end of the bar. I recognise a few faces and give a few nods, and arrive at the junction between the toilets, the back room and the beer garden. I take a look in the back room and see some of the usual crowd standing by the bar. Eddie's in conversation with Sonya; he's looking around while she's talking, and sees me just standing here. We acknowledge each other, and he says something to the barman. Next to them, near the bar, is a group of six, deep in conversation. Stopher is doing the talking, and he appears to be enthusiastic about the subject matter. He's probably talking rubbish as usual, bless him, but he does it with such enthusiasm you get drawn into it. His captive audience are Lionel, Sandy, two of their workmates I recognise but don't know, and María. Lionel's been part of the crowd for years. He's a good guy and has a dry sense of humour. He looks like a darts player but he works for a recruitment company; a job he claims he doesn't like, but he's been doing it for years. Sandy Brook is Lionel's friend from work. Sandy does like his work, and will talk about it if you let him. I don't let him. His hair is a sandy colour too, and parted in such an arbitrary way that I wonder why he bothers. María's looking bored, and she takes another sip from her drink; rum and cola. She has wavy, shoulder length chestnut hair framing her quite beautiful face. There was a time, years ago, when we flirted. We were a bit pissed at the time, and while I was single, she was going out with Gordon Chops. What she saw in Chops, I still can't decide. We agreed that the timing was wrong, but the topic resurfaced a couple of times. When she finally realised what a buffoon Chops was and told him to sling his hook, I was going out with Hilary Teeth. So the timing was wrong then too. After a few of these episodes, we kind of forgot about it, and we're just friends now. Which is great, because there aren't many real friends out there. To the side of that group are Binky, Dalton and Lucy. They all seem to be involved in their conversation, in fact they're all talking at the same time. Dalton was originally a mate of Eddie's, but we became friends too after I met Eddie. He's a good bloke, and has helped me and Eddie out several times. Lucy is his wife, and it's good to know that they are genuinely happy together. It's easy to see that they love each other, but thankfully they avoid the pitfalls of public displays of affection. Like hearing, "get a fucking room", "fuck off with that behaviour", "we know you do it, we don't want to see it", that type of thing. It took us by surprise when they announced their plans for marriage, but the reception was one hell of party. The bits I remember were great. Binky has been around for years. She was originally introduced to me when she was seeing an old friend of ours, Colin Broody. She's always been popular, so when she and Colin broke up, everyone remained friends with her. I've always got on well with her, though there was one time when we had a blazing row about testicles outside the book shop on Cow Shed Road, but we were both tremendously pissed at the time. We both felt a bit silly about it after, and apologised. Drunkenly and overdone, but we were genuine. She's about five feet two and has lots of blond hair, and smiles more than anyone in know. She sees me looking over and gives me a wave, along with her customary and warm smile. I return both, and finally start moving. I'm wondering if Binky's presence indicates Miriam's too. By the time I walk over to the bar and get through all the greetings with the assembly, a pint of Fiery Griffin is waiting for me on the bar.

'Thought you might need this,' Eddie informs me. Fiery Griffin is a dark ale, and while it's only 5%, it makes up for that with a soothing effect on the stomach.

'Just what I need, cheers Eddie. Hi, Sonya,' I say, looking at her. She looks slightly corvid, she has long black hair scraped back along her scalp, and a nose that is a little bit bigger and pointier than the average. Sonya Posture is friendly with most people, but she's a good friend of Ingle's. We get on fine, she thinks he can be an irritating tossbag sometimes too.

'Hi Laz, how are you?' She tilts her head back slightly as she speaks, and it does look like she's going to peck me.

'Good, thanks. I hear your project on traffic pollution levels near primary schools was well received. I'm pleased for you. I know you put a lot of hard work into that.' She did indeed work hard. She is dedicated to her projects, and she likes talking about them too. I take a swig of my pint and ask, 'Are the Council going to implement your findings across the city?'

'Yes,' she says, beaming. 'We're implementing some initiatives almost immediately, and others are being planned simultaneously. It's very exciting.' She's smiling at me, then Eddie, and we're smiling back. This is great, and I'm pleased for her, but I want to talk to Eddie. 'Ingle said he was out with you last night,' she says, suddenly changing direction, 'He said you were drinking faster than a steam train. Have you got any charlie, Laz?' I've noticed that with some people, when they want something, they ask for it. There's no beating around the bush, they cut straight to the chase. She's on the hunt again.

'No sorry, I can't help you.' I think I'm looking suitably disappointed that I can't help her, but I don't mind if I'm not pulling it off. She can sort out her own fucking coke instead of sniffing around me all the time for a free line. She seems distracted when the anticipated party talc doesn't materialise, and makes her excuses while joining Stopher's conversation. Which, I think I can make out is about the speaker system he has set up in his car. María looks at the new addition to the group with a look of hope. I assume she's hoping the conversation might take off in an interesting direction. She sees who has increased their ranks, and looks even more bored. I wish I could help her, but I need to talk to Eddie. 'I've got the coke on me, let me know when you want it,' I lean in so only his ears hear the news.

He looks at me casually, 'How about now?'

'That's what I was thinking.' I reach into my pocket, pull out one of the wraps and hand it to him. He pockets it while I take a swig of my pint.

'Cheers, Laz,' he too opts for a quick swig of his pint before heading across the room towards the door. Sometimes I have some of his stuff, and other times he has some of mine. I follow him out, and we're back in the main bar, we turn left and he pushes the door open to the toilets. We walk in and while I'm scanning the cubicles, Eddie walks straight into one and is shutting the door behind him. I dash over there and in a series of fast events I block him shutting the door, slide through a gap only slightly wider than I am, grab Eddie to stop him falling over due to the door knocking into him, close the door behind me, and manage to slow down my breathing after that sudden exertion. 'What the fuck are you doing Laz?' He's rubbing the side of his head. I think that's what the door knocked into. 'It might arouse suspicion if someone hears us in the same cubicle. We have a wrap each, let's have a cubicle each.'

'I don't have anything to cut it with.' I rotate my wrists and open up my hands, palms faced up, in a suggestion that I should also be shrugging my shoulders and offering a face of regret. But I imagine I'm looking as impatient as I feel.

'Fucking hell, Laz, lock the door,' he says laughing, and gets out his wallet. He takes out a note and hands me the wallet. I take out one of his cards, put his wallet on the cistern and unwrap my coke. I tip about half onto his wallet, wrap up the rest and pocket it. I roughly spread the coke into two lines with the edge of the card; they're not straight or remotely even. They look like an aerial view of two mountain ranges, but it's all going to get hoovered up the same, so what the fuck. Eddie has tightly rolled the note during my preparations, and hands it to me while I look at him with gratitude. He looks at me with amusement when he clocks my attentiveness to the perfect line of coke. 'Is that the Matterhorn there?' He's pointing at my lines, and laughing at his own joke.

'Yes,' I'm laughing too, 'My miniature coke sculptures are going down a storm,' and I hoover up the micro sculptures with two deep sniffs. I give Eddie a look that tells him Con has done all right again, and he looks pleased, then starts to look impatient. We swap places and he tells me the latest instalment in the life of a prosaic pillock he works with while he's sorting out his lines. I'm engaged in regular sniffing and going for deep inward snorts through my nose that carry that burning sensation down my throat. My throat is going a little numb, is that my sinuses too? This guy at Eddie's work, his name's Stewart, Eddie mentions him often and he's a source of constant amusement for me. I know working with Stewart frustrates Eddie, but he also sees the funny side of it, and that's how he tells it to me.

'I was talking to him today about the symbiotic relationship between sea cucumbers and cleaner shrimp.'

Eddie reckons Stewart is the most boring man alive, so his tactic is to get in first and start talking about something. 'And he said to me, "They do a good job, the cucumbers look clean in the supermarket".' When speaking as Stewart, Eddie puts on a voice and adopts a stance that are ridiculously exaggerated. I've never met Stewart, but I doubt anyone on the planet talks like that. 'I thought he was joking at first, then I realised he doesn't know there are two things called cucumber. I tried to tell him that you can't buy sea cucumbers in supermarkets. I know some people do eat them, but I wasn't going to confuse him more by telling him that.' He's got his lines perfectly straight and even, so I hand him a tightly rolled note. He snorts one line and clears his schnoz with some powerful sniffs. He's using the rolled note to point at me as he carries on, 'I probed him with a few deft questions, and it turns out he thinks cucumbers grow on the seabed, that's why they're called sea cucumbers.' We're laughing at quite a volume, if someone comes into the toilet now, we'll definitely draw attention to ourselves. We remind each other of this and quieten down. 'I asked him how he thought these cucumbers were harvested, and he said, "Probably deep-sea divers".' We both crack up at the combination of Stewart's interpretation of the world around him, and Eddie's preposterous impersonation. I say I'd like to meet this Stewart character, and Eddie tells me I'm welcome. He takes care of his other line, and conducts several sniffs of varying strength while rehoming his card and note.

'Let's get the fuck out of here,' he suggests, and I agree.

Back at the bar, we resume our positions next to the remainder of our pints. I order two fresh ones, and we finish our current pints in a few gulps while waiting. We're both still sniffing at the bar, trying to be discreet, but the barman looks over each time one of us sniffs. 'If Sonya hears us sniffing, she won't leave us alone,' I tell Eddie, and he nods. We agree to try our best to keep the sniffing to a minimum, several of the gathering would show interest if news of a line got out. I pay for our drinks, while giving the barman a friendly smile, which he doesn't return. We stand at the bar chatting for a while when Binky comes over to order a round. She's in a good mood as usual. I don't know how she does it. She's talking to us about a new film called "Aliens and Werewolves" starring Berk Scaffold, who saves humanity by fighting all the baddies to death. I feel like asking whether the aliens and werewolves are in cahoots, or fighting against each other too, or unaware of each other's presence, because I'm having trouble understanding the ridiculous plot. She suddenly breaks off and starts talking to the barman. I give Eddie a confused look and he starts laughing. The barman shoots a look over, and the cunt gives *me* the dirty eye. She finishes giving the barman instructions and she's back with us. I fear more confused plotlines for my brain to deal with, and as it's already having fifty thousand thoughts per second, I decide to say something that will involve a much simpler plot. 'Is Miriam out tonight?'

'Yes, she is. She's meeting us here.'

'Great, now I just have to convince her that Con works in the morgue.'

'Done,' she says, giving me a big smile to look at. In response to my puzzled expression, she says, 'I spoke with her this afternoon, after you messaged me, and we spoke about Con.' She's looking quite pleased with herself and continues, 'And I told her that he really does work in the morgue.' She stands there smiling at me, but also looking expectant; waiting for my response.

'Did she believe you?' I'm not convinced.

'Of course, we're friends. She knows I wouldn't lie to her. She sounded interested, but that doesn't mean she'll find his seduction technique bearable.' She laughs for a good few seconds, and Eddie and I involuntarily join in. Binky has experience of Con's seduction technique; he tried to charm her each time they met at first, but as each attempt was unsuccessful, he eventually gave up. She described him as being like an eel in a sock.

'That's okay, it's over to Con now. We've done our bit. Thank you, Binky.'

She looks over at the barman when he brings over the third drink, and she's away again. He asks her for payment, which she duly provides. I can see her thinking of the best way to carry the three drinks in one trip, and I'm about to suggest something when Eddie pipes up.

'I'll carry one of those drinks, Binky, and we'll join you with Dalton and Lucy,' and he reaches for one of the drinks. The three of us head over with an assortment of an empty hand, and hands carrying drinks. All the drinks make it. I have a sneaky couple of air sniffs walking over, and I'm reminded of the streaky burn in my throat. I'm getting a nice buzz off the coke, and I notice I'm nearly half way down this pint already. I'll slow down a bit. I don't want to be pissed out of my head when I talk to Rosie. There's lots of chatter between the five of us, and I appear to be responsible for quite a bit of it. Eddie's talking more than anyone, and he's just spent four minutes talking about shirt buttons. There are translocations of personnel between the two groups, but we are standing right next to each other, so that's easy and inevitable. I go to the bar, and some friend of Lionel starts talking to me. I ascertain quickly that he's a dick, and listen to his talk for as long as I can stand it, maybe eight or nine seconds, before I join in, then I'm talking ten to the dozen. Surely, that's dozen to the ten? Well, it's a damn sight more than a dozen anyway, I know that. I'm talking about something I don't give a fuck about, but quite enthusiastically. I look at him while I'm jabbering away, thinking I don't even like you, why am I talking to you. But more to the point, why are you tolerating me? It's the fucking coke, the fucking snow. One shit conversation after another. I look around the room and see people talking; they're blabbing about themselves, spilling themselves onto each other. They're excreting their inner thoughts to whoever will listen, exposing themselves, letting their essence leak out and evaporate. Surely, that makes them more vulnerable? Some people are pretty fucked. As for me, I'm jabbering away exuberantly like some swashbuckling snowman, but I too am talking nothing but shite. I should be ashamed of myself.

After a while I catch up with Eddie. We're chatting and I'm taking opportunities to look over towards the door, to see who's arriving. Eddie must have spotted this, as he says, 'Maybe she'll be at the party?' He doesn't miss much does he?

'Yeah,' I leave it at that. 'Talking of which, I need another drink. Do you want another one here, or should we go to the offie and get some booze for the party?'

'Let's head off,' he decides quickly. He announces to the others that we're heading to Anton's now, and asks if anyone wants to join us. Most people indicate they still have drinks on the go, and Binky reminds us that she's waiting for Miriam.

María knocks back the remainder of her drink, 'I'll join you,' she says with a sweet smile, but the relief is clear in her eyes. She puts her empty glass on the bar and the three of us head out.

In the offie, Baldwin's Booze, Eddie and I head towards the beers, and make our selections. I've gone for four ales; two bottles of Hairy Stoat at 5%, and two bottles of Chicken Lips at 5.5%. Eddie's gone for four bottles of a strong German beer, Wolff Stark Bier, but he still seems undecided about something. I suggest to him that our current haul might not be enough, and we should get a bottle of whisky to be safe. He tells me that's exactly what he was thinking, and I must have read his mind. I politely remind him we're standing in an offie.

'I'll buy the whisky, as you bought the coke. In fact, put all the booze together, I'll get this.' There's no point arguing and trying to force money into his hand, he wouldn't have offered if he didn't want to. Baldwin keeps his expensive booze behind the counter, so we head over to appraise the selection. María is there buying a bottle of rum, the old guy is clumsily putting it in a bag for her while she's holding out an Ayrton. Eddie's already spotted something that's taken his fancy, 'How about a bottle of Jerry Greyhound?'

'Good idea,' I tell him, to his delight. I've drank Jerry Greyhound many times, it's one of the more expensive whiskies, but it is wonderfully smooth. I put my bottles on the counter while Eddie asks the old man for the whisky. He's telling the guy about the party, but Baldwin's just working the cash register, looking at Eddie occasionally, and not showing any interest at all. Eddie's telling him who's going, and what kind of a night he reckons it will be. He's asking the guy what his night has been like. Has he been busy? Now he's talking about the retail business, supply and demand and economics. He tells the Baldwin that he likes his cardigan. María gives me a concerned look, and I must admit Eddie is jabbering on quite noticeably. Looks like another wave of coke has hit him, he just can't stop talking to the bloke, and he's talking faster than an auctioneer. I could help out the slow way, or the quick way. 'Eddie!' I shout at him. Not too loud that I startle the Baldwin, but enough to snap Eddie out of his patter. He was in the process of asking the bloke where he got it from. María gives a laugh, and the old Baldwin looks extremely fucking relieved. Eddie silently pays, picks up the bags of booze which clink noisily in the silence, and we exit the shop with a polite "thanks". We walk along, not saying anything, pretending nothing had happened, waiting for Eddie to say something, and trying desperately not to laugh.

After a short distance, Eddie asks, 'Was I talking a lot to the old man?' and María and I immediately release our barely contained laughter. Eddie joins in, and the three of us take a left down Fishy Grove towards Anton's, with Eddie back to talking like he's working in one of those stock exchange trading pits.

Chapter Six

María knocks on Anton's door and we're still laughing. As we turned the corner, the conversation moved on to dinosaurs; I don't know how, but that's the current topic. As we're waiting for someone to answer the door, Eddie says, 'I know why dinosaurs went extinct.' There's no point asking him why, he's definitely going to tell us. 'They munched themselves into extinction. The carnivores had a feast, munching on all the herbivores. Smaller carnivores took care of the smaller herbivores, while the larger herbivores were attended to by the larger carnivores. Big herbivores had no place to hide, they couldn't very well scamper up a tree. You know those goats that forage in trees in Morocco, you couldn't have a whole stegosaurus family up a tree. The first one could hug a tree and act as steps, so the others can climb up its plates and into the branches. But then, that one's fucked, how does *it* get into the tree? Anyway, after a while the carnivores depleted the herbivore stock, and as they were too big and cumbersome to catch birds and small mammals, they had to eat each other. Some of them would turn cannibal, and chomp on each other's heads, mantis style. Until there was only one left.'

'Lonesome Deano, that's what they called him,' I say, in complete sarcastic agreement.

'That's right, they did,' Eddie confirms. 'He died of starvation unfortunately,' and the three of us are saved from any more of that conversation by the door opening, and Anton greeting us, waving us in.

'How the fuck are you guys?' he asks all of us, then kisses María on the cheek and tells her she looks beautiful. He leads us down the hallway towards the kitchen, talking quickly; he can't get some of those words out fast enough. Some are overlapping, others get lost somewhere, their contribution deemed unnecessary. I think Anton's has had a line or two of his own. Anton Grüber works for the Forestry Commission, and has a nice house. He's earned it. He has a job with responsibilities, and he gets paid accordingly, but with responsibility comes long hours. He loves it though, he's turned his interests into paid employment, so I don't suppose he cares how long the hours are. Anton's boyfriend, Maxwell, is in the kitchen and greets us all with a flamboyant display of air kisses. I like Maxwell, but he is rather theatrical. Anton's favourite pastimes are sports, drinking heavily and taking skipfuls of drugs; three things Maxwell doesn't like doing. I take the opportunity, the occasion of being in the kitchen provides, to put three of my beers in the fridge. María is pouring herself a glass of rum and cola and I open a Hairy Stoat, while Eddie is already taking a swig from his bottle of Wolff. I didn't even see him open his bottle. 'Guys you know the usual rule applies, you are welcome to smoke in the garden and the conservatory but not in the house please make yourselves at home. I have to get Barb a gin and tonic.' There are rows of bottles lined up on the kitchen counter, and Anton clatters a few of them before finding the gin.

I look at Eddie and María, and suggest a smoke. They look pleased with my suggestion, so we leave Anton behind us, making hard work of a gin and tonic. We walk into the conservatory and I see the doors at the opposite side are open, revealing the large garden with quite a few people chatting, drinking and dancing. Anton's into some good music, not much of our tastes overlap, but some of the bands we like, we're both well into. Like The Stones, Zeppelin, Pink Floyd, Sabbath, but I don't know what this song is. I've ever heard it before. It's awful. But there are a fair few revellers dancing out there, and a few singing along too. There are a few people seated on the other side of the conservatory, near the doors to the garden, two women and a man. I don't know who they are. We spot some comfy looking seats right where we're standing, so we decide to sit down for a rest and check out who's here in a bit. As I'm rolling a bifta, Anton comes through smiling at us, but muttering something about bloody Barb. Maxwell is close behind him, informing him that he should slow down with the drugs and the booze, but Anton isn't listening. I watch them disappear within the slew of partygoers outside, and return to the bifta.

'Did you know it's highly dangerous to attempt to fart and whistle at the same time?' Eddie asks, looking serious. María and I quickly smile, as we know he's making this up as he sits there, but we play along and look serious too.

'I didn't know that,' María sits forward as she speaks, 'Have you tried it?'

'No. And don't you try it either. It's something to do with wind being pushed out of both ends simultaneously. It creates a false vacuum inside you, and as the bubble increases in size, you explode.' All three of us experience a burst of laughter. I light the bifta, and the conversation moves on. The bifta gets passed around a few times, and by the time it's extinguished, we've mainly spoken about teddy bears, women's tights, the latest face lift on Clifford DeRange and satsumas. Eddie is currently telling us that the kernel of a Brazil nut looks like a miniature orca, and I'm in the process of agreeing when there's a knock at the front door. Eddie gets up, 'I'll get it.'

Anton must have the hearing of a bat, as he's walking through the conservatory towards the front door, with Maxwell in tow. Maxwell wants to discuss whether it's Anton's fifth or sixth vodka, and Anton's telling him to fuck off. They disappear into the kitchen, but I can still hear them arguing. Another fucking diabolically awful song finishes, and a new one starts that I don't recognise. This one's terrible too. All different singers, this must be a mix tape for the party. I'm going to suffer listening to this shit all night. Looks like I may have to get pissed after all. While María and I are chatting, the noise level increases with the sound of many people talking at the same time. It sounds like our guests have reached the kitchen. People filter into the conservatory, bringing their chatter with them. It's the guys from the pub, and more greetings ensue. Lionel, Sandy and their workmates head out to the garden, followed by Binky, Miriam and Sonya. Eddie's talking to Stopher and Anton, while Maxwell stands by the kitchen door eyeballing them. Dalton and Lucy pull up some seats to join us as Eddie returns, and I see Stopher and Anton walking into the garden, but Maxwell hasn't moved.

There are a few murmurings of conversation as people settle down, when I hear Maxwell's worried voice asking, 'Eddie, was Anton obtaining more drugs?' There's a pause while we all exchange glances with each other, with Eddie and Maxwell receiving more glances than the rest of us. Eddie hasn't spoken, and doesn't look likely to, when Maxwell hurriedly says, 'Look, I know it's none of my business, he can take what he wants, but he gets totally fucked…and he's already quite fucked. He's been doing coke all evening…and knocking back the voddies.' He stops, and composes himself. 'Sorry Eddie, I don't want to put you in a shitty position, I should just ask Anton.' And with that he too joins the garden throng.

'Was he obtaining more drugs?' Dalton enquires of Eddie.

'Yeah, Stopher has some pills. Anton said he wanted some. I don't know what he bought, they were walking out as they discussed it.'

'Did you obtain any of those pills?' Dalton enquires again.

'Yes, thanks. Do you want some? Stopher has a bagful, but they won't last all night.' Eddie clearly has a point, as there is an immediate resumption of murmuring, as people discuss their requirements for the evening. Conclusions are made, and Dalton collects money from people before fucking off to find Stopher. People set about chatting again, when there's a knock on the front door. The chatting ceases and the glances recommence.

'The last time you got out of your chair to answer the door Eddie, Anton heard it too, from the garden, and followed you through. He must have highly developed auditory powers, more sensitive than other humans. Maybe he's part bat. That's probably why he likes the nectar so much. And he'll be through here any moment,' I tell him, and María nods her agreement. He should also be good at detecting Doppler shifts in whatever he's on, as waves crash around in his brain. We're all sitting here waiting, in silence; all of us unsure about starting a conversation until we know what's happening. There's another knock on the door, and Anton comes striding from the garden into the conservatory.

'Can't one of you answer the FUCKING DOOR,' he enquires without breaking stride, and disappears into the house.

'He didn't look happy did he?' Lucy notes. 'I hope he's not pissed off with us.'

'I don't think it's us he's pissed off with,' Eddie says matter-of-factly.

Anton returns and stands by us, I notice he's alone. 'I'm sorry for my outburst guys but Maxwell is really getting on my tits. It's not your fault.' He looks around the room and smiles at the trio sitting on the other side of the room. He turns back, saying, 'Remember to help yourselves to the booze in the kitchen, and the buffet is in the garden. I paid a small fortune for it and I couldn't eat a fucking thing.'

'Outside catering? Anton, can't you even make a sandwich?' María teases him. It's got us all smiling, including Anton.

'Of course I can make a sandwich but there's no way I'm making thirty of them. You'd want tabbouleh, various salads, olive fritters. I'd have been in the kitchen all fucking day. No chance. I ordered it all in so get stuck in. My stomach's the size of a marmoset's fist so I won't be partaking.' His mood has improved considerably, so I suggest he grabs a seat and I knock up a bifta. 'Thanks Laz, I will in a bit. I should go outside and circulate among the people I've invited,' he gives us a self-mocking smile, 'And make sure Maxwell isn't pissing anyone else off.' He moves off and gets a few "see you later Anton's" for his courage. You can't just let the man walk off to face that, being the host and ensuring everyone is having fun. A party round my place consists only of friends, Anton included, and sometimes acquaintances get invited. If someone isn't having a good time, it's okay if they go somewhere else. Anton invites friends and acquaintances from different spheres of his life, and he worries that people aren't enjoying themselves. A party round my place consists of everyone bringing their own stuff, everyone getting wasted, people passing out or going home. There's the occasional spillage of a drink, but I always put a few rugs down when people come round, and they take the brunt of the spills. Anton has a nice house, and when there's just a few of us getting quietly wasted, we chill out inside or outside depending on the weather. But with larger gatherings he doesn't want puke over his nice curtains, so the party is outside. There is always the danger that someone could spill red wine, but drink spillages and puke are more easily dealt with in the kitchen, the marble floored conservatory and the garden. It rarely happens, but I agree with his logic. He has a lot to think about. I reach into my pocket and retrieve my weed tin. In my tin I have weed, tobacco, skins and cardboard. As I'm doing this, I notice Eddie is already knocking up a bifta, two won't hurt, so I carry on.

I open my tin as Con walks into the room, it must have been him that Anton opened the door to. What's he been doing for the last five minutes? I can guess, but I don't want to know. He's just standing there by the door to the kitchen; I think he wants to be noticed. He's looking around the room, not making eye contact with anyone, giving us all time to get a good look at him. Lucy shouts out, 'Hey Con,' to get this over with, and starts dramatically waving her arms at him. He's about three metres away, she's hilarious. He walks towards us confidently, when a fart emerges. Everyone must have heard that. It was sufficiently audible to dampen anyone's confidence. But not Con, he strides purposefully forward as if it was his theme tune.

'Hey guys, how's everyone doing?' He looks at us all, each of us getting a look at his smile. He's greeted with a chorus of, "Good thanks", "I'm fucked", "How are you?", "Do you want a drink?" I tell him I noticed Anton has a load of beers in the fridge. 'Good, I'll grab one of them. Anyone else?' While María and Lucy say they have drinks, Eddie asks for a Wolff. Con signals with his eyes that he wants to talk to me, so I get up, put my tin away and go into the kitchen with him. 'Is Miriam here yet?' he asks as we're taking bottles out of the fridge.

'You're not wasting any time are you?' It would be good for Con to be distracted with Miriam all night. If she knocks him back, he's bound to try his luck with Rosie. If she turns up I think it would be unlikely that Rosie would go for Con, but he'd be using up precious time. 'She's in the garden with Binky,' I happily inform him, and he gives me a smile and a wink. 'Please don't do that again,' I tell him. 'And the good news is, she is fully convinced you work with stiffs all day.'

He grabs both my upper arms, 'You are a hero Laz, thank you.' In grabbing me, he's a little closer to me, we're about the same height, and I get a good waft of his breath. Semi-digested salty food, smoke and mint, he's making an effort. He lets go and looks around until he spots the bottle opener.

'It isn't me you should thank, Binky convinced her.' He opens his drink and offers me the opener, so I open a Wolff while Con tells me he certainly will thank her, and that he has more coke if I need any. That reminds me; I pay him the money I owe him. I grab Eddie's Wolff and we head back to the conservatory. Dalton has returned and is sitting down, passing out pills to the congregation. I didn't put an order in, I'm not in the mood for a pill tonight. He sees Con, and the two exchange greetings. I give Eddie his beer, sit down and get my tin out again.

'I like your goatee,' Con tells Dalton with sincerity, 'You look like Childs in "The Thing".' And he does, and we've all told him too. Childs is plural, shouldn't he be called Children?

'Keith David, yeah I know…thank you,' he says graciously. 'You're looking good as usual.' Before that gives Con the opportunity to talk about his outfit or hair, he carries on with, 'I just bought some pills off Stopher, if you need any he's in the garden.'

Miriam's in the garden, so I assume Con will take this opp… 'Good idea, I'll go and find him,' Con says quickly. 'See you in a bit.' As he walks out of the conservatory he looks at the three sitting by the door, waits for them to look up at him, nods his head at them, and exits. He's got a nerve attracting their attention, they must have heard his fart. He's probably forgotten about it though.

There's a knock on the front door and María jumps up, turns towards the garden, and shouts, 'I'll get it,' and walks off laughing into the house. I'm sitting here with my tin in my hand, thinking this might be Rosie. And Ingle following her around again. I'm trying to tilt my head to allow as much sound coming from inside the house to be channelled into my right ear, while trying to contract the muscles of my left ear to narrow the hole the noise from the party is trying to get down. I'm not having any success. Eddie tells me that he bought a few extra pills in case I want some, so if I change my mind, just ask. There is noise coming from inside the house, quite a few voices by the sound of it. It's difficult to make out individuals. This is useless.

'Cheers Eddie, not sure I'm in the mood tonight, but I'll let you know if I decide to head down that route later.' If Rosie isn't coming, or if I get knocked back, I might just get wasted instead. 'Are you looking to get fucked tonight? How many are you taking?' I notice him take a drag of his bifta, I didn't notice him spark it up, and my tin is still in my hand.

'No, just having one,' he hands me the bifta and I take a drag. 'I'll see how the party goes, if it's an all-nighter, I might take more.' I take a few more drags while he tells me about a new type of cardboard he's invented. I can hear chatter from the kitchen, now María's voice, sounds like she's informing people of the booze stock. That's definitely Ingle's voice too. Maybe? I pass the bifta to Lucy, who takes a drag and carries on a conversation with Dalton about garden sheds.

'It's paper,' I tell Eddie, 'Cardboard's made of paper, you can't invent cardboard.'

'It's a special type of cardboard,' he's looking pleased and excited, 'Wait 'til you hear this.' He's about to amaze me, when a gaggle of people enter from the kitchen. María is leading the chattering crowd straight at us. Following her is Ingle; a woman I don't know; that bloke Teak from last night talking to a bloke I don't know; Susan Conifer, another of

75

Ingle's new work mates; Rosie; and someone I don't know. Rosie's here. My breathing's getting a bit faster. I don't know if Eddie's still speaking, but I can't hear him. Rosie looks right at me, we both smile, she waves, and I wave back. Fuck. The signs are looking good already, or maybe I'm confidently thinking how wonderful things are going to work out because I shifted some fucking coke earlier.

The "someone I don't know" at the back is speaking to Rosie, so her attention is diverted, but I can't help looking over at her. The "someone" is a bloke; good looking, but not her type. How the fuck would I know that? He's tremendously clean shaven, and his hair is trendy. I'm hoping he's not her type. She looks over again, and I'm still looking at her, we both smile again. She's fucking beautiful, and her black hair is loose over her shoulders. Last week she had it tied back, revealing her beautiful neck. She caught me looking at the curves of her neck while we were talking, but she didn't seem to mind. She's wearing a short, dark green denim jacket, with a black top underneath, and a pleated, patterned skirt. I can't tell what the pattern is, but it stops above her knees, and her legs are sensational, ending where her black boots start. I look up and she hasn't seen me looking. That guy from a boy band is talking to her again. Ingle hasn't stopped fucking talking too, introducing all his new friends. Teak and his conversational companion are introduced then resume their chat. I catch Teak informing his eager listener that a friend of his fucked a woman from behind while she sucked off a labrador. Who are you Teak? Is bestiality the only thing you can talk about?

Some people have already met Susan Conifer, and Rosie, but Ingle's milking each introduction so we get to hear how amusing he is. He gets to end of the introductions and we meet Craig. He works in a different department, but they don't hold it against him. Really amusing. Craig has no choice but to break off his conversation with Rosie when Ingle shows his new friend to everyone, so Rosie takes the opportunity to ease away from him. I see everyone has a drink, so they should be ready to hit the party. Apparently, the introductions and greetings are over because Ingle is instructing his troop to follow him into the garden. Eddie must have noticed my shift of attention, and change of mood. He gets out of his seat and joins the moving troop. He moves quickly, and immediately engages Ingle in conversation, talking earnestly about something, utterly engaging his attention. Leaving his seat empty.

I watch Eddie walk into the garden, with his hand on Ingle's shoulder, leading him away. He's still doing the talking; I must remember to ask him later what topic he chose. Ingle's troop is filing out too, but María and Rosie are speaking to each other and remain where they stand. María was down The Wooden Octopus last weekend when Ingle introduced Rosie to us, and the two seemed to get on. She gives Rosie a personal introduction to Lucy and Dalton, and the three warmly greet each other.

Rosie turns to me, 'Hey Laz, how are you?' Her smile is beautiful.

'Good, thanks.' I indicate Eddie's vacant seat opposite me, 'Join us if you want.'

'Okay.' She walks past Lucy and Dalton and sits down, as María reclaims her seat. We're all sitting comfortably, and I'm sitting directly in front of Rosie. Eddie, you are a genius. Quick thinking and straight into action.

I ask her how she is, and I find out that she's feeling good. Lucy asks her about her job and how long she's known Ingle for. I discover that they work in the same department, but not on the same team. She's seen him around since he started last month, but they've only recently spoken. So Ingle didn't waste any time asking her out to the boozer and to Anton's party, and for that, I thank you Ingle. I knock up a bifta, take a few drags, and pass it to Rosie. It goes around a couple of times while we all chat. The conversation is easy, with everyone chipping in and having a laugh. I keep looking over to Rosie when others are talking, and I'm often rewarded with her looking back. I ask her a few questions so I can engage with her for longer, and I'm thinking she's the most attractive woman I've ever seen.

Nobody notices Ingle enter the room until he speaks. 'There you are Rosie, we were wondering where you'd got to.' He tries to sound casual, but there's a hint of uncertainty in his voice when he realises she's having a good time without him. 'You should join us in the garden,' he says to her, and gestures to the garden with his head, 'It's pretty lively out there.'

'Yeah, I'd like to check out what's going on in the garden. I need to sort myself out a drink first. I'll pop out in a bit,' she says this so sweetly, but Ingle's face is squirming slightly as he can't figure out whether this has gone well or not. He waves as he retreats, telling us he'll see us in a bit.

Dalton looks at Rosie, 'I know he's your new friend, but Ingle can be a massive fart hole at times.' At this, Rosie bursts out a laugh, which takes us all by surprise, including herself. We all join in, and there's a sense that she sees the point.

'I've only socialised with him twice, and both times I've enjoyed the company of his friends more.' She shoots me a glance. 'So you guys say what you like about my new friend.' She picks up her empty glass, 'Does anyone want a drink?' and I see her looking at my empty.

'I need one. I'll come with you.' The other three decide as we move towards the kitchen; Dalton and Lucy want beers, María wants rum and cola. We move around the kitchen getting drinks. We're checking each other out as we move, both when the other isn't looking, and when they are. Just different angles. I fetch two beers from the fridge while she mixes the rum. I take it from her, and with the beers in my other hand I tell her I'll deliver the round, and leave the kitchen.

When I return she's pouring a red wine, so I go to the fridge and crack open a bottle of Hairy Stoat. The chat is easy, and flirtatious. We're making each other laugh, and I can't keep my eyes off her. I'm not sure how long we've been chatting when Maxwell enters the kitchen looking bothered. I might change that to stressed, he's looking stressed. He greets me, almost pleadingly, and greets Rosie politely. I introduce the two, and ask him if he's okay. He tells me that Anton is dancing around in the garden. 'It is a party, Maxwell. Is no one else dancing?'

'Yes, but he's dancing around like a madman. Laughing all the time.' He takes a seat at the kitchen table and pours himself a vodka. I'm about to tell him that Anton's simply having fun, that's what people do at parties, but he'll get annoyed with me, so I decide against it. He necks the vodka and winces, 'He's already fucked, and I think he's taken a pill. Can you talk to him Laz? He listens to you.' He looks at me imploringly, and while I don't feel much sympathy, I sort of agree to talk to him.

'I'll ask him what he's taken, and what he's drunk, and ask him if he feels in control. I'll assess his behaviour and if I think he's making an arse of himself, I'll tell him. If after my advice, he decides to carry on, that's his decision. I can't do any more than that Maxwell.' He's looking calmer, I assume it's because I've just offered hope, everyone else is too busy partying. I'm aware that people can party too hard and overdose, but I don't want to talk in those terms with Maxwell, it will only stress him out more. Besides, Anton's getting wasted, that's all. 'My advice to you,' I'm looking him right in the eyes, 'Is to stop worrying about Anton, and try to enjoy the party yourself.' I give him a smile and suggest we all head back out. We file out the kitchen and I usher Maxwell into the lead position, while I bring up the rear. I'm walking behind Rosie and I can see the shape of her cheeks moving beneath her skirt as she walks, so it's worked out quite well. We find the guys still seated in the conservatory, 'I'm going to have a word with Anton, apparently he's enjoying himself too much. Either that or he might need medical attention.' The three of us walk into the garden. I see a few people dancing, but Anton isn't one of them. I see him to the right, standing by a table, not dancing. Maybe he's knackered himself out. He's talking to someone who looks like a young Barry Manilow. Barry has a full head of brown hair, it cascades backwards off his head and onto his shoulders, like the hair of a woman in a pop band in the '80s. He's wearing a crimson suit and is accompanied by a woman who could be attractive, but is far too thin. To the left, standing by two long tables of food, are Binky, Miriam, Con and a guy in a suit. Anton must be pleased that his different sets of friends are socialising. Binky waves us over, so we join them. Rosie and the three recognise each other from last weekend, and they exchange greetings. The suit knows Maxwell, and introduces himself to Rosie and me as Richard Farnborough.

When it appears the greetings are over, Farnborough looks at me with undisguised distaste and asks, 'What do you do?' He smiles, anticipating he's going to like my answer.

What? We've only just met. It's one of the worst questions you can ask someone. It's essentially asking, 'How much do you earn?' The question does not care about your gender, race, sexuality or anything else. It's a way of quickly sorting everyone out into monetary order. Why do it? Why not just meet someone and find out if you like them, instead of putting barriers in place before you start? I look at his smug smile, and resist the urge to slap it off his face.

'I read books, I listen to music, I go on holiday, I go to work, I enjoy cooking. What do you do?'

'I'm an IT consultant.' There's no humour in his response, that's what he wanted to tell me, and it's serious stuff.

'Is that all you do?' There's an exaggerated look of puzzlement on my face and Con is laughing. Farnborough doesn't seem to know what to say next, I'm not sure he understands where the amusement is coming from.

There's movement and noise approaching from the right; Anton is joining us, bringing Barry and his companion. 'Hey guys...' he does look and sound quite fucked, '...this is Rory Hyde, an' Cynthia.' We all say hi to each other, and Anton carries on, 'Rory's a sausage farmer,' he informs the group, and nearly topples into Miriam.

'So Rory's gay too,' Con says, utterly unimpressed with being told.

Anton has a brief fit of exuberant laughter, and Rory joins in with a hearty bellow of a laugh. His mouth was open so wide, I could see his clacker wobble.

'No, Rory's a pig farmer,' Anton is finding the whole thing funny, but Maxwell is looking anything but amused. 'He owns Hyde Farm in East Bamfor'. Yooar funny Con.' Anton looks a bit unsteady on his feet again, and as Miriam attempts to steady him, he tumbles into her sending them both crashing to the ground. Miriam is holding a drink and as she falls backwards the liquid splashes into her face and hair. Several people shout "Anton" at the same time. Some out of concern, others expressing annoyance. Miriam is not happy, she's on the ground with Anton's leg across her, and sticky booze covering her head. She's asking Anton what the fuck he's playing at, and he's desperately trying to apologise, but he's quite wasted and it's difficult to make out what he's saying. Binky helps Miriam to her feet, and escorts her tearful friend into the house. Anton's still lying on the ground. Nearby people are coming over to see what the commotion is all about, but as it's all over now, we just stand here watching Anton trying to get up. Rosie and I help him up and sit him on one of those expensive padded garden chairs. Maxwell has fucked off somewhere; I don't think he's in the mood to be sympathetic. People are going back to their conversations, so we ask him a few questions to determine how fucked he is. He's speaking more clearly now, and given the evidence, we're both happy that he's just wasted and having fun. 'I must find Binky's friend and…apologise to 'er,' he informs us and sets off towards the house. There are a few mistimed steps, but he's heading in the right direction.

I look at Rosie, 'Shall we go for a walk?' She smiles and tells me that's a good idea. She points out Ingle ahead of us; he has his back to us so he hasn't seen us. 'Out of curiosity, do you speak to Teak much?'

'I see him at work sometimes. I've had the pleasure of his conversation on the odd unfortunate occasion.'

'What kind of stuff does he talk about?'

She's laughing at my line of questioning, I assume it's because she has experience of speaking to him and has correctly guessed that I find his conversations unpleasant. 'I was making a drink in the staff room recently, and he came in and started talking to me. The conversation was ordinary enough to begin with, but then he asked me, if two fifteen year olds had sex, would they both be paedophiles.' She's stopped laughing and is looking a little disgruntled. 'I quickly said yes, and left with my drink. Who casually asks questions like that in polite conversation? Apart from Teek.'

'I think sex is the main topic of conversation with his thoughts. I would prefer avoiding him and Ingle.'

We head over to the other side of the garden and wander through the mêlée of people chatting, drinking and dancing to the outskirts of the crowd. There's a huge sycamore tree here, and beyond there is some open space with a few partygoers here and there. The light has been fading for a while, but it seems a lot darker now. I see Eddie sitting on the grass with Mila. She's a friend of Anton's. I've only met her a few times, she's really nice, and Eddie has taken a shine to her. I'd better not go over and get in his way, that wouldn't be the best way to thank him for his heroism earlier. He sees us and waves us over. Well, that's decided that then. We sit down on the grass and Rosie and Mila are introduced. It's quieter over here, that shitty music isn't quite so invasive. Eddie's smiling at me, he can see his plan worked. I take out my tin, and proceed to make a bifta. Mila asks what the commotion was, and Rosie gives a brief, but accurate, re-telling of the incident. She can't help laughing at a few points, and I'm joining in. We apologise for finding the incident amusing, but we're laughing while we're apologising. Eddie and Mila are laughing too, and asking for more details of how Miriam poured her drink over her own face.

Rosie suddenly looks serious, 'The poor woman was quite upset after she managed to get up off the ground.' We're all laughing again. I light the bifta and take a drag. 'Her hair was ruined. I think that might be the end of her night.' She's smiling like she's knows she's being naughty, but there is concern for Miriam's plight too. After a few tokes, I pass the bifta to Rosie. She takes a drag and tells us that she recently fell over walking past a primary school. 'It was lunchtime and the playground was full of children running around. I was walking past the wire fence when I tripped and hit the pavement with a thud. The group of children near me all laughed, but then I saw the teacher supervising them, and she was laughing too. She didn't even ask me if I was all right, just laughed along with those horrible children.' We too are laughing along with those children, but she doesn't mind one bit. 'I'd have to fall about four hundred and fifty metres to hit terminal velocity, so I wasn't going particularly fast. But I only just had time to get my hands out in front of me, to prevent my nose from being flattened against my cheek. When I was lying on the ground, I saw a cat sitting under a car watching me. It was probably thinking my landing technique was rather primitive compared to its own. I got up and walked off with those little shits and their big shit teacher still laughing at me.' She passes the bifta to Eddie, as María, Dalton and Lucy join us.

'It's all kicking off in the house,' María informs us. 'Anton and Maxwell are having a row, and Miriam's crying her eyes out in the bathroom.' She looks solemn, 'Some people aren't having a good night,' and drinks some of her rum.

'Con's buzzing around the place, trying to show how concerned he is for Miriam.' Dalton likes Con, he's not taking the piss. 'But he is being helpful. Though he was just standing there laughing at Anton at one point, and that wasn't helpful.'

Rosie holds up her empty glass, 'I'm thinking of getting a refill, is it safe to go in the kitchen?' I announce that I need a drink, so we'll check it out together. We walk past the sycamore, sticking to this side of the garden, to avoid Ingle. I look over to where he was standing earlier; he's still there, still talking. Anton is amongst the dancers, looks like something has kicked again. We walk into the kitchen and it's deserted. I retrieve a Chicken Lips from the fridge, open it, and stand leaning against the kitchen counter. The coke's had me knocking back the beers, but the numerous biftas I've participated in have taken the edge off the high. I could do with another toot, but I won't, things are going well with Rosie, I don't want to mess it up by drinking a load of whisky, and doing an Anton. Rosie pours her drink and comes over to where I'm standing. She stands next to me, leaning against the counter, and leaning against me. We stay like this for a while, enjoying the contact. People come into the kitchen for drinks while we're chatting and laughing. They sort out their drinks, smile at us, and leave us alone to our conversation. 'There's no way you can break an apple in half,' she's shaking her head at me. Her hair is dancing and I have a strong urge to take her in my arms and kiss her.

Anton comes bursting into the kitchen and staggers to the sink. He pukes loudly, several times. We put our drinks down and move towards him. He's half slumped to the floor; holding onto the sink prevents him from hitting the deck completely. He's trying to pull himself up, so Rosie and I get a hand each in an armpit and lift him up. He immediately bends forward and pukes again. It stinks, and Rosie and I instinctively move backwards. He's not looking good. We sit him in a chair, and Rosie fetches him a glass of water. 'How are you feeling Anton?' I ask, because I have to start somewhere. He shakes his head. I think that means "no", he's not feeling good. 'You've changed colour Anton. You've gone a sort of pale green.' He nods his head. I think that means he's aware he probably looks like shit.

'I think you should lie down Anton,' Rosie gives him a concerned smile, 'Before you fall down.' She looks at me questioningly, 'Do we put him to bed?'

Maxwell enters the kitchen with a fanfare of loud comments for Anton to deal with. 'Look at you…you're a mess…you're a disgrace…in front of all your friends…have you been sick?' He must have detected the smell coming from the sink, because he peers in as he crosses the room. '…you have…what a mess…time for you to go to bed, you drunken buffoon.' Anton struggles to his feet and while jabbing a finger towards Maxwell, he sprays out an intoxicated language only he understands.

I look at Rosie, and she has the same expression I have; what do we do next, can we leave them to it? I venture forward, 'I don't understand what you're saying Anton, but you're not happy are you?' Rosie smothers a laugh, while I try and conclude this episode. No chance of that, Anton and Maxwell are escalating this to another row, and we're in the middle of it. Anton has every right to enjoy his party the way he sees fit, but he has got tremendously fucked. As annoyed as Maxwell is about it, he's still trying to look after Anton. But they're not quite seeing eye-to-eye about that at the moment. The row has attracted attention, and Con and Binky appear from the hallway. No Miriam, she's probably still too upset to see what the fuss is about. We leave the arguing in one corner of the kitchen and have a quick meeting with Con and Binky about what to do next. It is agreed that I need to skin up a big fat bifta and give it to Anton and Maxwell. Anton is fucked, so the bifta will bring him back down. Maxwell doesn't smoke heavily, so it will calm him down too. The end result is that there's no more arguing. If Anton passes out, Maxwell can tell him all about the party tomorrow afternoon, when he re-surfaces. While the plan is being executed, and I'm rolling a Goodnight Vienna for Anton, Con and Binky fuck off to attend to Miriam's needs. The guys are still arguing and several people have emerged from the garden to make sure no one is being killed. The curious see Rosie and me chatting several metres away from the argument and are satisfied there's no bloodshed. They still look perturbed, but that doesn't stop them returning to the party. While we're chatting, I suggest to Rosie that we bail out of the party and have a drink somewhere else. She asks where, in an encouraging tone. 'My place,' I suggest. 'We can have a drink and a smoke....and it doesn't have two people shouting at each other in the corner of the room.'

She laughs, 'Sounds good.' There's a full scale barney going on now between the lads, and we're sitting here flirting. Life feels good. She points at the bifta I've prepared, 'Let's give these two their medicine, and we can make a move,' there's lust in her eyes. I spark up the bifta and take a drag. 'Isn't that for the quarrelling lovebirds?'

'They won't finish it,' and I take another drag. Rosie helps herself to a drag, then I approach the two quarrellers, talking loudly to get their attention. I hold up the bifta, 'You two should carry on your discussion with this,' and hand it to Maxwell, 'Stick this in your word pouch.'

'Thank you Laz,' he takes a drag and turns to Anton and resumes. 'You see, he's a nice person, Laz, not like you…' I stop listening. I leave them to it.

I look at Rosie, 'Shall we go?'

'Yeah, come on,' and we both head out the kitchen and down the hallway to the front door. I can still hear Maxwell and Anton in the kitchen, but I hear another voice, a lot closer.

'Are you two leaving?' It's Con, he's appeared out of the downstairs bathroom, and is closing the door behind himself.

I stop and turn around, he's about five metres away, but I say, 'Yes, Con…' without approaching him, '…enjoy the rest of your night.' He's having a weird night, not one he could have planned for, but it might be working out for them in the bathroom.

'I need to speak to you, Laz.' He's beckoning me over with small, subtle waves of his hand. Like a conspirator.

'Can't this wait 'til tomorrow?' I start to turn away.

'No, I need to speak to you now.'

I know what he's like; I should get this over with quick. 'I'll be back in a minute,' I say to Rosie, and walk over to Con. 'What?' I ask, not showing any subtlety or co-conspirator behaviour.

He moves in close to me and lowers his voice so Rosie is out of earshot, 'I made some enquiries about your need for a fence.' He lets that hang there, reminding me that I asked him for a favour. 'I've got a guy for you, his name's Tony. Tony Bicep.' He looks pleased with himself.

'What?' He can't be serious.

'Yeah, he's a boxing trainer.'

'What?' He's making this up.

'He runs a gym in Ripton Vale. Call me tomorrow and we can go over and talk to him.'

I can't be bothered to think about this now, so I change the subject, 'How's Miriam?'

'She was quite upset, so she and Binky left.' He sees me looking at the bathroom door. 'I wouldn't go in there Laz, I gave birth to a baby otter. The stench is quite horrific, it could break your nose. I'd go upstairs Laz.' He turns and walks down the hall to the kitchen. Apparently, I can go now.

Chapter Seven

I catch up with Rosie waiting by the front door, and she's giving me a look of curiosity. From her perspective the conversation I just had with Con largely consisted of me saying 'What?' three times. Once impatiently, and twice in puzzlement. She doesn't ask any questions though. She simply opens the door and I follow her out. 'You didn't tell Ingle you were leaving.'

'He'll figure it out,' she's smiling and has that naughty look on her face again. Fuck, she's stunning. My heart rate has increased again, and the urge to hold and kiss her has returned. We're walking down Magnesium Lane, by the haberdashery, when I stop her with the intention of going for this kiss I keep thinking about. She stops and looks at me wondering. I guide us off the pavement into the doorway of the shop; the shop front is glass, and so is the recess doorway. We are surrounded by buttons, threads, ribbons and fabric in a multitude of colours as I pull her towards me. She realises why we've stopped and smiles. I place my hands gently on the sides of her neck, lean forward and place my lips on hers. Her lips are soft and they grasp mine with tenderness. We kiss sensually for a few moments, and I notice her lips grasping mine more eagerly. I respond, and we've gone from sensual kissing to passionately making out in no time at all. We both wanted this since last weekend.

'Filth,' I hear from behind me, 'Filth…filth.' It's putting us off, so we break to see what the fuss is about. We turn and see two old ladies staring at us. They're not happy by the looks on their miserable faces. The one that looks a bit like Roy Hodgson points a finger, 'You filthy heathen, you have the devil inside you. The devil…' She looks over at her friend, who looks a bit like Eric Idle, for support. Eric's not saying anything, so Roy decides to carry on, presumably to make it look like she has a point. '…Satan…you have Satan inside you…get thee behind me, Satan,' she says the last bit triumphantly, but only because it's recognisable and is something to hold onto while she's floundering. Eric senses Roy's growing confidence and joins in with the recommendation. As the pair of them are working themselves up into a frenzy of instructions as to the position Satan should assume, I hold up one finger in the air and step forward from the doorway. Both women fall silent.

'I have a question for you.' I'm looking at them kindly. The two women look terror stricken. 'Why would you want Satan behind you?' I let the question formulate in their minds for a few moments. 'If it was up to me, I'd want him in front of me. So I could keep an eye on him. If he was behind me, I'd be looking over my shoulder all the time, checking what he's up to. It's not like he'd be doing a crossword, he'd be up to no good.' I look at them questioningly, but they don't have an answer. Their mouths open and close, but they neglect to include any words during the procedure.

Rosie's hand appears in mine and she pulls me down the street, away from the disapproving faces of Roy and Eric. She's laughing and pulling me towards her with her arm around my waist as we walk. We collide a few times, and use the excuse to use our free hands to steady each other. We're touching, making contact, reassuring each other, getting aroused.

We could be back at my place in fifteen minutes if we cut through Fathom Park, or twenty if we stick to the streets. Granted, I want to get back sooner, but if we go via the park, we might encounter night time park users. If it's a bunch of kids looking for mischief, we'll tell them to fuck off. But what if some guys come over asking for money, or our phones, and making lewd comments to Rosie? I wouldn't want to look like a pussy in front of her, so I'd no doubt say something and get punched in the face for it. What happens then? A brawl? I don't want the evening to go like that, so I decide against the park. I'm walking down familiar streets, but they feel different tonight. Recently, I've become disenchanted living in Stumpton. My work, my flat, my life, nothing changes. I walk down the same streets every day, and they stay the same too. The same dirty grey. But tonight they seem lighter, less full of the accumulated grime and misery. We're walking with our arms around each other's waists, chatting away, slowing down considerably every now and then, to exchange kisses. At one point, on the corner of Barzovian Road, this leads to a complete stop as we re-engage in passionate kissing and use our hands to explore each other's bodies. After a while we move on, thankfully my place isn't far. As we near my flat, I start to worry about where I left the diamonds. I know they're still in the pint glass, but I can't remember where I put it. In the cupboard rings a bell, but I can't be sure. It might be on the living room table. I might have tidied up and absentmindedly put it by the sink. I'll need to get in ahead of her, put the light on and scope the rooms. If it's on the table, I'll have to hide it. She'll see me and ask what I was hiding. I can't say diamonds. I could say dirty porn. What if she asks to have a look? I haven't got any that I could whip out quickly; the internet has done away with the need for that. I'm not looking forward to this. I could run ahead, and shout out what number I live at. No, that wouldn't work, it's too weird. I could tell her that I fancy a quick game of hide and seek first, so if she waits outside the flat and counts, I'll hide in the flat. I could take care of the diamonds, and I'd know how much time I'd have too; I could ask her to count out loud through the letterbox. What about when I've taken care of the diamonds? I'd actually have to hide somewhere. No, this is even weirder. Well, we're fucking here now, so running off's out of the question. Rosie says something, but I have to ask her to repeat it.

'Why have we stopped? Do you live here?' She's laughing at me, fuck knows what look I've got on my face right now. 'Are you all right Laz?' she's still laughing.

'I was lost in thought for a second,' I give her a smile back. 'Yeah, this is where I live.' I walk down the path, fishing for my keys in my pocket. The building is divided into five blocks, each three floors high. Each floor has one flat, so there are fifteen flats in total. I live in Block B, Flat B3 to be exact. Each block is detached, spreading out from the centre in the shape of a star. In the centre is a communal garden with a lawn, a few trees, various bushes around the edges, and several benches. It's a relaxing place to sit, and most tenants use it. Rosie follows me through the reception block with the pigeon holes and recycling boxes, and out the door on the other side into the garden. I know it looks beautiful at night; I sit out here for a bifta occasionally, looking at the stars. I can see the delight on her face as we enter the garden, and she links her arm with mine as we stroll across the lawn. I steer us to the entrance to Block B, and when inside we're presented with the choice of the stairs or the lift. She doesn't seem to mind when I suggest the stairs.

'I always take the stairs anyway,' I inform her as we climb, 'But a few weeks ago, Mrs Barnacle, who lives in Block E, got stuck in the lift. She was in there for six hours.' I give her a look of horror, 'She was in a terrible state when they released her. She was approaching floor two when the lift broke, but people were able to talk to her if they stood by the lift doors on that floor. She spent six hours complaining apparently. Jaya, who lives on the ground floor of Block E, went up the stairs to see if she was okay, and found an empty hallway with Mrs Barnacle complaining away. When she paused, Jaya asked her if she was okay. Mrs Barnacle said, 'Is that you Jaya? I was just telling Frank about my varicose veins.' Frank had clearly had enough at some point and fucked off. Jaya said Mrs Barnacle then proceeded to tell *her* all about her varicose veins, thinking Frank was still there, thinking he wanted to hear it twice. Thankfully, he didn't hear it once.'

'How long do you reckon she was talking to an empty hall?' Rosie's face was looking concerned for Mrs Barnacle's plight, but that's been replaced with a barely contained smile.

I return her smile, 'Most of the six hours, I imagine. I bet it wasn't the only time it happened.' We arrive at the top of the stairs, reaching the lift hallway. As I'm the only one living up here, I've placed a dragon tree by the window and a poster of Van Gogh's "A Wheatfield with Cypresses", 1889 on the wall. I find my keys again, and unlock the front door. I flick on the light in the hallway. I move in a couple of steps, turn and smile at Rosie, 'The door locks automatically, just push it to.' As she turns to close the door, I move quickly, I dash to the right, into the living room and turn on the light. I see zero pints of diamonds on the table. I scan the room with feverish intensity, no diamonds. As I turn, Rosie is standing beside me. Come on Laszlo, you need to do a bit more quick thinking, then the both of us can carry on with our night. 'If you need the bathroom, it's across the hall,' I turn and indicate the first door on the left as you enter the flat. 'Do you want a drink?'

'Yeah, what do you have?' As I'm about to answer, she has another thought, 'I'm going to the bathroom, I'll meet you in the kitchen.' She walks off slowly to the bathroom, she knows I'm watching. The bathroom doors clicks shut and I'm off to the kitchen. No diamond pint by the sink. The glasses cupboard! I open it and there's the diamond pint, right at the front in full view. As I have no place better to hide it, and I don't know how much time I have, I push it to the back of the shelf above and put some cups in front of it. I can't see it, perfect. I take out two glasses and set them on the counter. I close the cupboard door and see Rosie leaving the bathroom.

'Whisky, gin or red wine? That's all I can offer you.'

'Attractive selection. Red wine please,' she leans on the counter, looking hotter than ever.

Good idea, I was about to hit the spirits. I open a bottle of wine and pour us a glass each, into whisky glasses. We have a few sips, talking about my collection of spices, when we're suddenly at it again, kissing and touching each other. We're practically wrestling with each other in a desperate attempt to get our hands on each other. I stop, take her hand, instinctively grab the bottle of wine with the other, and move out of the kitchen into the bedroom. We're kissing and feeling and clawing at each other's clothes. I'm pulling at edges of clothing. I'm trying to passionately rip her top open. I'll buy her a new one. I'm trying to tear the material, but I can't get a decent grip on it.

'What are you doing?' She's laughing, throwing her head back, running her hands though my hair, kissing me, laughing, looking full of lust.

'I'm trying to dramatically and passionately tear your clothing off, to show you how manly I am. What's this made from? You should tell NASA about this material.'

She removes her top in one graceful movement, and we're in an embrace again. I'm trying to take my trousers off without falling over, and after an initial struggle, I get the fuckers off. We're kissing, I'm caressing her ample breasts, kissing passionately, I caress her neck, I slide my hands over her pert arse, she's got her hand on my cock. We break, to remove the remainder of our clothes. We stand here naked, and I grab the bottle of wine from the bedside table and take a swig. She takes the bottle from me, takes her own swig and puts the bottle back. We climb onto the bed and straight into an enthusiastic embrace. After sometime of kissing, touching, wanking each other off, and telling the other how hot, sexy and fucking gorgeous they are, Rosie decides the time is right to suck my cock for a bit. Fine by me. Fucking hell, she's particularly good at it. There's only so much writhing and moaning a man can take, so after a while I retreat and move into a different position. She knows what I have in mind; I want to return the gesture. I start slow, before building up a head of steam. She's writhing and moaning, and after a while, she pulls me up and onto her. I slide into her, and we're off.

This is fucking incredible, our hands are everywhere too. We're kissing, and talking a lot. I've never talked this much during sex. We're talking about what we're doing, and how much we like it. It's great. There's also a fair exchange between us of "you're beautiful", "fuck me", "you asked for it", "you fucker", "you cunt", "fuck me with my legs up like this", "you dirty bitch", "you dirty bastard", and the like. We're moving about a bit, wrapping ourselves around each other in interesting ways, eager to show each other our favourite positions. She digs her nails into my back, my spine arches with the exquisite pain. We're slamming into each other now, sweat is pouring off us. She moans, contracts her muscles, thrusts and screams out her orgasm. After a few more thrusts, I come and we both flop onto the bed, devoid of any strength.

We lie here embracing and I'm still inside her, slowly deflating. I reach over and grab the bottle of wine. It's empty, we had a swig each between some positional manoeuvres. 'Do you have another bottle?' She sounds sleepy, so I tell her I'll fetch one in a bit, and we carry on embracing. I slip out of her while we're lying here, and we shift our positions.

'I'll get the wine, and do a bifta.' I slide my arm from under her and get out of bed.

A second later, she gets up too, 'I need the bathroom,' she informs me. What a body! She sees me looking and gives herself a shake. I growl at her, and she walks slowly out of the room, slapping my cock as she walks past. I can't feel a thing at the minute.

I open a bottle of red wine, fetch my tin and take them to the living room. Back in the bedroom I find my phone; eight messages. No missed calls; people know not to call me. I scan through them; two from Eddie, one each from Dalton, Lucy, María, and three from Con. I'll read them in a minute; I'll knock up a bifta first. I'm just finishing the job, when Rosie walks in. 'You might want to check your phone, you've no doubt got a few messages.' I put the bifta on the coffee table, next to two unfinished glasses of wine, and a fresh bottle. Picking up my phone I see that Dalton, Lucy, María and Eddie's first message ask where I am. Have I left the party?

Rosie returns, 'Six messages and two missed calls. All from Ingle!' She looks a bit annoyed and disgusted.

'I didn't hear your phone ringing.' That doesn't contribute anything, but I say it anyway.

'I turned it off.' Her expression changes to that naughty look I find so sexy.

'What does he want?'

'Let me have a look.' She's concentrating on her phone, brow furrowed. I'm smiling, I can't wait to find out what that tossbag has to say.

Eddie's second message asks if I had any luck and left with Rosie. I send Dalton, Lucy and María a message apologising for the delay, and that I went home, hope they are having a good night, blah, blah. I message Eddie, 'I left with Rosie. Thanks for your chair-emptying quick thinking. How's your night?' Rosie's listening to her voice messages now, walking to and fro across the living room, and she doesn't look impressed.

'What a creep. He's worried about me apparently. But eight messages, that's seven too many.' She sits on the sofa, 'I'm feeling irritated that he's infiltrated our evening here.' She looking serious, but I love her sense of humour.

'What are you going to do?' There's no disguising my pleasure in her predicament. I hand her a glass of wine.

'I'd better message him, or he'll keep calling. I'll tell him the truth. I'm fine thanks, I've been in bed.' There's that look again. I leave her to it, and go to the bathroom to wash my dick and have a piss. I return to the living room and Rosie's still on her phone. I light the bifta, take a few drags and knock back a shot of wine. I refill my glass and pass the bifta to Rosie, sliding the ashtray over to her.

I check my phone and Eddie's messaged, 'Went home with Mila. Good night for both of us. Speak tmrw.' He knows I can't stand all these message abbreviations. Or should I say abbreves? So he types normal English to me, sometimes shortened, knowing that I'll accept the occasional abbreve. My main objection is that I don't understand them. Sentences are rendered incomprehensible. I usually inform the sender that a slightly longer form of communication is required, one that uses words. I couldn't give a shit how other people communicate with each other, but friends do appreciate that I need special care. I simply won't understand the message if it uses unfamiliar abbreves. Abbreviations! Rosie throws her phone on the sofa, and knocks back her wine. She refills her glass and I ask how things are going with Ingle, smiling all the time.

'He's a sweetheart, isn't he?' She's got that straight face again. 'Maybe I should be kinder to him. Take him out for a meal? Suck his cock?' Neither of us can keep a straight face at that, and we're laughing, touching each other, caressing each other. We chat for a while, the conversation is so easy, it's frightening. Sitting here naked, I'm naturally looking at her body whenever I'm not looking at her face. We've been passing the bifta, she takes a drag and nubs it in the ashtray. She takes a swig of wine, puts the glass on the table and kisses me passionately. It takes about point two of a nanosecond before I'm responding. We have sex again, smoke another bifta, and return to bed to get some sleep. I lie here feeling Rosie's back press into my chest as she breathes, thinking that is the best sex I've ever had. The previous number one was Sally Worship, who I met in The Staunch Farmer. She's from Australia, and was in the country for a year. She spent two months in Stumpton, and I met her after she'd been here two weeks. We spent the next six weeks shagging each other's brains out. But sex with Rosie felt different somehow.

Chapter Eight

I wake up and stretch. It feels great. I stretch my legs as far as they will go and arch my back. There's a considerable amount of pain there, but that feels good too. I feel the weight of Rosie's body on the mattress as I move, and the memories of last night come flooding into my consciousness. What a night! And I'm waking up next to Rosie. I don't even feel like I have much of a hangover. I should be suffering. It's Sunday morning and I try to organise my thoughts. I need to do something with the diamonds, but what? Talk to Aubrey, he'll have good advice. I could make some hash cakes. I should speak to Con and find out what the situation is with Tony Bicep. But all that can wait 'til later, I'm in bed with Rosie and I'm going nowhere. I need a piss. As I'm walking towards the door, I hear a sleepy voice behind me, 'Morning, where are you going?'

I turn and see her propped up on her elbows, and she gives me a big yawn. Her hair is a little messy; she looks beautiful. 'Morning. For a wazz.'

'Good idea,' she gets out of bed and joins me. We have a kiss and a cuddle before heading to the bathroom. She's standing next to me while I have a piss, leaning against the sink, watching. 'Are you going back to bed or do you have stuff to do?'

'I'm going back to bed. Are you joining me, or do you have stuff to do?'

'Back to bed, that's the only sensible option.'

The stream is starting to peter out now. I give a few pushes to get the last of it out, and shake the last drops off. We swap places. Rosie puts the seat down and sits down. I stand at the sink and wash my hands, and my dick. I lean against the sink facing Rosie, and ask her what her plans are later. She tells me she's free all day while stroking my cock and my balls. My cock responds quickly, and she's giving me that look again while stroking. She pulls me forward and takes me in her mouth. She's gently kissing and licking, then just holds me as she finishes pissing. She washes her hands and leads me back to the bedroom, giving me an occasional squeeze. We have slow sex for some time before it turns into a passionate fuck. Knackered, we both drift in and out of sleep for an undeterminable length of time. When I feel sleepiness receding, I roll over and stretch. Rosie stirs and rolls over too, she offers me her beautiful smile, and I accept. 'Are you hungry?'

'Yeah, what have you got?'

'Rye toast and black coffee.'

'Sounds great.'

I get out of bed and look back to see she's already having another snooze. In the kitchen, I attend to the coffee machine and turn it on. I drop four pieces of rye bread into the toaster and get a plate, a knife, the soya spread and two cups. The coffee machine starts gurgling and I look at the glasses cupboard. I already feel that I can trust Rosie, and I'm tempted to tell her about the diamonds, but I don't know her that well. I need to speak to Aubrey before I do anything else. The toast pops up, and I'm snapped back to the kitchen. I spread the toast and pile in on the plate, fill two cups with coffee, and go back to the bedroom. I put the breakfast on the table and get back into bed, Rosie wakes and smiles. She joins me sitting up, and I hand her a coffee, putting the plate on my leg. We eat hungrily, devouring the toast in no time; gulping the coffee to wash it down. We're chatting with toast in our mouths, it doesn't matter. We lean against each other as we talk, enjoying the feel of each other's skin. It's not long before a few kisses are exchanged, and she picks up the empty plate and throws it onto the floor. She lifts her leg over mine, grabs my hand, and puts it on her arse cheek. And we're off again.

Later, when we're lying in bed talking, she asks, 'What time is it?'

I laugh, 'I have no idea. I haven't looked at the time once today.'

'Me neither, I've been kind of busy.' She's looking at me with such innocence.

'That kind of look might keep us both busy for some time.' She gives me a squeeze as I reach over for my phone. It informs me that it's 13:17. 'One seventeen.' There's a note of surprise in my voice, and on my face. But I don't know why, I don't have a reference point today. I have five new messages; one from Eddie, and four from Con. I still haven't read his messages from last night. Eddie wants to know if I want to catch up today.

'Here he is again. I've got two messages from Ingle this morning. That's an improvement on eight, but still too many.' I don't need to ask what he says; she knows I want to know. She's reading, shaking her head slightly, and making barely audible snorts from her nostrils. 'First message, he hopes I had a good time last night, blah, blah. Second message, he's suggesting meeting up today.' She looks at me with no emotion on her face. Blank face, blank eyes. We both erupt into laughter.

'You could give him that blow job you suggested. He'd like that.' I'm still laughing, but I make it sound like I think it's a great idea.

'Great idea, what are you going to do today?'

We lay around in bed for a while longer, making each other laugh. 'I'm going to have a shower,' I announce. 'I stink.' I ask her if she wants a shower too, then we can make the hash cakes I was telling her about. She says she'll head home so she can shower and get changed; she doesn't want to wear the same clothes from last night. She says she'll come back here in a couple of hours. I'm perfectly happy with that, even though I was hoping we could have a shower bonk. There's plenty of time for that. We get up and she dresses quickly, kisses me passionately, grabbing my hair, and then she's out the door. I tidy up a bit, make the bed and do some washing up. I still haven't looked at the diamonds today. I know they're there, I don't need to keep looking at them, I need to stay focussed. I take a shower, and soreness on my shoulder alerts me to teeth marks. I hadn't forgotten there was some biting, but I didn't realise she'd had a chew. It's not too bad, the skin's only broken in a few places. I find clean clothes and set the coffee machine in motion again. I message Eddie, telling him that meeting up is on, I'll get back to him later. I pile through all the messages from Con. The gist of it is that he's keen to get a meeting on with Tony Bicep, and he can set that up any day next week. He's keen, he must think there's something in it for him. Maybe a cut of my deal. Maybe getting in with the Bicep crowd.

I pour a coffee and take a well-earned rest on the sofa. I decide to have a look on the internet, and type in "tony bicep". Shit, Con was right. He's a boxing trainer, and he owns a gym called "Tony's Gym". He's an imaginative guy. Where is it? It's on Fungus Street, in Ripton Vale. Wait, that's in the south of the city, does that mean it's in Figg territory? What if they know each other? I scroll down, he trained some lad that won a title. I scroll, there are few news reports of his involvement with criminal activity. Stolen goods, money laundering, and fraud. Well, he does sound like the kind of guy that could help me shift the diamonds, but he might be an associate of the Figgs. It's too risky. If my name gets mentioned to the Figgs in the same sentence as diamonds, I'm going to be put in a shredder feet first until I tell them where they are. I need to find out if Con's said my name to Bicep, or anyone else. I call him, he picks up after four rings. He's keen, but he doesn't want to appear to be.

'Hey Laz, how was your night with Rosie? Did you have a dirty fuck?'

I'm curious, 'How would it have been dirty?' Actually, I've changed my mind, I don't want to know his thoughts on that. So I answer for him, 'I suppose we could have done it in a bin.' Get him off the subject and onto his favourite. 'How about you?'

'Awesome.' There's a silence.

'Did you catch up with Miriam?'

'No, I hooked up with one of Anton's friends. She's a secretary in a law firm. She has great big—'

I have to cut in, 'Why are you telling me what she does for a living?' I'm not in the mood to let the conversation head off in that direction, so I move on quickly. 'About this fence, thanks for your help but I don't need him anymore. My mate, who I was enquiring for, doesn't need him anymore.'

'That's a shame,' he does sound quite regretful.

I don't give him time to ask questions, 'Did you speak to Tony yourself?' I'm sitting forward now, on the edge of the sofa, concentrating on the table.

'No, some guy I know suggested him as a good option. Said he has connections and can move anything. I was hoping to be involved in a deal with him, make contact.'

He has connections. Sounds like he might indeed know the Figgs. I think Con got a lucky escape there, making contact with Tony is one thing, but getting in with the Figgs is a different bucket of snakes. 'Sorry Con, wish I could help. Did you mention my name to the guy you spoke to? Or to anyone else, about needing a fence?'

'You're getting a bit paranoid Laz, you should go easy on the weed.' He's laughing away down the other end. I want an answer, but if I push him, he might get suspicious.

I relax my body in the hope it will relax my mind. 'It's like you said, I've never been involved with this type of activity before. I'm nervous my name is out there attached to Tony's reputation.' I think that sounded plausible, and it did acknowledge his streetwise superiority.

'Don't worry, I didn't mention your name. I told the guy that I had some stuff to move.'

'Didn't he ask questions?'

'Are you kidding?'

'What sort of people do you know?'

'Let me know if you hear of anything that needs moving?'

'That's not really my style.'

He laughs, 'Listen Laz, I gotta go. Speak soon.' And he's gone.

I toss my phone on the sofa and try to clear my head. The Tony Bicep avenue is closed, and Con didn't mention my name. What a fucking relief. Time to move quickly on, and find a better option. I message Aubrey, 'Are you in later, are you up for a visitor?' I'll make some hash cakes, if I don't see him today, I'll give him some next week. I put my phone on the kitchen counter, turn the oven on, and put on "Obscured by Clouds" by Pink Floyd. I cut the piece of hash up into a several pieces, and select the few I will use for the cakes. It's important to get the measurements right. One time I put far too much hash in; it was so strong, it felt like I was tripping. That has its time and place, but once I've made hash cakes, I want to eat them every day. I can't trip my tits off every night, but a nice strength batch can be consumed over a fairly short period of time. I grate the chunks into a powder, and put some soya spread in a dish in the oven. When the spread is nice and gloopy, I mix in the hash. I grind some flax seeds and pour boiling water over them in a bowl. In a large bowl, I chuck in some sugar, flour, soya milk, and squeeze a lemon over it. I mix it thoroughly, then add the hash spread and the flax mixture. I mix again until my arm's burning, the bite is on this shoulder, so that's throbbing too. I chuck the mixture in a tin I bought especially for this activity. It has twelve cups indented in the tin, I think it's called a cupcake tin. I fill each cup, and put it into the oven. I pick up my phone, a message from Aubrey, I didn't hear it, might have been when I was rocking out while I was mixing. "I'm out for the day. Come around after six". I check the cakes after about half an hour; I'll give them five more minutes. I sink another coffee and take the cakes out of the oven. I leave them on the hob to cool off. My buzzer sounds. I walk to the front door, and speak into the phone. 'Hello.'

'It's Rosie.' And there's a crackle.

'Come on up,' I press the buzzer that sounds like it's in pain. I open the front door and return to the kitchen. I'm checking on the cakes when I hear the front door click. As I look up, she's walking straight for the kitchen. She's wearing tight jeans, her black boots, and a dark red T-shirt under a short black denim jacket. Her hair is loose behind her shoulders and on her chest. 'How's your afternoon been?' I ask as she nears, not slowing down.

'Fine thanks.' She'd closed right in, and puts her lips on mine and her arms around me. I don't need any more encouragement than that, so I join in. During a convenient break, she says, 'Good choice of tunes, I've got this album.' "Physical Graffiti" by Led Zeppelin is on now. 'That smells nice,' she moves to the oven, bends towards the cakes, and takes in a big sniff of the warm steam coming off them. She stands and looks at me, 'I got something off that.'

'I licked the bowl. I'm feeling something off that.' I give her a big smile. 'Are you hungry?'

'Yeah, I haven't eaten since breakfast. What have you got?'

'I'm thinking of noodles in black bean sauce, with stir fried veg and tofu. What do you think?'

'Sounds delicious. Do you want a hand?' I tell her that would be great. The tunes finish, so I put disc two on. We're chatting, washing and chopping vegetables. She suggests a drink; a glass of red wine perhaps. I retrieve the glasses, as she opens the wine. I look up, still can't see it. Broccoli, mushrooms, spring onions and baby sweetcorn all get chopped up and fried. I have some tofu in a container in the fridge. I made it last week, roasting it in a mixture of oil, turmeric, cumin, salt and pepper. I've been snacking on it, but it will go great in this stir fry. And it does. We both agree that the meal is quite delicious. She doesn't bother with all this "thanks for the meal" bollocks, we did it together. She doesn't bother with all this "it's unusual to find a man that can cook a meal without burning the house down" bollocks; she's lived a bit more than that. The cakes are cool now, so I wrap four in tinfoil and put them in the freezer. 'Are the rest for Aubrey?'

'No, four for Aubrey. Do you want one?' She smiles and nods. 'Do you want to take one with you, or have one today?'

'One today maybe, if you're having one.'

'Yeah, I'm thinking of dropping some off at Aubrey's, then meeting Eddie for a drink, maybe have some then. What do you reckon? You can meet Aubrey.'

'Yeah, I'd like to.'

I wrap four cakes together in tinfoil, these are for Aubrey. I wrap the other four in foil for us; me, Rosie, Eddie, and he might be with Mila. I ask Rosie what time it is, and she tells me its ten to six. I suggest we go to Aubrey's now, and she's happy with the idea. We grab our jackets, and I put the two foil parcels in a paper bag and fold it up. I message Aubrey, "Setting off now, be at yours in half hour". I close the door behind us and we walk down the stairs. It usually takes me thirty minutes to walk to Aubrey's. I could take the bus, but the walk takes me through Diligent Square, and past the old college buildings and Parsons Green. So it's quite a pleasant walk, the bus journey isn't. Today the walk takes us forty-five minutes, but Aubrey doesn't give a shit what time we arrive. He opens his door and invites us in. I introduce Rosie, they greet warmly, and we follow him into the kitchen.

'Would you like a drink? I'm about to make coffee.'

'That would be good, thanks.'

'I'll have one.'

'Sit down,' he instructs us, pointing at the stools by his breakfast bar. We sit down and I put the paper bag on the counter. While Aubrey's preparing the coffee, I ask him what he's been up to today. He tells me it's none of my business, and I smile at Rosie. I ask him if he was out with a lady friend, and he slowly turns to me and says, 'What did I just tell you?' and smiles at Rosie. She's smiling too. He finishes making the coffee, 'Would either of you like something in your coffee?' He reaches for something behind him on the counter and holds up a bottle of whisky.

'Yes please,' Rosie and I say together.

He improves our drinks, and suggests we go to the living room, where we will be more comfortable. We chat on the sofas, sipping our drinks, and the conversation is easy. Rosie and Aubrey are getting on well; they're asking each other questions, and talking about themselves. I give Aubrey his cakes, and he takes a look at them while expressing his gratitude. Rosie asks to use the bathroom, and Aubrey gives her directions; down the hall, up the stairs, first door on the left.

When she leaves the room, he looks at me, 'Nice young lady,' he looks pleased.

'Yes, she is,' and I'm smiling at him.

'You like her, don't you?'

'Yes,' that's all I can think of to say.

'Good.' Now that we've established that, he moves on, 'I bumped into Maureen Turnip last night.' He remains silent, giving me the opportunity to try and remember who that is. I remember the name but... He can see me struggling, 'Her maiden name was Maureen Figg.'

'Oh, Maureen! You used to date her. Are you trying your luck again?' It's an innocent question, but I am about to start teasing him. He must have noticed my amusement, as he's giving me a serious look. I straighten my face, this is serious, and I am hoping he can help me.

'I spoke to a friend yesterday afternoon, after we spoke at work. He knew that Big Joe was murdered and that his body is at Partridges, so we spoke about the Figgs briefly. I casually enquired if he knew much about Maureen.' He's talking a little faster than usual, presumably because he wants to tell me something before Rosie returns. I keep my mouth shut and let him get on with it. 'Well, I hit the jackpot, Laszlo, he happened to mention that she goes to the Legion on Saturday nights. So I went to the Legion last night, and bumped into her.' He looks at me a moment, then carries on, 'We ended up having a few drinks together, and quite a long and interesting chat.' He's silent.

Why the dramatic pause now, I thought he wanted to get on with it. 'Well, what did you chat about?'

'She thinks the Figg name has gone to ruin, since the younger members of the family are all mixed up with criminal activities. When she was younger, everyone cut corners, and took something for themselves, but it wasn't organised. Since the Figgs have become known as gangsters, she has little to do with that part of the family. She doesn't want to be associated with their mischief. And the feeling is mutual, they don't have much to do with her. She lives in a bungalow in Washley, it's a modest home, and she doesn't have much. She said all the local community know who her family are, and she's sick of the gossip.'

'That's dreadful,' I say without any conviction. 'Is that what you wanted to tell me?'

'She said she was at Partridges' yesterday afternoon to view Big Joe, and she heard talk between family members and associates of a missing package. On the drive back, she heard two young members of the family in the front of the car, speak about diamonds.' That's the first time the word "diamonds" has been mentioned, and while I haven't yet officially admitted I took them, he's talking like he already knows. He pauses again, looking at me with concentration. 'She told me it serves them right. If they're going to be involved with crime, they deserve to have their things stolen.'

I'm not sure what any of this means, and I'm about to ask him when Rosie walks in. I think I have a strange look on my face so I quickly try for different expression, but I'm not sure that's any better. She's not stupid, she senses that something was happening. The way the conversation stopped as she walked in was a hint. She sits down, and I ask Aubrey what his plans are for tonight. He says he might watch a film, but I tell him we're going out for a drink with Eddie, and ask if he wants to join us.

'Good idea Laszlo, shall we eat one of these too?' He's unwrapping his cakes again.

Rosie and I are in agreement, and as she sorts out two cakes from the other foil parcel, I message Eddie, asking what he's up to. The two commend me on my new batch; tasty, they agree. I eat my cake and get a message from Eddie, "On my way to the sticky pud, be there in 30". I message back, "See you there". The Sticky Pudding is probably about a half hour walk from here, back towards town. I tell the guys the news, and ask Aubrey if he wants to get a taxi.

'It's a nice evening for a walk,' Aubrey's looking in a good mood, and it makes me feel good too. 'I'll put these in the fridge,' and off he goes with his remaining cakes. I wrap up the two for Eddie and Mila, and put them in the bag.

'Is everything okay?' she asks when I've finished.

I nod and smile, 'Yeah.'

She looks at me a little longer, 'Okay, let's go then.' She walks into the hallway and I follow; we see Aubrey putting on his coat and wait by the door for him. The walk to the boozer is nice. Aubrey and Rosie like each other, and I'm being my usual ridiculous self with both of them. I ask them if they've heard of a South American tree frog that rapes tarantulas. I go on for about three minutes, and they let me! They're laughing, while I maintain a straight face throughout. We walk past Parsons Green and the old college buildings, then head along Marmalade Street towards the Police Station. After a while, we reach the Wellington Canal, and follow it across town enjoying the warm evening. The Sticky Pud isn't far, it's a cosy boozer on the canal, with plenty of benches and tables out front. We approach the pub and I see Eddie and Mila sitting at a table outside. We all exchange greetings, and Aubrey and Mila are introduced. I ask them if they want another drink and they decline, so the three of us enter the pub to get our drinks. I put the bag on the table as I leave, and tell Eddie they're for him.

We're inside the pub, leaning against the bar. We put our order in and the barman goes to the other end of the bar to pour our drinks. 'I think I'm feeling the cake kicking in now,' I'm speaking to them quietly, even though the barman can't hear, and wouldn't care. 'A few colours seem brighter, and I feel a few tingles.' I smile broadly, and start to laugh quietly.

'I'm feeling a few tingles too,' and Rosie starts laughing. Also quietly.

'I started to feel the tingles when we reached the canal,' Aubrey has a big smile on his face, and the three of us crack up laughing, not quietly this time. We seem to realise at the same time that the barman has returned with our drinks. He's silently watching us laugh.

'I'll get this,' he composes himself and pays the barman. Rosie and I compose ourselves too, while Aubrey waits for his change. We collect our drinks, and head back out front, already laughing again, for some reason. We sit on the benches at their table still laughing a little. Eddie suggests to Mila that we've already eaten our cakes. I point at the paper bag.

Eddie squashes the bag flat with his hand, 'Already taken care of, thank you Laz.'

'Thanks, Laz,' Mila concurs.

The evening is going well, the conversation is light and freely flowing. Rosie, Aubrey and I are laughing over silly things, while Eddie and Mila humour us until their cakes kick in, and when they do, we're all giggling at each other. We order some pub food; chips, flatbread, olives, falafel and a pine nut salad, and we all tuck in as the evening sun fades. There are several trips to the bar and toilet, until it gets a bit chilly outside, so we move indoors en masse. We sit at a round table in the corner, by a window. I'm watching the boats bob up and down on the canal outside. They're not bobbing in a graceful synchronised dance, each boat has its own bob going on, making for an erratic display. I don't know why they're bobbing, there's no wind out there. I hear Eddie speaking.

'I take it you're not driving tomorrow, Aubrey.'

'No, I'm not in work until Wednesday,' Aubrey takes a sip of his whisky.

'What's happening then,' I ask, looking over at him.

'It's the Figg funeral.' I look at him and feel the humour escaping from both of us, but it wouldn't be good to let that show. Though if anyone asks what the matter is, maybe we could put it down to professional grief.

'Oh yeah, I forgot. Does anyone want a drink?' Everyone is immediately distracted with the contents of their glasses. They're thinking, "How long will it take to drink the remaining contents?" "How long will Laz be at the bar for?" After a remarkably short deliberation time, everyone says yes.

'I'll help you with the drinks, Laszlo,' Aubrey gets up and follows me to the bar. 'Keep walking,' I hear him say, so I keep walking. 'Carry on,' he says when I start to slow down. I carry on to the far end of the bar.

'Will here do?' I turn to face him.

'Here's fine.' This end of the bar is deserted and the barman has disappeared too.

'Won't it look suspicious that we've come all the way to this end of the bar?'

'I don't care.' We're both quite high and a little drunk, and I don't mind his brusqueness. He clearly has more to say to me, so I let him get on with it. 'I had lunch today with Maureen.' There's no one near us, but he speaks softly. 'We talked more about an idea we have. Most of the old timers in her family have passed on, and as she does not want the association with gangsters, she's looking to move out of Stumpton for good. She says she has her own contact from way back. She says she will be able to help anyone that is in possession...' he looks around, no one is any nearer to us, '...of the diamonds.'

'Why are you telling me this?' I ask plainly, I don't act puzzled; I'm not going to bullshit him. I just don't know what else to say.

'Come on Laszlo,' he looks around again, 'We both know you took the package.'

'What makes you think that?' He just looks at me, expressionless. Has he blinked yet? Why doesn't he stop staring at me? Why doesn't he say something reassuring and nice? Stop looking at me! I scan the room, 'Yeah, okay, you're right.' I straighten up, the barman appears from out the back. I ignore Aubrey completely and look over his shoulder, so he understands we have company. We give him our order of five drinks, and he busies himself further along the bar.

Aubrey waits until the barman is making some noise before continuing, 'Her contact moves the package,' he's practically whispering now, 'And she takes her cut.'

'What makes you think you can trust her?' I'm whispering too.

'Do you trust me?'

I straighten again as the barman brings over two drinks. I nod my thanks and wait for him to go away again. 'Of course I do.'

'Good. Trust me now. We can trust her. She wants to move to Florida, and not tell any of the scoundrels in her family anything about it. This is her chance to make a new life, change her name. So she won't rat us out to her family.'

'Okay, but how do we know she won't rip us off?'

'She won't.'

'How do we find out how much they're worth? And how much does she expect her cut to be?' The barman brings over the remainder of the drinks, and I give him a few Ayrtons. He returns with my change, and disappears again.

'Laszlo, there are lots of questions, and we need to discuss this soberly. Let's talk more tomorrow.'

'Okay.' I think of something else, 'Earlier you said you spoke to someone about the Figgs and about Maureen. What if that person talks?'

'No need to worry Laszlo that was an old friend of mine, Wiggy Wiggins. It was a casual conversation, during which he did most of the talking. It was a conversation I could have had with a number of people. Besides, I didn't mention your name, or the package.'

'Wiggy Wiggins? Who's he?'

'We go back years, he's one of the old crowd. His name is William Wiggins, but we've always called him Wiggy. Some years ago he started wearing a wig, but never spoke about it. We're not supposed to know, but of course it's obvious. The rest of us have chatted about it and concluded that if we stop calling him Wiggy, he'll want to know why. We can't mention his wig, and we can't think of a plausible lie, so we've all had to continue calling him Wiggy, it's absurd. One time, a few of us were having a drink in the pub one afternoon, and Wiggy left to go home. He hadn't got half way to the exit, when Errol noticed Wiggy's phone on the table, so he shouts out "WIGGY". Well, Wiggy's as deaf as a squid, so he didn't hear Errol. I joined in, and so did Gallon; all three of us shouting "WIGGY" at him. Some people laughed, which was dreadful, but most tried to burn holes into our flesh with their eyes. We finished our drinks and went to a different pub.'

I can't help but laugh. He picks up two drinks, and I pick up the other three. We return to a chorus of 'About fucking time,' and much laughter. Rosie too, even though I saw her looking over a few times when Aubrey and I were in secret discussion. After some chatter, Aubrey tells us he's going home, and calls a taxi. He asks if anyone wants a lift, but we all tell him we'll walk. Less than ten minutes pass when a guy appears in the doorway asking, 'Taxi for Obrey?'

'I think that's you Obrey,' Rosie tells Aubrey, who finishes his drink, and gentlemanly bids each of us farewell. I tell him I'll call him tomorrow. The rest of us set about finishing our drinks and head out too. We're walking about ten minutes when our paths diverge, so we say goodnight to Eddie and Mila, and walk on. Eddie told me, in the toilets, that he and Mila were so fucked last night, they couldn't do anything. They sat around smoking weed and drinking that bottle of Jerry Greyhound, and passed out in the morning. They woke up in the afternoon, and had a mad banging session. I said, 'Nice one,' to him.

As we're walking, I ask Rosie if she wants to stay at mine tonight. She says she has to get up early in the morning, would that disturbance be a problem? I tell her I have to get up early too.

'I'll stay at yours then,' and we hold hands as we walk. We're silent for a little while, when she asks, 'Laz…what are your thoughts on seeing each other after tonight?' She sounds a little tentative, nobody likes rejection.

'I was hoping we could catch up next week.' I think of saying something else, but I don't.

'Good, me too.' We walk in silence again, both with our own thoughts. We cross over the road and I ask her if she likes living in Stumpton. 'Not really,' she doesn't sound impressed. She tells me that she's not from Stumpton. Her dad died when she was six, some years later her mom married a guy called Donald. Donald Crabb. Her mom changed her name to Crabb, but Rosie kept her dad's name, Park. Donald was adequate in raising Rosie and her older brother, but they just didn't like him much. When her brother was sixteen he moved away, and when Rosie was sixteen, she did the same, years later ending up in Stumpton. She says she misses her mom, but rarely goes home. I won't tell her about my childhood right now, I get the feeling she doesn't talk to everyone about hers. It's nice that she's opened up to me, so I don't want to cloud over her intimate revelation by telling her my story.

Chapter Nine

I'm woken by the sound of Rosie's alarm on her phone, and her fidgeting to turn it off. I sleepily ask her what time it is. 'Six twenty,' comes the equally sleepy reply. I'm woken again by the alarm, and hear Rosie enjoying a good stretch. I ask her what time she needs to get up. 'Ten minutes, one more snooze.' I wake up again to the sound of Rosie urgently saying, 'Shit, shit, it's ten past seven. Fuck, how did that happen?' She dashes into the bathroom, and I have a good stretch too. I don't need to get up yet, but I might as well. I get out of bed as Rosie returns hurriedly putting her clothes on. I find my boxer shorts on the floor and step my left foot into the leg hole. My heel catches onto the material at the back, and the material at the front get hooked under my toes. I'm pulling the shorts, but my foot's stuck and I'm losing balance. Instead of putting my foot down and starting again, I persist in tugging on the shorts in the hope that I will successfully pull them up before my balance is lost. I'm too optimistic and fail in my attempt. I topple forward and crash onto the floor, with my face in the carpet. Rosie stops what she's doing and seeing me spread on the floor with my shorts wrapped around my left foot, asks, 'Are you okay, Laz?' I assure her I haven't broken any bones and gingerly get to my feet. She's dressed and comes over to me, kisses me, and says, 'I'll see you soon.'

'I'll message you,' I rub my sore face as she closes the front door behind her. I do the usual; have a shower, get dressed, make coffee and toast, go to work. I say 'Good morning' to Henry as I pass the office and get the same greeting in return; there doesn't appear to be any further fallout from the Figgs at this end. I'm about to walk on when Nicholas appears, and stops me.

'Good morning Nicholas. How were the rest of the Figg viewings on Saturday?' He looks tired. He enters the office and gestures for me to follow him.

'Unsettling; the entire afternoon was spent entertaining one agitated party after another. It was not a satisfying ordeal.' He strolls over to the desk, 'There are no further viewings, and the funeral takes place on Wednesday morning.' There is a sense of relief in his voice; relief that this episode will soon be over. It will be for the Partridges, but it certainly won't be for me. He hands me a piece of paper from the desk, 'There is another pick up for you this morning.' I'm thinking his sombre mood is simply due to tiredness until I look at the paper. The pickup is from the Children's Hospital; these jobs can be heart-breaking if you let them get to you. But it's still satisfying to make them look peaceful for the family.

I return to work, and store the body in the fridge. It's an eight year old boy, non-Hodgkin lymphoma. I go to my shed, I need to compose myself for this afternoon's work. As I'm putting out the bifta, there's a knock on the shed door. This is unusual. I slowly open the door, and it's Nicholas standing there. He looks at me, then past me, scanning the shed. I don't think he's been out here since I took residence. It doesn't look like it's to his taste, but he doesn't mention the smell thankfully. He'll be able to tell I've been smoking, but probably doesn't recognise Lebanese hash. 'Laszlo, there are two policemen in the office, they would like to speak to you.' I don't say anything, I'm just standing, looking at him. 'I will take care of the boy this afternoon; you can attend to other duties.' He looks more than tired, but if he's working in the prep room, he won't be dealing with any more visitors. I thank him, and tell him I'll be right there. He heads inside, while I take my chunk of hash and hide it inside the cushion on the armchair. Seems to be my new place to hide things.

Feeling quite stoned, I enter the office and see two men sitting talking to Henry, both wearing civilian clothing. They stand when they are aware of my presence, and introduce themselves. The first guy, neat blond hair and a barely visible blond moustache, says, 'Detective Phobian,' and shows me his ID. It reads Alexander Phobian, and the photo shows him without the moustache. I wonder what made him grow it. The other guy, neat dark hair and a short neat beard, says, 'Detective Biscotti.' His ID reads Raymondo Biscotti, and he looks identical in his photo, clearly his preferred look. While the introductions are taking place, Henry is making his way towards the door, quick thinking to start off as soon as he could, but his frail legs can't keep up with the decision making. 'You must be Laszlo,' Detective Biscotti informs me. I already know that. There was one time when I forgot my name, but I haven't got time to think about that now. I tell him he's right. They both seem relaxed enough, but why the fuck are they here? Henry has reached the door, and silently leaves the room. 'Please, take a seat,' Biscotti gestures to Henry's vacant seat. I sit down and look at the two detectives, it feels strange sitting in this chair, facing the room from this angle. It sort of makes me feel in charge. I'm trying to look calm, and I think sitting here helps.

'Are you aware of the gang war between the Figgs and the Dancers?' Detective Phobian asks.

'I've heard of it, but only since Mr Figg was brought here. I'd never heard of either family until last week.'

'The violence between the two families increased over the weekend. We are not at liberty to divulge the nature of the violence, but several attacks have taken place,' Phobian reports.

'Was anyone killed?' What if someone was murdered, is that my fault?

'No, but we want to stop this war before more people are.' Biscotti's looking serious now, I think he wants to get on with it.

'The Figgs are under the impression that the Dancers murdered Big Joe…' Phobian is about to carry on, but I speak before I know I'm going to.

'Did they?'

Phobian and Biscotti look and each other and shift in their seats, 'The exact individual responsible has not yet been identified,' Phobian ventures. Which means, yes, the Dancers did kill Big Joe, but they don't have evidence to prove which one.

'Mr Partridge informed us that you embalmed the body of Big Joe on Friday,' Biscotti is getting to work, 'When you met members of the family, and you returned on Saturday, again when members of the family were present. As the gang war has escalated since the murder of Big Joe, maybe you overheard something, talk of revenge for example. Maybe you saw something suspicious?'

'No, I wasn't around for the family viewings, I was in briefly on Saturday, but when the main viewings took place I'd already left. So I wasn't around to hear any conversations.'

'And when you spoke to Tyrone and the others, did they say anything suspicious?' Phobian asks.

'He's quite intimidating, so I was concentrating on making sure I didn't say anything to displease him.'

There's a gentle nod of appreciation from both men, but Biscotti is quickly back at work again, 'Mr Partridge stated that Tyrone and a few others were quite agitated on Saturday, claiming that something had gone missing.'

'Yes, that's right. It was quite unnerving, they were quite angry.' The two detectives exchange a brief glance with each other. 'I told him that I take my job seriously, and I would never jeopardise that by stealing jewellery or watches or…'

'Yes, yes, Mr Partridge explained Tyrone's accusation, and assured us you would never steal from the body,' Biscotti sounds impatient now. 'He said Tyrone became more agitated, and left, when you informed him that you saw a visitor leaving after hours.'

Fuck, did Henry and Nicholas tell them everything? I was hoping to decide what to disclose to the detectives myself, by somehow deducing what would be best for me. 'It wasn't after hours, it was when I was locking up, just a late visitor.'

'Can you describe the person?' Biscotti doesn't sound like he's enjoying being here.

'He was male, and was wearing the usual black suit…and had ginger hair,' there, I said it. I could have left that out. Maybe Henry or Nicholas already said it. I don't want to appear to be leaving out information. I need to avoid suspicion. I can't have the police thinking it's a good idea to poke into my business. The two exchange a look again, stand up and thank me for my time. They leave the office and I sit in Henry's chair wondering if that makes things better or worse. Both the Figgs and the police think the Dancers stole something valuable from the Figgs. Hopefully, both parties will never think of casting suspicion in my direction, unless it becomes known I have some diamonds for sale. The Dancers are unaware of the whole situation. Or are they? They might be fully aware of the diamonds. Maybe they'll be after me too. I need to get rid of them. I need to speak with Aubrey.

I message Aubrey, "Can we talk this afternoon?", and leave the office. I'm in the dressing room when he messages back, "I'm in until five". I sneak back out to the shed; I know Nicholas is in the prep room, but I don't know where Henry is. He might have something for me to do. I'm officially attending to other duties, and I'd like to honour that request. I retrieve my hash and make my way to Aubrey's, undetected. I'm sitting in Aubrey's living room, and he hands me a whisky flavoured coffee, and sits down. I take a swig. Fuck! I nearly cough. How much whisky did he put in?

'Where shall we start Laszlo?'

'Well, there is something else you probably should know.' I pause because I don't know where to start. He isn't saying anything either; he's looking at me with concern. 'When the Figgs asked to speak to me about the missing parcel on Saturday, I told them that I saw a man leaving the building when I was locking up. A man with ginger hair.' I'm looking at him for reassurance, but he's refusing to change his expression.

'Why did you say that?' his voice is as steady as his face.

'I don't know.' We're just looking at each other, so I feel compelled to say more. 'I think it was because I was shitting myself. I had the diamonds for less than twenty-four hours

117

and I was already being accused of taking them. Not exactly a master criminal, am I?' His face softens, and he smiles at me. 'I didn't plan to say it; it just came out under pressure.' I pause and steady myself for the next thing I have to say. 'Two detectives questioned me at work today. They'd already spoken to Henry and Nicholas, who informed them about the mystery visitor, they asked me about him and I had no choice but to confirm that's what I'd said to Tyrone.' He's looking thoughtful, but not too worried. 'It might work to our advantage if the Figgs, and the police think the Dancers took the diamonds. After all, they did kill Big Joe, so there was always going to be revenge. As I've thrown the missing diamonds into that mix, it might help me remain undetected.' I give him a pleading smile, almost demanding that he agree with me.

'I agree, it takes the suspicion away from you, but if the Dancers deny taking the diamonds, the Figgs could come looking for you. That depends upon the Figgs asking the Dancers, and the Figgs believing them. I don't think we're at the dialogue stage in this conflict, the Figgs want revenge for Big Joe.'

I take another sip of my drink; fuck, that's strong. 'I think we need to shift them as soon as we can.'

'Have you thought more about my suggestion?' He asks casually, not trying to sway my decision.

'I like it, and not just because it's the only plan we have. My understanding of the plan is, I give the diamonds to you, you give them to Maureen, she gives them to her contact. The contact exchanges them for a large sum of money, of which, Maureen takes her cut. I assume the contact will want a cut too.'

'Exactly right.'

'Who's the contact?'

'Verb Stanley. I know him from years back; he was married to Maureen's sister, Morag, when we dated. Excellent chap, Verb. We got on well when I dated Maureen, we used to go round their house quite often. After Maureen and I separated, I remained good friends with Verb, we used to meet up in The Drowning Mackerel. That's not there anymore; a raging fire tore that place down. We met one time and he was in a terrible way. He told me Morag was dead; he was devastated. She was killed by a cow. She had taken their dog for a walk and gone past a field with some grazing cattle. The dog got excited and ran through a gap in the gate, chasing the cattle, and she went in after the mutt to stop it getting hurt. Mrs Cake was walking her dog at the time and witnessed the event. She said Morag's dog was running around one poor cow, barking at it. Morag was trying to catch it and ran behind the cow. At this point the distressed cow's back legs gave way, and it landed on the grass, trapping Morag underneath it. Apparently its buttocks were on her face, and she died of suffocation.'

'Suffocation by buttocks, doesn't sound like the best way to go. Do cows have buttocks?'

'Yes, they do. After a while, living in the house without Morag was too much for him, so he sold up and moved away. I haven't seen him since, but Maureen stayed in contact with him. He remarried and had a few kids, which is nice for him.'

'How do we know we can trust him? You haven't seen him in over a hundred years, and he used to be part of the Figg family.'

'All the crime and violence came years later when Big Joe set up the business. Verb wasn't innocent, who amongst us is? But he's not a gangster and he's not associated with the Figgs, he simply kept in touch with Maureen. Morag and Maureen were close, and I think by keeping in touch, they feel they won't let her be forgotten.' He sups his drink without a flinch.

'Okay, so you reckon we can trust him. Why him? What's he got to offer?' I didn't have chance to eat lunch, and I'm feeling the whisky.

'He was a lapidarist.' I'm looking at him blankly, and he gets the message. 'He was a craftsman of gemstones.' I nod my head in understanding. 'He worked for PJ Hoffenheim in London for thirty-five years, and knows a lot of people in the trade. He also worked in their offices in Amsterdam for several years, and has contacts there too.'

My eyes have widened, and I'm just staring at him. After a while I come up with, 'Are you having a giraffe?' He remains silent; of course he wouldn't make that up. 'This sounds perfect,' I purposefully put suspicion into my tone. 'He might rip us all off. He and Maureen might rip us off. What if he tells the Figgs?'

'He won't tell the Figgs. Maureen has told him about Big Joe's business, and how the Figgs are regarded as gangsters. He was married to Morag for several years, they were truly in love, and it saddens him too that the Figg name has been tainted. He said he would enjoy putting one over the younger generation.'

'Have you spoken to him?' I ask quickly.

'No, Maureen spoke to him last night. She tried calling me after, to let me know what he said, but I saw her call and didn't answer it. We were in The Sticky Pud, and we were all laughing, and I was high, so I didn't want to talk to her then. We met this morning and she filled me in. She told Verb that Tyrone has had a package of diamonds stolen. He thinks the Dancers stole it, but she knows who really took it. She didn't say your name, or mine. She asked him if he would be prepared to find a buyer. If he agrees, she would consult with the person holding the stones, and get back to him. He agreed.'

'How do you know he won't rip us off?'

'Verb and Maureen have kept in contact all these years. There's a bond there that he values.'

'Large sums of money can compensate for breaking some bonds.'

'She told him they'll both get their cut, and he's happy with that. He wants to help.'

'What if she screws us over?'

'Maureen won't do that.' He's knows I'm going to say something else questioning the validity of trusting these two people, two people I've never met, so he indicates he hasn't finished. 'There's a bond there too.' Now he sits silently looking at me, maybe not sure if he should carry on. 'In the Legion on Saturday night, we'd had a few drinks and Maureen told me that I'm her true love. She married that Turnip idiot, and she loved him, but her heart has always been with me. That's what she said, and I admitted that even though I've been married three times, I've never stopped loving her. And it's true, Laszlo; all these years later and I still love her.'

He's looking at me with an expression I've never seen before, and while I'm tempted to look at it a while longer to figure it out, I tell him what I'm thinking. 'So, you told her about the diamonds, she told you that you're her true love, and now you want to give her the diamonds.'

'No, you goose. I didn't tell her about the diamonds until the following morning.'

I recognise that expression easily enough, and I get the picture. 'Okay, what do we do about valuing the diamonds?' I'm trying to move on and get that image out of my head. I don't even know what she looks like, but I've got a fair approximation.

'Verb will need to examine the stones. Then we'll know what we're dealing with.'

'And the cut they'll both want?'

'Nothing has been agreed yet, let Verb value the stones first. You should meet Maureen. We should all get together, I haven't seen Verb in years.' He's smiling and lost in thought. If the worst that comes out of this is Aubrey reconnecting with an old friend, me ending up with broken legs, and the Figgs walking off with the diamonds, I'll be happy enough. 'I have a dinner date with the lovely Maureen this evening. I'll tell her that you are content with the plan so far, and she'll contact Verb to give him the go-ahead. We'll discuss the best way forward from there, and I'll talk to you tomorrow to see what you think about our discussion.'

'You two are seeing a lot of each other; is this getting serious?'

'You're seeing a lot of Rosie too, as I understand it. Are you getting serious?' I don't answer, I don't know what to say. He sees my discomfort and ploughs on, 'Are you seeing her tonight?'

I look at him for a while, and eventually say, 'Hopefully.' I take his point.

'I remember our first date…' he's lost in thought again.

'Did you take her scrumping for onions?' That snapped him out of it, and he's giving me a puzzled look.

'No, we went to the picture house. I can't remember what film we saw, it was delightful simply to be sitting next to her, in the dark. I'd glance over at her, and see her face illuminated by the screen. The light flickering and dancing on her face. I remember she was wearing a green dress, and she had a blue cardigan over her shoulders. She was such a beautiful woman. She still is.'

Now it's my turn to look puzzled.

We have another coffee and chat for a bit, but we both have stuff to do, so we get on with it. I walk back to work, they might need me to lock up. I receive a message from Rosie on the way, "Hey, how's your day?" I could say that I was questioned by two detectives, and discussed plans to sell stolen diamonds with Aubrey. But instead I say, "Good thanks, and you?" I stop off at the local supermarket and buy a bagful of fruit, nuts, crackers and humous. I'll leave them in the kitchen at work, and snack on them during the week. Back at work I find Henry in the office and we have a chat about the police visit and the Figg saga. He's a good old lad, and talks humorously about the whole affair.

'Gangsters…' he's shaking his head gently, but smiling too, '…gangsters, running amok in our place of work. It's like a Rufus Chaffinch crime novel with items going missing, or stolen, and detectives on the scene.' We talk a while longer, and go over the details of the Figg funeral on Wednesday. He tells me Nicholas will lock up this evening, and I should go home. I thank him, but don't tell him I spent the afternoon at Aubrey's drinking whisky.

I fetch my bag from the dressing room, and exit by the back door. As I'm walking around the building towards the front yard, my phone lets me know I have a message. Rosie. "Busy, but good. What you up to later?"

I have a think and message back, "Staying in and having a wank. What you up to?" I cross the front yard and walk down the driveway, leaving work behind me. My phone. Rosie. "Coming round to watch".

I message back, "I'm going to start at 8".

Phone. Rosie. "I'll be round at five to, to get a good seat". I'm getting hard reading this. I get home and message Rosie, suggesting that she come round mine earlier, for dinner.

I've already got a tarka daal on the go, and I'm preparing some mushroom rice when my buzzer sounds. It's Rosie, I let her in. She shuts the door and throws her bag on the floor, she embraces me and we're kissing. I look at her, she simply does not stop knocking me out. The usual "how are you"s are asked, and we chat about our days. Her day sounds busy all right, and she sounds like a hard worker too. She could do with a change in her pace of life, before she burns out. She's asked me about my work on a few occasions, and she's asked me some interesting questions. I told her about the embalming process in detail, and she was fascinated. I don't find her work particularly interesting, and I told her that. But she didn't mind, she agreed. I serve dinner, and she tells me this is the best tarka daal she's tasted. I tell her it's good, but we should try Mohan's sometime. Rosie pours some drinks and suggests we watch a film.

We're having a smoke, discussing what film to watch. We can't decide between "Dog Day Afternoon" and "Scarface". It's a difficult choice. I remember the half a gram of coke I have left over from the party. Where is that? I don't think now is the right time; maybe at the weekend? Maybe buy some more off Con? I'm in the middle of a good point, when Rosie starts coughing, looking at me. I carry on talking, and she coughs again, a few times. She's smiling, but I don't understand, I'm missing the point. She coughs again and looks at an imaginary watch. 'What time is it?' I dumbly ask, still not comprehending.

'Eight o'clock. Wank time.' She sits back smiling at me. That look is on her face.

I forgot I told her I'd be buffing the baldigan at eight. 'Thank you for reminding me,' I say with convincing gratitude. 'Do you have a preference? I could unzip sitting here, pull my cock out, and get going. Or I could disrobe, full nudity, and get going.' I'm about to carry on, I don't know what I'm about to say, but Rosie has clearly made up her mind.

'Full nudity,' she says quickly. 'And standing up.'

I take my clothes off while she watches, and stand here already hard. I get to work, and she's being tremendously encouraging. Praising my action, making suggestions. She lets me go on for some time before joining in. Later, we're lying on the sofa, embracing, sweating, panting. We smoke a bifta, drink some wine, and I don't know why, but I tell her that I feel completely relaxed in her company. And I do, I can just be myself. She kisses me sweetly, and walks to the bedroom. I close my laptop, take the last drag, nub it out, finish my drink, turn the light off, have a piss and get myself in the bedroom. Later, she rests her body against mine as we lay in bed, this feels good.

Chapter Ten

'Laz, wake up.' She gives me a shove, 'Laz, wake up.'

I wake up. I don't have any fucking choice do I? 'What's happening?'

'Nothing, I want to ask you a question.'

I haven't moved a muscle, or opened my eyes. 'What time is it?'

'Six.'

'We don't have to get up yet, let's sleep.' I feel sleep returning; well, I hadn't let it get too far away.

'I want to ask you a question.'

'You woke me up at six o'clock to ask me a question? You've got the time it takes me to fall back to sleep to ask it.' I still haven't moved.

'I've stayed here three nights in a row, do you mind?'

'You woke me up to ask me that? Get out.' I roll over and open an eye, she's on her side, propped up on one elbow. Her hair is hanging over half her face, but she doesn't seem to mind. She puts her hand on my cock, which responds immediately. 'Am I being shown the benefits of you staying over?' We're shagging doggy when she comes, she's really pushing back hard with some force, while I thrust. She shouts out her orgasm, and with just a few more thrusts I too come hard. We lay in bed together a while, until we have to get up. We get up, she dresses, kisses me and she's off like a shot. After she leaves, I shower, and the hot water stings my back; must be some more scratches there.

I receive a message from Aubrey, "Meet at lunch? My place?"

I reply, "Yeah. I'll message when I'm leaving". The morning is a drag, my mind isn't on my work. I'm doing some paperwork, but I'm not getting into it for some reason. I keep thinking about a big Figg hand around my throat. I've already had a chat with each of Henry and Nicholas, so I've exhausted that avenue of procrastination. I've made several coffees too. So I sit here in my little office staring at the paperwork, feeling my throat tighten. The paperwork doesn't seem particularly important considering I might be dead soon, but I distract my thoughts by getting some work done. Lunch time arrives, thank fuck for that. I tell Henry I'm off for lunch, and message Aubrey that I'm on my way.

I'm with Aubrey in his living room, and he fills me in with the developments. He did offer me a coffee, but I don't need any more caffeine, and I probably shouldn't have another afternoon drinking whisky. I'm supposed to be on my lunch.

'I told Maureen that you are happy with the plan to give the diamonds to Verb, who will find a buyer. I said you may back out if you become unhappy with how the plan develops, but at the moment you're in.' I'm nodding gently, all good so far. 'She called Verb, and told him you are interested, and suggested that we all meet. Based on your description that the diamonds fill about three quarters of a pint glass,' he stops to look at me for a moment smiling. When we chatted yesterday afternoon, he asked how many there are. I said I hadn't counted but they fill about three quarters of a pint glass. He found it hilarious that I keep them in a pint glass. He carries on, 'Verb estimates they could be worth a considerable amount, so he's keen to have a look, and move them quickly. Verb is driving to Stumpton today. He'll catch up with Maureen first, and they will come here later. Can you come here this evening?'

'Yeah, of course.' I've gone from not having a clue what to do with the diamonds, to getting involved with Maureen, who used to be a Figg, and Verb, who used to be in the diamond trade. Because of Aubrey. He hasn't once mentioned taking a cut. I'm going to give him a generous cut, but he's behaving like he's simply doing me a favour. He must know I'm going to sort him out. I hope he does. 'Are you not concerned that we'll be seen together? Maybe we should meet out of town somewhere?'

'If Maureen and I are seen together, we'll state romance as the motive. If Verb is seen in Stumpton, none of the younger generation of Figgs will know who he is. He's been out of town many years. You are often around here, so if all four of us are seen together, it will simply be friends catching up. We have to make sure no one sees the diamonds, that's all.'

'I'll try not to get mugged on the way over.' We both laugh. That's the first time we've laughed since I got here.

He tells me he'll message me later to confirm the time. I walk back to work, and Nicholas informs me there is another pickup, this time from Saint Catherine's. I make myself some lunch and drive over listening to "Soul Rebels" by Bob Marley and the Wailers. In the morgue, Con is talking non-stop and asking about Miriam. I ask why he doesn't call her, and he says he didn't get her number at Anton's party. He didn't want to ask her while she was crying; I'm actually impressed with him. I tell him to get Binky to pass his number on to her, and he tells me I'm a genius. It was fucking obvious. I ask where the stiff is; Con tells me he's a forty-two year old male, who got pissed and thought it would be a good idea to climb a wall. He made it to the top and was drunkenly celebrating, when he fell three metres and broke the fall with his head. We reach the table, and Con pulls back the sheet. Fuck! This is going to be a closed casket. His head is a mesh of scars. That was nice of him to make the jobs of the emergency services more distressing, by making them clean up his mess. I tell him I'll contact him about going out at the weekend, and ask him to let me know how he gets on with Miriam. I drive back to work, and put the body in the fridge. I smoke a bifta and spend a few hours preparing for tomorrow's funeral, and cleaning the hearse. The funeral is first thing, and Aubrey won't have time to do it in the morning.

I go home and cook some roast potatoes, parsnips, vegetables and a lentil pie. I wait for Aubrey's message. I don't even have a bifta. Aubrey messages, "My place at 8?" Right, this is happening.

"Okay", I message back. I need to find something to put the diamonds in, I can't carry them there in a pint glass. What did I do with the bag they were in? I have no memory of that. A sock! Fucking great idea. I go to the bedroom, retrieve a sock without a hole in it, and go to the kitchen. I open the cupboard and get the diamond pint from the top shelf. I try and open the sock end with one hand, and pour the rocks in with the other. About three rocks go into the sock and about eighteen slide out the edges and tumble onto the counter. I put the glass and sock down while the rocks bounce and settle down. This could get frustrating, but putting them in a few at a time sounds like an agonising chore. I have a plastic funnel knocking around somewhere; where did I put it? I rummage around the kitchen cupboards several times until I concede I might not find it. I know. I get another glass from the cupboard and put the sock in it, closed end first. I open the sock and fold it over the lip of the glass, and pour the rocks into the sock. I scoop up the loose rocks on the counter and chuck them in there too. I tie a knot, and throw it up and down in my hands a few times, even though I don't know why. It does feel nice though. I sling it in my bag and grab the rest of my shit. I message Rosie saying I'm meeting up with Aubrey tonight, and I'll message her tomorrow. She says she hopes I have a good night, and to say "hi" to Aubrey. I tell her I won't be saying "hi" to Aubrey, because he'll say "hi" back, and if I go ahead and act as middleman for that pointless conversation, I'll have succeeded only in wasting my own time. I tell her to say "hi" to him herself when she sees him next. She tells me to fuck off, then sends, "Have a good night, I'll message you tomorrow lover". I lock up and get a taxi to Aubrey's. There's a small kitchen knife I use for cutting vegetables. The blade is fairly short but it is dangerously sharp, and can cut through hash without being a hot knife. It's in my jacket pocket. My plan is to wave it about if anyone asks, 'What's in the bag pal?' But I have no intention of using it. I'm quite nervous having it on me. The walk from the taxi to Aubrey's front door is event free, so I knock and put the knife in my bag. Aubrey answers and leads me to the living room, where he introduces me to Maureen and Verb. Maureen has straight grey hair to her shoulders, and Aubrey was right, she's still attractive. I had her down as one of the many permed and withered grannies that roam this land. Verb's a baldigan. He has some liver spots on his scalp and forehead, and a grey goatee. Neither of them get up, the energy expenditure it would involve can be used more effectively elsewhere. Like keeping the internal organs ticking over.

I sit in the empty armchair and Aubrey asks me if I want a drink, pointing to the coffee table in the middle of the room. There's a bottle of whisky and four glasses. Three glasses contain an amount of whisky, the one nearest me is empty. I rectify that immediately. Maureen and Verb ask me a few questions, and I return the politeness. They seem like nice people, and they both have a good sense of humour. The conversation is friendly, but I'm not going to do my usual and drink several large whiskies and talk about some nonsense, like conjoined orangutan twins, thinking everyone's interested. Which is a shame, because I could have got several minutes out of them being joined at the waist, swinging through the trees, pulling in different directions, having a row about it.

Verb sits opposite me and talks about being back, and how much things have changed. He talks of his time in Stumpton, of Morag, how the four of them would play cards and drink moonshine in the old house. He sounds like a good bloke, I feel at ease listening to him. Maureen too, I see what Aubrey sees in her. The three of them get to reminiscing, so I fall out of the conversation. I'm happy to, I feel tired and not in a chatty mood. After a while, Aubrey apologises for leaving me out of the conversation.

'I don't mind. It was a nice conversation. I enjoyed listening.' They all smile, we're all smiling. It's clear to see that Aubrey and Verb are happy to see each other again. Verb's like Aubrey, he's ancient but he's compos mentis. His mental agility hasn't decreased. Well, it might have done, but it's still more agile than mine. Maureen clearly has all her faculties working at a high level too, and she's really quite amusing. I see her and Aubrey exchanging glances occasionally. Old love, it doesn't matter how old you are, does it?

'Shall we move on to the reason we're here tonight?' Aubrey suggests. Our faces change, the mood changes, we've all become more serious. 'Do you have the diamonds, Laszlo?'

'Yes.' I put my drink down and reach for my bag. I see Verb reaching for his bag too. I pull out the diamond sock and hold it up by the knot. I look around to see what expressions are looking back at me. Aubrey has already started laughing; I look at him and join in. The other two do as well; that's broken the growing tension. 'It was this or a pint glass.' I undo the knot and see that Verb has taken a small briefcase out of his bag. It looks like it might be a luxury travel backgammon board. He opens it up and it's lined with black felt, empty. I hand the sock to Aubrey, who hands it to Verb. He gently pours the rocks onto the felt, and the air pressure in the room changes as the three of them participate in a sudden intake of breath. I breathe normally, as I've seen them before; I should tell them about looking at them in a pint glass. They look great as they dance in the light. I think Aubrey might have already told them, he did find it funny, so I could remind him. I hear them speaking, they're talking about the diamonds. I should listen. Verb takes out his eye-piece magnifying glass, which I just found out is called a loupe. He examines one rock after another, putting them to the side, muttering to himself as he works. The three of us daren't say a word, we sit in silence watching him examine the rocks. I pour myself another drink and top up the other glasses. I take a few sips. Is he going to look at all of them? This is fucking taking forever. Thankfully, he stops about half way through, clearly excited with what he's seen so far. He's composes himself, and has a drink.

'Each gem is a two carat diamond. The cut is of high quality, the symmetry and polish demonstrate a high standard of expertise. None of them are perfectly colourless, but some of them have a slight blue hue,' he sounds professional, I don't understand what's he's talking about. But he looks pleased, so it must be good. 'The internal characteristics are barely visible in most, and absent in others.' He pauses, contemplating his next words. 'I would suggest VVS1 grade, maybe more, but I'd have to make a complete examination of the entire collection.' He looks at each of us, but we don't say anything. 'VVS1 grade is high on the clarity scale, so these are worth a lot of money.'

'How much?' Aubrey asks tentatively. 'Approximately.'

He thinks about it for a few moments, and tells us. The three of us sit here open mouthed, looking at each other. I don't know what to say. The others aren't saying anything either, so I guess they're equally as stunned. He puts the open case on the coffee table for us all to look at; the diamonds flicker as my head moves, as different surfaces catch the light. No one speaks for some time until Verb breaks the silence, 'That's their potential value, but that's not what you would get for them.'

It's agreed that Verb takes the diamonds in his case. He's staying here tonight, driving back tomorrow morning. Aubrey's made up the bed in the spare room for him, I've crashed here several times, it's a comfortable bed. He says he'd already identified several potential buyers, but considering the value of the gems, there's a contact in Amsterdam he thinks will be interested. He's going to make contact tonight, this is moving fast. I could stop it, but I don't want to. I'm actually happy to pass the rocks on. I should have been showering in diamonds, pouring them over myself, smoking a cigar. But whenever I looked at them I thought of the Figgs, so fear was the overriding emotion. And I'd have to pick them all up again. Covered in cuts.

Aubrey brings up the subject of Verb's cut for selling the gems, and Maureen's for involving Verb. Maureen and Verb agree that I should get the lion's share, as they wouldn't be in a position to make any money if it wasn't for me. 'You took the risk in taking them, and storing them,' Aubrey joins in.

'So what do you think my cut should be?' I ask them, not wanting to suggest a number myself.

They exchange a few looks, this could be awkward. Maureen is brave enough to speak first, 'At least fifty per cent. Sixty per cent?'

We all look at each other, I certainly don't know what to say. 'That would leave forty per cent,' Aubrey's says, following this one through to see how we feel about it, rather than deciding something. 'Twenty each for you and Verb.'

'It would be nice to receive something for being part of the plan, but Verb is selling the diamonds which involves more, so he should get more,' Maureen generously proposes.

Verb starts to disagree, but I quickly speak up agreeing with Maureen, 'Verb, without your contacts we won't be able to sell the diamonds, and you'll be looking after them from now on. You'll be taking the risks now. You should get a good chunk.'

'No,' he immediately objects. 'I'll drive the gems home and put them in a drawer. If my contact in Amsterdam wants to buy, he sends his representative to London to collect them. There's no risk to me. I'm not doing so much.' He smiles genuinely, I recall Aubrey telling me Verb just wants to help.

I lean forward, 'Are we all trying to give each other percentages? Not very good at business are we?' We have a laugh that breaks the tension, but doesn't remove it. I decide to throw an option out there, to see how they like it. I have to say something. 'If...I take fifty per cent, you two can take twenty-five each. It has always been my intention to give Aubrey half of anything I make, so that gives Aubrey twenty-five per cent too. What do you think?' They were looking at each other intently as I spoke, gauging each other's reactions, but now the mood had changed. They look surprised, interested and hesitant.

'That could work Laszlo, but now it looks like the risks you took are not being rewarded adequately.' Maureen's looking concerned, but I like her, she's not greedy.

I smile at her, 'Look at the four of us, sitting here making plans to sell diamonds. I think we're in this together.' We ease into an agreement that it's the best idea, and I feel different about Maureen and Verb now. I've only just met them, but I don't feel like an outsider, the four of us are joining forces. I notice Aubrey isn't saying too much though. I pour another round of drinks. Verb suggests he proceeds with the valuation of the entire collection, and informs his contact. If the contact is interested they will negotiate a price. He'll then report the price back to us, and if we're happy with it, he'll make the sale. Fine by me, if I get out of this with no money but my kneecaps intact, I'll be delighted. But that kind of money is fucking ridiculous.

I finish my drink, and knock up a bifta for the walk home. Verb tells me it was nice to meet me, and I will be informed as soon as there are any developments. I shake his hand, gently, and kiss Maureen on the cheek. Fucking hell Aubrey, she's actually quite hot. What am I thinking? Aubrey walks me to the door, and tells me there's no way he can take half my share. We argue quietly by the front door, both stubbornly standing our ground. We end up laughing as we're arguing, but still neither of us backs down. He tells me we'll continue this conversation tomorrow, and I tell him I can't fucking wait. 'Damn,' he says suddenly. 'I forgot to wash the hearse; I planned to go in this afternoon to do it, but I've been somewhat distracted.' I tell him to sleep easy, I've already done it. Now I wonder if Maureen's staying over too. Aubrey thanks me, and I tell him it was my pleasure, even though it wasn't.

I'm walking home and my phone tells me it's ten o'clock. I could message Rosie, see if she wants to meet up. But it's the Figg funeral tomorrow morning, so I should get an early night. Shit, I forgot my sock, I need that one, it doesn't have any holes in it. I light the bifta and make my way past Parsons Green. I feel relieved I don't have the diamonds anymore. If for some reason Tyrone knocks on my door, until its hinges snap, he won't find any diamonds in my flat, and I can play dumb quite convincingly. I get home and have a nightcap; a few whiskies and a few biftas. I watch a few episodes of The IT Crowd, and laugh a lot.

I wake up before my alarm goes off; I feel awake, so I get up. I decide to mix up my usual routine by having coffee and toast first, then having a shower. It didn't feel right, but I'm in a pretty good mood as I walk to work. I get in early in case I'm needed, or there's some trouble. I plan to be visible to the Figgs today, but keep out of their way. It would be suspicious if I'd had the day off. I need to show the Figgs it's business as usual for me. I find Aubrey, Henry and Nicholas in the office. They're discussing the funeral. The Figgs will be here in an hour, which is plenty of time to make preparations, but we all want this one to go smoothly. Aubrey's looking at me like he wants to talk, flashing his eyes at me. I make my excuses and tell the lads I have stuff to do and I'd better get on with it. I wait in the dressing room for several minutes, thinking Aubrey wouldn't be far behind me. I take a peek in the office and see he's still stuck in a conversation with Nicholas. I do have stuff to do, so I'll catch up with Aubrey later. I retrieve Big Joe from the fridge and make a few small adjustments to his clothing, he's looking good. I put the coffin in the back of the hearse, and fetch the wreaths the Figgs want put in the there. I put the coffee machine on, and take Henry and Nicholas a cup each, they say thank you, but whether they drink it or not is none of my business. I find Aubrey in the dressing room and give him a cup.

'You did a good job cleaning the hearse, thank you Laszlo.' I nod, but I don't think that's what he wants to speak about.

He gets on with what's on his mind. 'Verb got in touch with his contact in Amsterdam last night, and told him what we have. He called Verb this morning with a deal.' He remains silent for a few moments before telling me what we've been offered. Fuck, that's incredible. It's not as much as Verb's initial valuation, but we expected that. What's that each? Fuck, I never expected this sort of money. Aubrey breaks my thoughts, 'Do we want to go ahead?'

'Fuck, yes.' I must be looking a bit dazed, I certainly feel that way.

'Good, I've spoken to Maureen and we're both keen to take this deal. So as you're happy too, I'll tell Verb to go ahead.' There's excitement in his voice, and in his eyes. I'm starting to feel the reality of it now, and I'm feeling energised too.

'Yes, let's go for it. I don't care if they're worth more, with this money we could buy a mansion each in Florida.' I see a flash in his eyes, but I don't question him.

'I'll call him now,' he says hurriedly. I hear him telling Verb that all three of us agree and we should take the deal. They chat briefly, then he hangs up and turns his attention back to me, 'I cannot accept half of your share. I cooked up a hare-brained scheme with Maureen to sell the diamonds, but I wouldn't have been able to get Verb involved, that was Maureen's idea. I really can't take half, but thank you.'

'You can and you will. Without you, there's no Maureen and no Verb. You're as important a cog as the rest of us.'

'I'm old, I won't live long enough to spend that kind of money. You're young, you can make good use of it.'

'You'll outlive me. Besides, Maureen and Verb are old too, and you seem happy for them to get twenty-five per cent.' I can see he's about to protest again, so I carry on, 'If I end up broke I'll ask you if I can stay at yours until I find a job. How about that?' I know he hasn't finished, so I stand up to get changed, and change the subject too. 'Did I tell you there's a spider in my bathroom with nine legs?' I talk about that for a bit, while he drinks his coffee. He knows I'm making it up, but he doesn't stop me. He's clearly prepared to wait until later before he resumes the allocation of shares conversation. I change into my funeral clobber, and tell Aubrey I'll meet him at the hearse.

I spend about fifteen minutes in my shed, and find him standing by the car, Nicholas will let us know when it's time to move out. He asks me if I've had a joint, 'I need it today,' I tell him. 'Evolutionarily speaking, we humans have perfected the harvesting and preparation of drugs and alcohol. Plenty of animals have developed a taste for drugs and booze, but none have taken it as seriously as humans. Wallabies eat poppies and get high on opium, deer eat fly agaric, gorillas eat the hallucinogenic roots of the iboga plant. Vervet monkeys get pissed on fermenting sugar cane, and plenty of animals enjoy the effects of eating fermenting fruit. It's most likely that humans learned of the effects of these natural highs by watching animals. Some animals, like elephants, are now watching us. They find out where illegal stills of fermenting fruit or alcohol are kept, and break in, get pissed and go on the rampage.'

'And jaguars,' he looks at me, 'They chew the roots of yage, a hallucinogenic plant. It is suggested that the indigenous people that also use the plant, learned to do so by observing the cats.'

'I didn't know that.' We're about to get stuck into that topic when Nicholas appears from the side entrance and tells us it's time. We get in the hearse and Aubrey starts the car; we're both hit in the ear holes with "Freedom Run" by Kyuss. I turn it off. 'Sorry Aubrey, I'm a bit forgetful sometimes.' When I get Alzheimer's, it will be seamless. He doesn't say anything, I don't think this is anywhere near his top five things he needs to talk to me about. We slowly drive around the building and down the driveway. There are a few people standing around, but most have already gotten into cars. I don't look at anyone, I solemnly look out the windscreen, but my vision only extends as far as the windscreen wipers, nothing beyond. The drive to Saint Timothy's should take about fifteen minutes, and the procession of expensive vehicles slot in behind us. Aubrey tells me that he and Maureen have agreed that they will acknowledge each other, and he will express his sympathies. After all, they do know each other. But that's it, they don't want to draw attention to their relationship. The less the Figgs know the better.

'Maureen plans to quietly sell up and disappear, and it's possible they might not notice, as she rarely sees Tyrone and the others. But it's likely they will notice after a while, and if they're curious as to where she's gone, they'll ask her last known associates. And that could include me. It's best not to leave them any trails.'

'Good idea. And in the spirit of things, that means I've never met Maureen before. Under these circumstances we may not even acknowledge each other, there are lots of guests by the looks of things.' I look in the wing mirror, at the giant metallic snake following us. It's not simply following us, we're its prey, it's after us. 'I'll stand, looking respectful, and nod at those that walk past me, if she's one of them, I'll just nod.'

'Perfect, we simply act naturally.' We drive the rest of the way in silence and pull into Saint Timothy's. We park to the side of the main door, and the guests of Big Joe file in behind us. The cars keep coming in until the car park is full. Some people are walking in on foot, they must have parked outside somewhere. We get out and stand by the hearse. People are milling about in the car park, moving from one pocket of folk to another, having brief exchanges before moving on. I recognise Maureen, Tyrone, Tommy, Marco, Frannie and Potato. There must be about a hundred people here, I've never been to a funeral this big before. Tyrone and Tommy approach Aubrey and I. We instinctively open the hearse and pull out the coffin on the trolley. The four of us exchange greetings, they don't seem agitated or cross with me, but I can't make out their expressions. They're not giving anything away. That might be because they're burying their dad today, and it's going to be a difficult day. Or they may still think I know something, and they're saving me for later. We're joined by Potato and a guy I've never seen before. He has a nose that looks like it's been broken several times. The four of them lift the coffin and carry it inside. The mourners have been gathering themselves, swarming near the entrance, people are still moving about greeting each other. A line of people emerge from the throng, and enter the building. It looks like a tornado hit the entrance, got tired and decided to lie down. Slowly, the gathering filters inside, leaving Aubrey and I outside.

I watch the darkness inside the building devour the last of the mourners and wait in silence until the door is shut. 'Were they looking at me funny?' I ask him quickly, and don't give him time to respond. 'I think they were looking at me funny. What do you think?'

'I think you're stoned.' There's a silence, which is fine because I can't think of anything to say. 'Are you still happy you smoked that joint?' He sees my fear, 'Don't worry, they weren't looking at you funny. Did you recognise the big chap carrying the coffin?'

'Who? Potato?'

'Who? The big chap with the damaged nose.'

'Oh him, no never seen him before.'

'I recognise him, that's not a face you forget. His mug shot was in the papers on and off for months last year. His name is Bernie Fingers; he was arrested and faced trial for the murder of a successful businessman. He strangled him with piano wire; with such force that his head was nearly severed. The prosecution claimed he's a freelance assassin, working for all manner of criminal organisations. He has done hits for many gangs, but never hits gang members. He's no doubt simply keeping himself alive adopting that policy, but the gangs think he's an honourable man. He gets paid well to keep his mouth shut, and that's exactly what he did during his trial, he never spoke anyone's name. News reports claimed that the prosecution had a key eye-witness, who could identify Fingers as the killer. The person's identity was not disclosed for security reasons, but as the trial progressed, news filtered through that the eye-witness had disappeared. The prosecution did not bring out an eye-witness, so it could be true. The evidence they were left with was circumstantial, and Fingers walked free.'

'Bernie Fingers,' I look at Aubrey with renewed fear, 'What's he doing here? As he doesn't hit other gang members, he's not being roped into the war with the Dancers, so why is he here? Is he here simply to pay his respects to Big Joe, or has he been hired to hit someone else?'

'Don't worry Laszlo, he's an assassin attending a funeral, that's all.' We chat, and Aubrey keeps the conversation light, steering me away from talking about having my head sliced off with piano wire. The door opens and a religious looking

138

person leads the pallbearers into the graveyard towards the big open wound in the earth they're going to lower Big Joe into. The procession of mourners files out slowly, and a few nod at Aubrey and I, so we nod back. Maureen exits the church and she and Aubrey exchange a few words. They're wonderfully convincing as old friends; Aubrey expresses his sympathies, but keeps it brief, a professional performance. We follow the last of the mourners to the grave and stand at the back. I can barely see what's going on from here, but I swear Tyrone looked over at me. I scan the backs of the people in front of me, the ground, my shoes. I look back to where the action is, to look attentive and professional, and Bernie Fingers is looking at me. My heart is beating too fast for comfort, and I think a bit of piss came out. I'm going to be assassinated. It's actually going to happen. I want to get out of here, I need to lie down. This is going on forever. Eventually, they finish and start to file back towards the church. Aubrey and I retreat to the hearse. A few more people pass, and nod and say thanks. Then Tyrone, Tommy, Potato and Fingers stroll over to us. Please don't kill me right here. Tyrone says thanks for the work I did on his dad, and Tommy says I've been helpful. What does that mean? There are handshakes all round, and I have to stop mine from shaking when I give it to Bernie Fingers. I know the hand is supposed to shake during the process, but an up and down motion is usually appropriate. I'm scared mine's going to be shaking like a one-armed bartender knocking up a daiquiri when I offer it to him. If he asks, I'll tell him I have the DTs. Survival mode kicks in and I offer him a steady hand and get through the ordeal without letting him know I'm shitting it. They walk off and get in their cars while Aubrey and I stand here in silence, watching them. They drive out of the car park, and it's just the two of us left. We get in the hearse without speaking and close the doors. I look at Aubrey and his expression is one of relief. 'I think we made it,' he sounds satisfied, but I'm still shitting myself.

'I swear both Tyrone and Bernie looked at me when they were lowering the coffin.' I'm looking for support.

'Don't start that again. They were simply looking around.'
He starts the ignition and we glide out of the car park.

I don't pursue it, he's probably right, and he doesn't want to hear me being stressed out about being assassinated. I should try hard to get the idea out of my head, I can't spend my time stressing about something that might not happen.

Chapter Eleven

Back at work Aubrey and I see Nicholas by the entrance to the prep room. He greets us and asks how the funeral went. Aubrey tells him it went like clockwork, I tell him it was as smooth as a velvet glove on your buttocks. He smiles at Aubrey, but only gives me a quick distracted look. He expresses his pleasure that our association with the Figgs has ended. I fucking hope so. He tells me that he will work in the prep room this afternoon, on the pisshead who thought he was Monkeyman I presume, and that Henry is dealing with viewings for the young boy. He still looks tired, the strain of dealing with the Figgs has not fully abated yet. He'll lose himself in his work when he's concentrating, and that's a welcome break after his recent stress. Aubrey and I leave him to it, and congratulate each other on getting through the funeral.

Aubrey hangs around for the remainder of the morning. He could fuck off somewhere, but he works on the hearse for a while. He's got his tool kit out but he's only checking the oil and other fluids, there's no repairs being done. Maybe he wants to be around company, maybe Maureen's busy, maybe he wants to pass on any news quickly and as I'm not great at answering my phone, it might be better if I'm in his vicinity. Lunchtime arrives, and we retire to my shed to eat. I bring a chair from the store room and sit on that while Aubrey takes the armchair. 'I like this place,' he looks around my kingdom, 'But you could do with a few pictures on the walls.' We eat lunch; Aubrey didn't know he was still going to be here for lunch and only has a packet of mints in his pocket. I brought some leftover roast potatoes and parsnips with me, so I've reheated them, and we have half each. Aubrey fetches two coffees while I make a bifta, and we're sitting drinking when his phone rings. He looks at me, 'Verb.' They chat briefly, but I can't make out what's happening, Aubrey's mainly giving one word replies. They finish, and Aubrey informs me that Verb's contact is sending a representative to London this evening to look at the gems.

'What about payment? How does that work? I don't think we can accept cash.'

'I don't know, I didn't ask. I'll call him back.' He calls, but Verb's line is engaged. 'I'll try him again later, and find out.' We drink our coffees and I smoke the bifta, Aubrey doesn't smoke. He puts his tool kit away after lunch and heads off, telling me he'll let me know if there's news later.

I head towards the office, to see if Henry's about. I hear crying coming from the Chapel. Loud, forceful crying, more like shrieking. I hear soft voices trying to calm the distraught person. The cry weakens, but it's only an intake of air, as the vigorous cry returns. There's so much pain in that sound, I can't face it, I turn around and go to my office.

I receive a message from Rosie telling me she's going down The Hefty Pigeon after work, do I want to join her. "Too fucking right I do", I message her. There are more viewings this afternoon and I keep out of the way, busying myself with paperwork. I offer to stay behind and lock up as Henry and Nicholas have a meeting at the Rotary Club this evening. I lock up, and grab a falafel wrap from Lord of the Falafel on my way to The Hefty Pigeon. I enter the pub, scan the room, and see Rosie sitting at a table with four people I've never seen before. I walk over and I'm introduced. I smile and say one "Hi" that covers everyone. I ask if anyone wants a drink and they politely decline. Rosie joins me at the bar, we're chatting, touching each other, leaning against each other. I get my drink and we rejoin her group. The conversation is easy and fun, but I'm not having a great time. Her friends are nice, but I wanted to catch up with Rosie, not talk to her via a six-way conversation. I'm drinking too quickly, and after a couple of hours I feel I might be getting pissed. I tell Rosie this, and say I'm going home. She's out for the night, on the piss with her friends, so she's staying in the pub. She comes outside to say goodnight, and we kiss passionately around the corner, by the vets with a poster in the window advertising treatment for worms in dogs and cats. 'I hope you have a good night, I'll message you tomorrow,' and I back away still holding her hand. I watch her walk back into the pub and I stroll home.

I get home and hit the nightcaps, listening to "Master of Reality" by Black Sabbath. I'm feeling quite pissed and stoned, when my phone rings. It's Aubrey. I say 'Hello,' and he tells me to turn the music down, he needs to talk to me. I lean over, and nearly fall off the sofa before I manage to press pause.

'The Amsterdam representative is pleased with the diamonds, and the sale is going ahead. He has also kindly advised Verb of the best procedure for payment. We need to set up a bank account in Switzerland.' I haven't said anything since saying "hello". 'Are you still there?'

'Yeah,' I try not to sound wasted.

'Good. Large deposits, particularly opening deposits, will require authentication to prove we're not money laundering. We will need to open the account with a smaller amount. The Amsterdam contact will provide us with a receipt of sale of a quantity of diamonds from one company to another. With the receipt we will be able to open a Swiss bank account without suspicion. Any subsequent large deposits may also draw attention, but if we deposit smaller amounts over a period of time, all with receipts, we can avoid suspicion. Verb's contact will pay us in instalments over a two year period. It will be easier for both parties.'

'What if they don't pay us?' I do sound wasted.

'Verb said he and the contact go back many years, and he owes Verb a favour. This is it.' I wasn't really in the mood for a conversation when my phone rang, and this one is requiring some concentration. 'We need to do two things, Laszlo. First, we need to set up a business. Can you do that? Apparently, you simply need to register a name. Second, we need to go to Geneva and open a bank account. We'll need proof of the company's existence, our passports, and the receipt for the sale of the amount of diamonds. Verb will be sent the receipt by email, you set up the company, and we go to Switzerland next week. Is that okay with you?'

What the fuck is he talking about? Switzerland? Setting up a business? It did sound like I'm involved in some way, but I'm not sure how. 'What do you want me to do?' He sighs and patiently runs through it again, and this time its clearer. I tell him I'll set up the business tomorrow; how hard can it be? And I'll look at flights to Geneva too and get back to him. I pour another nightcap and a drop of whisky lands on my foot. I hoist my foot up onto the opposite knee and lick the drop off, there's no point wasting any. I need to think about a name for the business, so I scribble a few suggestions on a notepad, and cross them out. What are our initials? Maureen, Verb, Aubrey and me; M. V. A. L. Mval? No, that's no good. I like Val though; it looks like it's short for value, or valuation. How about Verb, Aubrey, Laszlo and Maureen; Valam. That is genius, it sounds mythical. I message Valam as the company name to Aubrey. He messages back, "Valam on its own sounds like an antifungal medicine. How about Valam Gems?" That is fucking brilliant, I take a drag and message him, "Perfect, goodnight". This is all coming together nicely. I might have to go to bed soon though.

I wake up on the sofa, with my laptop on and the lamp on. I sit up, fuck my neck hurts. I check the time, 03:07. I feel like shit. I notice half a bifta in the ashtray, and spark it up. I smoke it while I turn everything off and pour myself a whisky. One nightcap later, I go to bed. My second attempt at sleep is more restful, and I get up with my alarm. I have a shitty hangover; I've had colossal hangovers before, but this one might be tolerable. I get up and go to work, spending the morning researching how to register a business, with a pile of paperwork next to the computer. It's not as simple as registering the name, and I've already identified a few problems; I hope this isn't going to be a traumatic experience. It's already giving me a fucking headache; running parallel to my existing hangover headache. Two of the cunts battling it out to see which one can ache the most. I'd like one of them to fuck off, to give me a fighting chance of getting through the morning; but in truth I'm just hoping a third one doesn't become aware of the commotion and decide to see what's going on.

I call Aubrey, a quick greeting and I get on with it, 'If I set up as a sole trader, it takes ten days to register and we don't get a certificate. If I set up a partnership, we do get a certificate, and I can pay for same-day service. The problem is that I need to put two names on the form. Shall I make one up?'

'No, definitely not. We don't want to falsify a legal document.'

'Isn't that what we're doing?'

'Put my name on the form.'

'I need a signature.'

'I'm on my way.'

I print off the form, and fill out what I can. Aubrey arrives late morning and joins me in my office. It's a small room off the back corridor, there's enough room for a desk and chair, a bookcase, an armchair, and a small filing cabinet, on top of which is a printer. My desk is fairly tidy, apart from the stacks of paperwork waiting to be attended to. We say "hi", and he sits in the armchair. I give him the form to look over, while I fetch two coffees. When I get back, he's written his name, Aubrey Wisp, and signed it.

He hands me the form and thanks me for the coffee, 'What happens now?'

'I send this first class, and pay for same-day service. As long as they receive it before three o'clock, they process it and dispatch the certificate the same day. It's sent recorded delivery, so I should receive it on Saturday. I'll have to sign for it, but I'll stay in 'til it arrives.'

'Good work Laszlo that is great. How much is the same-day service?'

'A hundred, or something like that. I don't have a chequebook, but I'll buy a postal order.'

'Let me give you some money,' he pulls his wallet out of his inside jacket pocket, and looks up to see me studying him intently, with an exaggerated look of puzzlement. 'Okay, good point,' and he puts his wallet back.

'I'm assuming that as soon as we receive all the instalments, we fold the business.'

'I have a feeling that we can fold the business way before then, so long as we have the Swiss account set up, we can receive payments that have corresponding receipts.'

'Where are the diamonds now?'

'The Amsterdam representative took them last night.' He pauses while we both appreciate the gravity of that statement. 'That means we no longer have the diamonds, and we haven't been paid.' He pauses again, 'And whoever this contact is, we're no match for him.'

'I wish I hadn't asked. Are we fucked?'

'Verb said that his contact doesn't simply owe him a favour, the chap feels like he's indebted to Verb. He wouldn't say why, he said it should remain between them. I haven't seen Verb in years, and people can change. But he was always a good man, trustworthy. Seeing him again I have the same thoughts about him, but my thoughts may be clouded with nostalgia.'

'What are you saying?'

'I'm saying that I trust Verb. He tells me his contact will honour the agreement of instalments, and I also think it was our only option.'

I agree without saying so. We finish our drinks, chat a while longer and leave the building. I'm going for lunch which will involve a visit to the post office to send this letter, and a trip to Cyril's cafe, The Sunshine Cafe, for a vegetable pattie. I've been going there for years, he knows my dietary choices. Aubrey says he's going round Maureen's, but I don't ask him what he's having for lunch. After a successful mission at the post office, I message Rosie asking how her night was. I'm eating my pattie on a bench in Crawford Green when she messages back, "Was a good night. Feel like shit. Work is painful", and then "How are you?"

I finish my lunch and send, "Serves you right, you were drinking faster than a thirsty dolphin". So was I. Then I send,

"Feel like shit too. Do you fancy a quick drink with Aubrey and Maureen later?" It was Aubrey's idea, he said we don't need to talk privately. We're not expecting news, we're waiting to set up the account. If Verb has any news he'll let us know.

She replies, "Yeah, I'll get to meet the gorgeous Maureen. Would you give her one?"

"Already have", I send, and walk back to work smiling.

The walk back has cleared my mind. I made a plan for this afternoon, and as soon as I get here, I implement it. I go to my shed first. Then I tackle a pile of paperwork. Once that's completed, I make another coffee and set about dismantling another pile of paperwork. I'm not going to leave work until I finish it. Getting through it all will require several breaks, as admin is so catastrophically tedious, that the brain can capsize under the weight of boredom. As the work is life threatening, breaks are mandatory. I notice the signs after doing admin for a while; it makes me want to tear down the nearest wall with my teeth. Then it's time to take a break. I've noticed that when reading the word admin, it likes to announce its presence with a capital A. Why has it assumed that privilege? If it's done properly, it can be done easily and quickly, what's the big hoo-hah all about? Why does admin get such a fanfare? It's people pushing paper around. Paper goes from hand to hand, folder to folder. Hand, folder, hand, folder, hand, forever.

Nicholas finds me beavering away at the computer, inputting data from the papers. He tells me Henry has already left to meet Alan Swetz, their accountant. Alan Swetz is a stocky man with dark curly hair. He laughs enthusiastically at his own jokes, but I've never found one of his attempts at humour to be even slightly amusing. He comes around from time to time; I get the impression he wants to be thought of as important, but he isn't to me. He's picked up on that, and he doesn't try conversation or small talk with me anymore. Apart from my general indifference towards him, he took umbridge with me one time and has barely spoken to me since. He was telling me how good he was at squash, and I let out an involuntary snort, which the lardy cunt took offence at. I told him I thought he looked so unfit; he'd get out of breath pulling his socks up. That's all I said, not much, and he got decidedly pissy with me. Granted, I was laughing at my own joke, but I assumed he'd join in. He didn't, and now he just keeps to greetings. Fine by me; the man bores me. I tell Nicholas I'll lock up if he wants to get away. He thanks me and dodders off, so I crack on with more data input.

I receive a message from Aubrey, "Sticky pud at 8?" I think of asking him if he enjoyed his Maureen pattie, but I decide against it. "See you there", is what I go for. I message Rosie with the news, and we arrange to meet at the boozer. I lock up when Nicholas leaves and finish the paperwork. I work about an hour later than usual and walk home enjoying the warm evening. At home I cook my world-famous pasta with mushrooms. I cooked it one time for a group of people when I stayed on a campsite when travelling around New Zealand. There were people of several nationalities tucking in, and they all loved it. It would come as no surprise to find out news of it has spread across the globe. While eating, I have a message conversation with Eddie and we agree to meet up tomorrow night; we don't say where or when, we'll sort that out tomorrow. Sounds like things are going well with Mila. I walk to The Sticky Pud and see Rosie, Aubrey and Maureen sitting at a table outside, they're chatting and laughing. I walk over and notice they all have drinks; we greet and I don't bother sitting down, I tell them I'll get a drink. I open the door, walk to the bar, wait, order a pint, pay, take a swig, wait for my change, walk back outside, sit opposite Rosie and look at her. She's beautiful. I enjoy her company, and I'm worried that I'm developing feelings for her. I think about her when I'm not with her. I could be assassinated within the week, and I don't want her getting dragged into this shit. Or I could be filthy rich, and where does that leave us? Maureen thanks me for making the hash cakes, she had some the other day with Aubrey, and she enjoyed the feeling. Yeah I bet you did.

Rosie looks at Maureen and Aubrey, 'Have you two lived in Stumpton all your lives?'

'Yes, I have. I grew up here, married here, and had children here. I've had some good times here, great memories.' Maureen stops, contemplating her memories. 'My husband died, and my children moved away. I have a son and a daughter, we're close and we keep in touch, but they have no intention of returning.' She pauses again, and looks around at us, 'I think maybe it's time for a change for me too.' She seems lost in thought again, so Aubrey steps in.

'I grew up in Corshon, and moved to Stumpton for work when I was a young man,' he looks at Maureen, 'And I'm pleased I did.' He smilingly turns his attention to Rosie, 'But I've lived in various places over the years. I returned to Stumpton about twenty years ago.'

'How exciting,' she looks to me to register her interest then back to Aubrey, 'Where have you lived?'

'Here and there,' Aubrey says, also appearing to lose himself in thought.

'This is what he's like,' I tell her, 'He's done so many things he can't remember them all. Then one day he'll casually mention that he used to work as a wildlife veterinarian in Zambia.'

Aubrey smiles, 'And maybe it's time for another move.' He's lost in thought again, so I carry on.

'I'm not so exciting, I've been here all my life, and I'm as bored as a captive animal.'

'What about you Rosie?' Maureen enquires.

'Well I'm not from Stumpton,' she hesitates for a moment, maybe thinking of her parents and deciding what to say, 'And I don't think I want to live here forever.' She looks at Maureen, 'Change is positive, it's good to see what different places have to offer. Good for you.' She looks at me with an expression I can't decipher, because it's comprised of several expressions rolled into one.

'Where would you like to live?' Maureen asks her.

'Oh, lots of places, but I can't afford to move somewhere anytime soon.'

I avoid glancing at Aubrey and Maureen, in case Rosie picks up on the silent communication and realises she's been excluded from something. But she's distracted by finishing her drink and looking for her bank card. She asks who wants a drink and we all say yes, so I go to the bar with her to help carry the drinks back.

We return with the drinks, sit down, and as there's a moment's pause I ask, 'Did you know astronomers have recently discovered that the Moon is hollow?'

'Yeah, that's what I heard. It's like a giant table tennis ball,' Rosie chimes in with.

'What's in the middle?' Maureen asks.

Rosie answers before I have chance, 'A scientist was explaining that it's full of gases, mainly helium. The plan is to siphon the helium because we need more balloons in our lives.'

'If the Moon's full of helium, why doesn't it float off somewhere?' Aubrey's enjoying himself, I can tell.

'It's because the weight of the rocky surface offers a perfect balance to the floating off properties of the helium inside. It's a bit like the tug of war in a dying star. The gravitational forces and the pressure inside balance each other out.' Rosie's taken charge of this one now; I started it, but I haven't spoken since. I must admit, I'm impressed with her knowledge, and her bullshit. She sounds like a natural. 'The problem with siphoning the helium,' there's more, and I start to gently laugh, wondering where she's going. She ignores my laugh and continues, 'Is that it will destabilise the tensional forces maintaining the rigidity of the rocky surface; which will eventually cave in on itself. The Earth's gravitational pull will ensure it remains locked into an orbit, but it'll be the size of a football stadium.' She takes a sip of her drink, so Aubrey pipes up again.

'It has a rather a thin rocky surface, the Moon.' He bats that one back to her and takes a sip of his own drink.

'Yes, that's right Aubrey, you've heard about it too, I see.'

He laughs, 'Yes, it's all over the news.'

We chat for a while longer, when Maureen asks what everyone wants to drink. Rosie says she's had a long day and is going home when she finishes her drink in progress. I agree, saying I'll walk her home. When Rosie and I leave, Maureen tells her it was lovely to meet her, and Aubrey says it was delightful to see her again. I think again how much I enjoy her company.

We walk along the canal and I'm lost in thought. She slips her hand into mine, 'What are you thinking about?'

'About how nosey you are.' I look at her, 'Which is quite rude?'

'I've learned something tonight.' I don't ask, I know she's going to tell me, 'That I really hate you,' she's looking serious, but we're still holding hands.

'I thought you already knew that.'

'I mean I hate you more.' She still hasn't cracked a smile.

'Why don't you say something nice to me?' I try to look hurt.

'Why don't you stick a dog turd up your arse?' She maintains her formal expression, but her eyes widen as she looks at me. I don't think she knew she was going to say that. I think I'm falling for her.

'Most people pick up their dog's turds these days, so we may have trouble finding one.' We decide to go back to mine, and thankfully make it all the way here without spotting a turd. We have the customary nightcap of a glass of red wine and a bifta, and go to bed. We have a long slow shag, except the last bit which is quite frenetic.

As I'm drifting off to sleep, she asks, 'Do you mind me staying over so often?'

'No, I like it when you're here. I like you.'

She leans over and kisses me, 'Good, because I like you too.'

We wake up before our alarms and make love. We're lying in bed chatting when she says she has to go. She dresses, kisses me and she's off. I shower, make coffee and toast, and go to work. I make a coffee and look at flights to Geneva. There are two each day, and the prices are fairly cheap. The first flight leaves at 07:15, which means getting up ridiculously early. The second flight arrives in Geneva at 22:50, which doesn't give us a lot of time to explore the city on day one, but an anticipated lie in would remain unharmed. How many days are we going for? Three should do it, one to arrive, one to open an account, and one to depart. Or we could depart after opening the account. There are two flights each day returning; I'll ask Aubrey what he'd prefer. Nicholas enters my office and tells me there's another pickup from Saint Catherine's. I tell him I'll go there straight away, when Aubrey appears at the door. I wonder what excuse he'll think of for his presence, the hearse's windscreen washer fluid doesn't need a top-up.

'Hello Aubrey, what brings you here today?' Nicholas and Aubrey get on well; they've been friends for years. They're different types of people though; Nicholas doesn't eat hash cakes and fornicate with the hot looking Maureen. Aubrey gets invited to all the Partridge family events, which he goes to out of courtesy, but he tells me I'm not missing anything. And he'll scarper faster than me if he sees Nicholas's wife. I've seen him trapped in conversations with her. Sometimes I'll get straight in there and tell him he's required elsewhere; he'll thank me, but he does the same for me if I get snared. Other times I remain mostly out of sight, I let him see that I've noticed his predicament, but I hold back, trying not to laugh. I can see him getting agitated as he sees the end in sight, but I'm being a cunt and make him suffer a while longer for my amusement. When I triumphantly emerge and detach him from another ear mauling, he thanks me, then reprimands me for taking so long. I remind him that he does the same to me sometimes, and we call it evens.

'I was hoping to talk to Laszlo.' Nicholas doesn't take offence; he's relaxed with Aubrey and walks slowly out of the room. As they pass, Aubrey tells Nicholas he'll catch up with him in a while. I ask him if there are any developments. 'Nothing spectacular, but I thought we could have a chat, and I could keep you informed.'

'I need to go to Saint Catherine's, do you want to talk before, or join me?'

'I'll join you. I haven't seen Doug or Con for a while. I'll catch up with Nicholas first, and meet you at the hearse.'

I wait for Aubrey in the car; in the passenger seat. I have driven with Aubrey as the passenger, but it didn't feel right. He gets in and we drive to Saint Catherine's. He tells me Verb has gone to Amsterdam. Apparently, the business deal has reignited an old friendship. I suppose that puts one of our team in their camp, to keep an eye on the rocks. But I'm not sure how much that helps us. I tell Aubrey about the flights. 'The early flight is better,' he says with no consideration. I try my best to convince him of the awful day ahead of us if we have to get up at four o'clock, but he's not fazed in the slightest. 'Go to bed earlier, then you'll be rested.' I try to convince him of the improbability of going to bed early, but he thinks it's better if we land early so we can visit the bank that day. We remain in Geneva for another day, in case there are any unforeseen problems; and we'll get to do some sightseeing. We fly out on the late flight on day two. I agree that's a good plan. I tell him I'll book the flights, but I need his passport. 'Can you come around tomorrow, late morning, to pick it up?'

'Yeah, no problem.' We listen to the tunes for a while, Johnny Cash is singing about being a worried man. Aubrey pulls into a parking space at the morgue, and turns the tunes off. We walk down the corridor towards the office, Doug is there and I give him a wave. He waves back, and Aubrey goes in to chat with him. I open the doors to the morgue and see Con sorting through some paperwork. We greet and he apologises for the radio silence over the last few days. Apparently he's been out of town to meet his contact and stock up. I don't have the heart to tell him I didn't notice his absence; I've been quite preoccupied.

'This stuff is really good, I promise you.' He rifles though his bag and hands me two wraps, 'Pay me when you want.'

'Cheers Con,' I put the wraps in my pocket, 'I'm meeting up with Eddie later, if you want to join us.'

'Thanks, but I'm meeting Miriam later,' he gives me another of his winning smiles. If I'm being honest, he's a handsome man, but he sure fucking knows it.

'Nice one, how's it going with Miriam?'

'Binky passed my number to her, but she messaged while I was out of town, so I haven't sealed the deal yet. I got back last night, and suggested meeting tonight. She's as keen as an icy wind.'

I screw up my face, 'Sounds a bit frosty, are you sure?'

'She's as keen as a sharpened blade,' he screws up his own face, 'That's no good either. She's as keen as a penetrating smell.'

That's terrible, maybe I should offer him one. 'She's as keen as highly competitive rates.'

I like that one, but he doesn't even respond, instead he offers, 'She's as keen as spicy jam.'

I'm spared any more when Aubrey walks in the room. 'Hey Aubrey, how are you?' Con once called Aubrey, Aub; and he was quite clearly told not to do that again. And bless him, he hasn't. Con can be a cheeky bastard sometimes, but he's told me he has respect for Aubrey, and he knows he's going to be cool too when he's an old timer. He's also tried to call me; Lazzie, Lazmo, Lazmatron, and one or two others, but I told him I'd pummel him into a Con Nest Soup if he said them again. He did, a few times, thinking he was hilarious. But now he sticks to Laz.

He offers Aubrey some coke, but the offer is declined. He suggests some hash, and Aubrey expresses an interest. The two speak in numbers and Con retrieves some hash from his bag, he says, 'Pay whenever,' but Aubrey has the money on him, so that's that sorted. We remember why we're here and load the body into the hearse. A thirty-three year old woman killed herself; pills and booze. I don't know what family she has, but I'll find out.

Back at work, I put the body in the fridge, and catch up with the lads in the office. Henry and Nicholas are leaving for a few hours; they have another meeting with Alan Swetz. The two leave Aubrey and I standing in the office.

'I don't believe there is a population of lizard people wearing human suits living on Earth, but if they do, Alan Swetz is a prize candidate.' Aubrey doesn't like Swetz either, he's previously described him as a forlorn squid, a greasy dog stool, a bucket of gizzards, a helminth heaven, Pustule Pete, the list goes on, he doesn't like the man. He once told me that if we filled a boiler suit with porridge, and put one of those polystyrene heads with a dark curly wig into the neck hole, it would have more personality than the real Swetz.

My plan is to have a bite to eat and work on the suicide this afternoon, but I'll lock up first. I walk to the front door with Aubrey and he tells me he's taking Maureen to the picture house tonight, to watch the new Stephanie Windmill film. I tell him I'll be round tomorrow late morning. 'Yes, not too early,' and he walks off the bus stop.

I message Rosie asking if she wants to eat out tonight at the new Thai restaurant in town, and go for drinks with Eddie after. She messages back in the affirmative. I find the number of the restaurant, and book a table for two at seven at The NeckThai. I complete my work in good time and decide to do some shopping on my walk home; if I can stock up the fridge today I won't have that chore haunting me all weekend. I get home and smoke a bifta while watching a documentary about orca hunting behaviour. I remember something Eddie said, and imagine giant Brazil nut kernels swimming effortlessly through the water, chasing down some poor seal.

Rosie comes around about six thirty, and we walk to The NeckThai sharing a bifta. I ask her if she wants to do some coke. She says yeah, but we agree to eat first. We get to the restaurant and it looks amazing; like little Bangkok in Stumpton. The room has lots of orange, red, yellow and gold greeting the eyes. There are statues of Buddha, dragons, elephants, fish and pheasants. We're shown to our seats by a friendly waiter, who takes our drinks order before leaving us alone. I have a speciality beer, and Rosie has a cocktail called Dragons Breath. We're discussing the difference between raisins and sultanas when the friendly waiter brings our drinks, and takes our food order. We have vegetable grilled dim sum and spring rolls for starters, which we're going to share. I order veg stir fry with salt and pepper tofu, while Rosie orders veg stir fry with noodles. We order some brown rice to share.

'Do you think they'll cook the food in a taipan?' she enquires.

'I'm not laughing at that.' And I make a point not to, but I have to bring my drink to my mouth to hide a developing smile.

'You are internally, I can tell. Have you been to Thailand?' I shake my head while taking another swig. 'You should go. I travelled around there with a friend, a few years ago. It's a beautiful country, and the people are really friendly.'

We chat about places we've been and where we'd like to go, when the food arrives. We scoff the lot, and agree it was delicious, but we don't bother with dessert. I ask for the bill, and pay for it, because I'm a fucking gent. Rosie said she'll get the first round in The Cloak and Dagger, Eddie said he'd be there from eight. We thank the staff, who thank us back, and I pick up a takeaway menu as we leave. We walk to Bosun Square and sit on a bench by a large hawthorn tree. There's no one around us so I cut up the gram of coke into four healthy looking lines on the menu, while Rosie rolls up a note. I have highly developed hoovering capabilities, and make two lines disappear with two hearty sniffs. I pass the menu to Rosie who takes care of her lines while I enter an imaginary sniffing competition. I was winning until Rosie joined in. I eventually found the half a gram I had left over from Anton's party; it was still in my jacket pocket. The idea is to save that for a top-up later; best to start off with the good stuff afresh. The other wrap is for Eddie.

We walk to The Cloak and Dagger and find Eddie and Mila sitting at a table in the back room. I ask them if they want a drink as we stand here occasionally sniffing. They're fine, so Rosie and I fetch our drinks. When we get back Eddie asks if we both have hay fever, and I slip him the other wrap of coke. He pockets it, 'How much is in there?'

'A gram,' I take a swig of ale.

'Sorry I don't understand what you mean. I'm no longer able to comprehend the imperial or metric systems of weights and measurements. It wasn't a gradual thing, it happened today. I don't know why but it has been replaced by the couscous system. Now I can only understand the volume or weight of an item in terms of a quantity of couscous grains. So could you kindly describe to me how much coke there is using the couscous system?' He's looking at me, expectantly, but I'm feeling quite high and trying not to laugh.

'I'd say, in weight, it's equal to a third of a teaspoon of couscous grains.'

'That's more like it, now I understand,' and he and Mila get up and walk off in the direction of the toilets.

We have a few drinks, pretty speedily, and I announce that I still have a sixth of a teaspoon of couscous grains of coke from last week. I take a dab; it tastes like shit. I pass it on and thankfully don't see it again. After a while we agree to call it a night, even though it's not last orders yet. Eddie knocks up a bifta, and we share it walking back through town. We arrange to have a picnic tomorrow afternoon at The Stumpton Rock. It's a tourist attraction in a field, and it can get quite lively there with people picnicking and drinking. Rosie and I head back to mine, and when we walk past Yoost Park, she suddenly drags me into the darkness. She's picking up the pace now, holding onto my jacket, pulling me with her. She runs up to a big tree, its dark over here and there's no one around. She kisses me passionately, grabbing my hair, and grabbing my dick. She undoes my belt and trousers, and pulls down my shorts. My cock springs up and she wastes no time in taking me in her mouth. She does this briefly, then stands against the tree, 'I'm already wet,' and she lifts her skirt up. I pull the gusset of her panties to the side, and feel how wet she is. I rub my knob against her wet lips, and she's on her toes trying to push herself down onto me, trying to engulf me. I stop teasing and push my cock into her. We're both thrusting and grinding, charged up by the coke. After I come, we stand here kissing, I haven't even pulled up my shorts. We walk home, and have sex for several hours, in a coke-fuelled fuck-frenzy. We have to have a few enforced breaks, but as soon as we recover, we're at it again. My dick looks red and battered by the time I knock us up a Goodnight Vienna. There are certain shades of red that are quite worrying, but it's the place that's taken the reddening that contributes most to the worry.

Chapter Twelve

I wake up and stretch; pains, the usual pains and new pains. On my chest. I look down and with blurry vision I see fresh bite marks in two places. Oh yeah, I remember now. I go for a piss and put the coffee machine on. I bring two cups back to the bedroom, and put one on her bedside table. Without opening her eyes, she murmurs something, but as she doesn't open her mouth either, I can't make out what it is. I put my coffee down and get into bed. She rolls over and looks at me through one eye, 'Good morning gorgeous, thanks for the coffee.'

'Good morning beautiful, you're welcome.' We have a lazy morning in bed cuddling and chatting. Neither of us shows any signs of arousal or a desire for sex. I'm a bit sore, and she must be too. We have breakfast in bed too, and another coffee, and get up after a few hours. 'I'm having a shower,' I inform her, keeping her up-to-date with my whereabouts. She tells me she'll join me. The water's warm and it feels good. We're washing each other, and becoming aroused. We kiss and she guides me to her. I enter her as we stand, and we both wince a little. We take it slow, but it ends up being a bit of a workout. She's backing into me again when she comes. When I come, my dick burns, I think I might have damaged it. We're dressing and I ask, 'Can you do me a favour? I need to go to Aubrey's, but I'm expecting a letter to be delivered today and it needs signing for. Would you mind waiting here for about an hour?' She shrugs her shoulders and is about to speak, 'You'll have to go down to the front door to sign for it. Do you mind?'

'No I don't mind. Ask them to come to the picnic; I'll get a few things ready while you're gone.'

I kiss her and put my boots on. I walk to Aubrey's and knock on his door. He leads me to the back garden, where he and Maureen are sitting in deck chairs drinking port. They offer me a drink, but I decline; I tell them I need to grab his passport and head off. 'It's on the counter in the kitchen,' I'm informed. I fetch it and stuff it in my pocket as I return. 'I've cleared it with Nicholas that we can both have Tuesday and Wednesday off next week, but we have to be back in work on the Thursday for a funeral,' he says, and I tell him that's brilliant, I'll book flights today. I tell them about the picnic, but they say they have plans for this afternoon, so we bid each other farewell and I let myself out. Port at eleven thirty in the morning? And he bought some hash off Con. I need to have a serious word with him before he's out of control.

I get back to my flat and Rosie informs me the postman has been and the letter is in the kitchen. She walks into the kitchen and I follow her; she indicates a rucksack I keep in the wardrobe. 'The picnic's in there. I have to go home to get changed; I'll meet you at The Rock at about one thirty.' She stops and is looking in my eyes, it feels like she wants to say something else, but she kisses me and leaves. I open the letter and find the certificate of registration of the company Valam Gems. It looks fucking legal; I don't have a reference point but this looks good. I fire up my laptop and check my emails; Verb has forwarded me the email with the receipt for the diamonds. I'll print that off on Monday. I search for the flights. There it is, 07:15 in the fucking morning. Aubrey told me he'll arrive at mine, in a taxi, at five thirty. Bastard. I find the Wednesday night return flights and book the lot; on my credit card. Aubrey again attempted to tell me he'd pay for half, until I again reminded him that we'll be stinking rich soon. His passport photo isn't as hilarious as his bus pass; his hair is combed down here, but his expression is one of utter boredom. I look for a hotel; two single ensuite rooms, with breakfast, in Hotel Pierre. It's a bit shabby, but it'll do; we haven't received any filthy money yet. Flights; done. Certificate; done. Hotel; done. Picnic; done. Bifta; not done. I skin one up; it's time to hit the road.

160

It's about a forty-minute walk to The Rock, and I have a smoke while I walk. I message Aubrey with news of the certificate, receipt, flights and hotel. By the time I reach The Rock, he hasn't replied. There are maybe twenty-five, thirty people here. I wander through a few gatherings; I can smell weed, Eddie must be around here somewhere. I see Eddie, Mila and Rosie waving at me. I join them and put the bag down; it weighs a fucking tonne after that walk. They've brought a blanket, a bottle of Highland Barley whisky and a bag of pistachio nuts. Eddie's smoking a bifta. 'Is that all you brought with you?'

'No, we were waiting for you to arrive to crack open the picnic.' He passes the bifta to Mila and takes a sip of whisky.

'I'm ravenous,' Rosie opens the rucksack and lays out its contents on the blanket. Eddie does the same from his bag. We end up with olives, bread, cashew nuts, crackers, humous, a bag of salad, blueberries, grapes, and five bottles of red wine; to complement the whisky and pistachios. Mila passes me the bifta; I take a few drags and pass it to Rosie. I'm munching on some bread and humous, drinking some wine, feeling stoned, looking at the Rock; The Stumpton Rock. Its 3.16 metres high, and 6.25 metres in circumference at its base. It's estimated to extend a further two metres into the ground. No one knows how it got here, or what significance it held for people in history. Its sarsen stone, so it's likely it was put here. Today, it's a hangout for people drinking, smoking, and at this time, eating lunch too. There's a great view out of the city from here; people like it here and keep it clean. There have never been any incidences of graffiti on the Rock, or someone throwing shit on it. People respect the tranquillity of the place, and some people claim to feel mystic forces here. But those people are either pissed, stoned, mentally unbalanced, or a combination of those factors. If there is a mysticism about the place, it's only what people have given it. I lay back on the grass, letting the warmth of the afternoon wash over me. I think I might have dozed off; my phone announced a message from my pocket, and it brought me back to where I am. I carry on lying down with my eyes closed.

'Typical,' Eddie says, 'His phone rings and he doesn't answer it. He gets a message and he doesn't read it.'

'Email me,' I don't move, it's comfortable here. I think I drift back to sleep for a while. I realise I'm Starvin' Hagler, so I sit up, rub my eyes, and tuck into some cashew nuts, olives and crackers. I'm listening to the conversation; Eddie's talking about training up to be an Olympic standard gymnast. Either that, or a concert pianist. What do we think? Rosie suggests that he combine the two. I stuff my face with grapes and remember I have a message. It's Con, "The eagle has landed". I inform the gang of Con's news.

'What does that mean?' enquires Mila.

'I think it means he and Miriam have finally shagged.' No one says anything. 'Which is nice for them.' We sit here for a few hours, filling our bellies, getting pissed and stoned. I occasionally look around to make sure there aren't any Figgs marching towards me with a look of thunder on their faces; but other than that, I'm happy this afternoon. We decide to go back to Eddie's to watch a film. We pack up the remains of the picnic, and carry the rubbish and the five empty wine bottles to the recycling bins. We walk back slowly; we're all a bit fucked. The talk turns to what film should we watch? There's a lengthy discussion, which took time because we kept finding ourselves talking about other random things, forgetting the topic of conversation. After a few reminders, it's been narrowed down to any film with Joaquin Phoenix; the guy's nothing short of fucking brilliant. Back at Eddie's, drinks are poured and biftas rolled. He's a film buff and has a big screen in his living room; and still can't believe I watch films on my laptop. The evening is relaxed and enjoyable; we eat more food, and listen to some tunes. We don't get round to watching a film in the end, and Rosie and I walk back to mine at about midnight, feeling quite battered. At mine, we use the bathroom, and undress quickly; get into bed and pull the covers over us. We cuddle and I feel her sleep breathing in just a few minutes. I lie here with her arm across my chest, looking up at the darkness of the ceiling. Hooking up with

Rosie simply couldn't have worked out better; she's fucking amazing.

I wake up and after a piss it's business as usual with the love making. We're on the floor when she comes; I'm on top with her ankles resting on my shoulders. The deep stick being one of her favourites. I come, and she wraps her legs around my back to keep me in her. We're a tangle of sweaty bodies, and we kiss passionately, even though neither of us can breathe properly. We shower and have lunch, and I notice my fridge is empty again. One picnic and one lunch and I'm wiped out. 'I've got no food again. I'm going to have to go to a fucking supermarket yet again,' I'm giving it plenty of anguish.

'There, there, it's all right. I'll come with you, but you are going to need to pull yourself together first.'

'Can we shag on the fresh produce?'

'What if a little old lady is out shopping for plums? She'll get quite a fright when she picks one up and finds it's still attached.'

'She might have a nice, gentle touch.'

'She could join in.'

'Let's go.'

We go and feed the ducks and swans on Yoost Lake instead. We buy some pellets from the kiosk by the lake, and head to the water's edge to prepare for our feeding assignment. We rustle the bags of pellets and we immediately gain the attention of local intended recipients. We throw a few pellets into the water and they come dashing over; this commotion attracts the interest of the wider community, and most ducks and swans are looking in this direction. We're soon surrounded by avian beggars, slapping their feet on the ground as they approach. They're extending their necks, and quacking, honking and grunting. They're noisy fuckers when they get going. There are nine swans and about thirty ducks, all out of the water encircling us, greedy for pellets. Both our faces show pure joy; this is fantastic. When the pellets run out and the birds lose interest in us, we take a slow walk through the park. I receive a message from Aubrey, "Sorry for the delay, great news. See you tomorrow". I don't bother replying, I'll see him tomorrow. We have a coffee in the large conservatory style cafe in the park, and I get a message from Eddie suggesting a pint. I put the proposition to Rosie, but she says she should probably go home. She hasn't been there much this week, and she has stuff she needs to sort out for work tomorrow.

'You have a few pints with Eddie. I'll do some washing and ironing, and get an early night.'

'Sounds great, do you want to do mine?'

'No, it's a chore doing my own.'

'What if I pay you?'

'Fuck off. I'm not a washing whore.'

'You're being provocative…' I look at her, with what I think is a stern expression; '…you're being an effing cunt, aren't you? Do you want a fight?'

'Yeah, right here in the cafe.' She smiles, and her naughty look is playing on her face, 'And I'd win. I'd hit you with a combination of jabs and uppercuts, and finish you off with a left hook. You'd be on the ground before you got your first funny comment out.'

'Okay, let's not bother then. I wasn't anticipating that. I thought you were just going to give me a Chinese burn.'

'Are you allowed to say that? Someone might take offence.'

'How about…an abrasion of Asian derivation.'

'You definitely shouldn't say that.'

We finish our drinks and walk back through the park, exiting through the north gate. 'I forgot to tell you, Aubrey and I are going to Geneva on Tuesday.'

'What?' She looks at me like she wasn't expecting that. 'What is it, a lads drinking holiday?' She doesn't give me time to answer, 'How long are you going for?'

'We're back on Wednesday.'

'What?' Doesn't look like she was expecting that either. 'You're going to Geneva for a day?'

'Tuesday plus Wednesday equals two days.'

'You're not teleporting there. With travel you'll get…I can't be bothered. Why are you going for that amount of time?'

'Lads drinking holiday.'

She just looks at me, she knows I'm hiding something, but she doesn't pursue it. 'Can we catch up tomorrow as you're away?'

'Yeah, come round after work.' We walk on and arrive at Bandium Road, where we must part ways. Eddie said he's in The Crooked Lobster, which at the end of the road. It doesn't look like I'll be going shopping, but I'll be away for two days anyway. We kiss and hold each other; she rests her head on my shoulder and breathes onto my neck. She lifts her head and looks at me, like she wants to say something. Maybe it's about Geneva.

I find Eddie talking to Con; they're both looking a bit wired. That reminds me, 'Sorry Con, I don't have your money on me.'

'Any time Laz, no rush.' I notice they're nearly on empties, so I offer to get the round in. I put all three pints on the table without spilling a fucking drop. I sit down, pleased with myself.

Eddie passes me a wrap, 'That's this afternoons edition, leave me some, but help yourself.'

I think about it for a second; it is still fairly early. There's a funeral tomorrow morning, but it won't harm to have a toot, I won't have much, just a small line, and a few drinks and biftas will bring me down. 'Nice one,' and I walk to the toilet. The blessed toilet cubicle, the refuge of drug takers across the globe. It may stink of piss and shit, and there may be half a centimetre of liquid covering the floor, but the toilet cubicle hides all our sins. I was once in a small cubicle with four other people; five of us trying not to elbow each other getting our gear out of our pockets. I open Eddie's wrap, there's not a tremendous amount left; it looks like they've had a few lines already. I open the paper fully and push an amount, less than half, to the side with my bank card and make a rudimentary line. I roll up a scuba diver and snort the line, its Con's new stuff, it burns. I neatly fold up the remaining coke and head back to the guys, checking my nose in the mirror for powder. I sit back down and hand Eddie his coke, a few internal snorts are dragging the burn down my throat. A few swigs of ale ease the burn, and highlight it simultaneously. Con tells me in extraordinary detail about his and Miriam's shagging rampage. I guess Eddie has already heard about it, but he lets Con get on with it. In appraisal, it sounds like they got on well, and the sex was good. That's all I can gather from the bits I'm listening to. Eddie has divulged that he and Mila got together recently, and I divulge that Rosie and I did the same; but that's all we say. Much to Con's irritation. After a few pints and smokes, I leave the guys in the boozer, and head home via Mohan's. I get home and eat some mushroom balti, knock up a bifta and pour a nightcap. I message Rosie, and she tells me she's in bed, stoned, watching crap on her laptop. I tell her I'm about to do the same. We message for about half an hour, and say goodnight after the chat gets steamy. I have a few biftas and nightcaps, and hit the sack.

I wake, shit, shower, dress and have breakfast. I get to work early, and I'm the last to arrive. Everyone's looking gloomy, and we don't say much after greeting in the office. Aubrey looks knackered; maybe I should drive. The grieving family and friends arrive, so I disappear to the dressing room to get changed. I wander out to the hearse; I don't feel like getting stoned this morning. Aubrey's already sitting in the driver's seat, and I look at the coffin as I open the passenger door. I get in and offer to drive, but he says he's fine. We don't say much during the drive to the church; I ask him how things are going with Maureen, and he says things are going well. We don't talk of Verb or the diamonds. We pull into the church, get out and wait for the procession to slowly pour in and find parking spaces. We slide the coffin out of the hearse when the pallbearers greet us. It always looks so absurd for such a small coffin being carried by four people. It could easily be carried by one person at each end, but then it would look like they were carrying a stretcher; and that doesn't give the right impression. People follow the coffin through the

166

door. The parents look in bad way. They all do. Aubrey and I wait outside. We chat, but it's only so that we're talking. The service ends and we adopt our respectful positions. People are moving out slowly, holding onto each other, clutching each other. The crying is almost unbearable. We stand observing the burial, but I'm not paying much attention, it's too difficult. When we drive back, we're nearly at work before one of us speaks. 'I'm going to retire, and I will not miss days like these.' There's another silence, there's no need for me to verbally agree. We pull in when he says, 'Thank you for booking the flights and hotel; and for all your work setting up the company. You're a good man Laszlo.' He parks the hearse, 'And for stealing the diamonds too, of course.'

'Can you steal stolen goods?'

'Did you pay for them?'

'No, I don't have that kind of money.'

'Yet.'

We find Henry and Nicholas in the office attending to paperwork. Henry informs me there's a pickup from the morgue at Stumpton General. I tell him I'll get changed and go straight away. Aubrey follows me to the dressing room, and we change out of our funeral clothes.

'Remember to bring the paperwork, remember to bring my passport, and remember not to get too drunk tonight.

'Rosie's coming over tonight, I'll probably only have a couple of glasses of wine. I'll see you at five fucking thirty.' He just smiles; he still doesn't seem to think that's appallingly early.

I drive to the General, and park outside the morgue. The attendant today is Susan, she's really nice. We chat for a while, and exchange some paperwork. I don't stop for long; I have a lot to do. I drive back to work; the new arrival is a ninety-four year old male, heart attack. A lot of old guys his age are nothing more than flesh and bone, shrouded in wrinkled, baggy skin. But this old boy looks healthy, he must have been getting plenty of exercise right into his nineties. I put him in the fridge and go to my shed for lunch; which is eighty per cent of a mushroom balti. As I exit the building, I see some old newspapers and take a few with me. The first paper, from Friday, has an article with the headline "Gangster War Sees More Bloodshed", and the piece informs me that Barry Dancer is in hospital with a gunshot wound. He's critical but stable; whatever that means. He's currently not getting any worse, I suppose, and that's good because I don't want anyone's death on my conscience. The article tells me that this follows of week of gangland attacks which saw the murder of Desmond Dancer on Wednesday, and that of Lance Figg on Thursday. Shit, fuck, did I do that? Have I got Desmond and Lance murdered? The article has their photos; I'm looking right at them. Did my ginger talk get two people, I now know the names and faces of, murdered? It probably did; but maybe it didn't. I'll ask Aubrey what level of guilt he'd be experiencing, and I can compare that to my own. If he tells me I shouldn't feel as bad as I do, I won't. I don't know Lance Figg; I never had the pleasure of meeting him, though I might still get my chance. I must ask Nicholas what the current policy on Figg funerals is. I would prefer never seeing them again, and I suspect he will agree.

I eat my lunch and go to my office to print off the receipt, before I forget. I put it in a plastic wallet and put that in my bag. Back in my shed, I prepare for the afternoon. Suitably stoned I wheel the old guy into the prep room. The paperwork tells me his name is William Meridian; and today William I am going to restore you to a picture of health. I put some tunes on "Brown Album" by Primus, and I boogie around getting my equipment ready. I message Rosie, telling her I might be late leaving work and I'll message her later when I know more. Larry LaLonde is ripping through his guitar on "Golden Boy", and I'm joining in; I'm probably note perfect. I look up and see Nicholas watching me; he doesn't seem impressed, and he gives the music player an uncomfortable stare. I press pause.

'I was looking for you to see if you wouldn't mind working on our new arrival, but you've taken the initiative. Good work Laszlo. Henry and I will be working in the office this afternoon; we'll be leaving at five. I'll leave you to lock

168

up if you are still working.' He looks pleased I'll be taking care of the old guy. Nicholas is old himself and he works hard; I was hoping he'd be pleased I'd cracked on with the job.

'I understand from the newspaper that a secondary Figg has succumbed to the rigours of criminal affiliation.' He lets out a laugh, it's not often Nicholas has laughed at one of my attempts at humour. 'What is the probability that we accommodate the latest Figg fatality?'

'Zero.' He must see my relief, as he smiles as he walks back out of the room. I wait until he's gone before I hit the pause button. It's still "Golden Boy", so I put it on from the beginning again. I take my time with William; I'm boogieing while working, but I talk to him all the time, speaking as friends do, telling him exactly what I'm doing, keeping him informed. When I finish, I wheel William back into the fridge for the night, and I'm buzzing because this might be my best work yet. I was in a zone I'd not been in before. I message Rosie, telling her I'm finishing up at work and will be home in forty minutes. She says she'll meet me there. I don't bother replying, I'll meet her there.

I get back and sling some potatoes in the oven; the only things left from my recent shopping trip. Baked potatoes, easily done, don't have to think about them. The fridge is still fucking empty, so I rummage around in the cupboards. There are a few cartons and tins, but nothing to put on a potato. I look in the freezer and see a lonely bag of peas; perfect. My buzzer sounds; it's Rosie. We sit in the living room drinking a glass of wine listening to "Maggot Brain" by Funkadelic, while I check on the potatoes every now and then. 'I hope you like baked potato.'

'I fucking love baked potato.'

'Do you like peas?'

'I fucking love peas.' She's smiling broadly; it does appear that she loves baked potato and peas.

'Well, you're in luck, because otherwise you'd be having a bowl of tomato puree for your dinner.' I return to the kitchen to stick the peas on, and check on the spuds. On my final return from the kitchen I inform her that dinner is ready. We eat at the kitchen table, so she gets up to join me.

After dinner we return to the living room for a drink and a bifta, and put on "Cosmic Slop". She doesn't mention the reason for the Geneva trip, but suggests attractions we could visit. 'Are you and Aubrey going to visit Lake Geneva and the Jet d'Eau?'

'I would imagine so.'

'Are you going to hold hands?' She's not smiling at all, she's great at this game, but I can detect the humour in her eyes.

'I hope so.' I pause before suggesting, 'Maybe we could go away for a weekend sometime?'

'I'd like that.' The wine and the weed have us both pretty relaxed, and we start kissing and taking our clothes off. One seismic bang later, we're sitting on the sofa, naked and sweating, dripping in each other's stink. Like two horses that have just steamed through a hundred furlong race. I remind her Aubrey's coming round at five fucking thirty, and an early night is on the cards. We retire to bed to stink the sheets out some more. I need to wash them when I get back. The bed sheet has changed colour somewhat under the recent activity. The duvet's usually on the floor somewhere. We make love and she drifts off to sleep. I finish the last bifta as I set my alarm. Four fucking thirty.

I wake up to my alarm and hit snooze. I hit snooze again ten minutes later; I need to get up. My alarm goes off again, shit, I'd drifted off. I stretch but don't bother getting up; I feel myself drifting off again so I drag myself out of bed and hit the shower. I get dressed quietly, and find my bag; time to pack. What's the time? Five twenty! How the fuck did that happen? I need to be out front in ten minutes. I find the documents we need, and both our passports, and put them in my bag. I stick my phone in my pocket, and the charger in my bag. What else do I need? Toothbrush, deodorant, bank card, keys. I put them in my bag. Anything else? I grab a pair of boxer shorts and socks and stuff them into my bag too. I kiss Rosie gently; she stirs and opens her eyes. As quiet as I'm trying to be, I've been dashing around the flat hurriedly packing my bag, so it's no surprise she's not sound asleep. She puts her arms around my neck and kisses me before flopping back into sleep position. 'See you on Thursday.'

'See you Thursday, have a nice time.' We kiss again and I leave her in bed.

I'm standing outside hunching my shoulders; it's still dark, and the morning chill isn't to my liking. A taxi pulls up in front of me and I get in. 'Morning,' I say flatly, still trying to get across to him that I don't like getting up this early.

'Morning, you look smart.'

'Thanks, so do you.'

'Do you have all the documents?' I nod, and he instructs the driver to continue to the airport. We head out of town past the houses, shops and parks. The buildings start to thin out and the greenery takes over the landscape as we merge onto the A632, which takes us in the direction of the airport.

'I didn't have time for coffee or breakfast.'

'You can get some at the airport.'

'Why are airports so gruellingly boring? They're not comfortable, they're not pleasing on the eye, and there's simply nothing to do. The selection of food is limited, and overpriced; and there's nothing to do. No entertainment at all. Tons of people sitting around looking bored, just waiting, and queuing, and sitting, and waiting, with nothing to do. I could go shopping and buy a tracksuit.' I look from the moving landscape to Aubrey, 'I don't want a tracksuit.'

'Don't buy one then,' he says matter-of-factly, and he's right.

'The only thing to do in an airport to ease the drudgery of time slowly passing in front of you, is to try and find a comfortable seat in one of their shitty bars, and drink pints of hideously gassy lagers followed by several whiskies to take the taste away.'

'We're opening a bank account today, we need to stay focussed. I don't think getting inebriated will give the right impression. Maybe we should stick to coffee.'

There's not much traffic at this preposterous time of day, and we're cruising to the airport; we'll arrive in plenty of time. Plenty of time to sit around doing fuck all when I could have been in bed with Rosie. 'A few drinks will help with the flight too, which eagerly competes with airports for the "monumentally boring" award. A few drinks, with any luck, we'll sleep the entire flight. Have a couple of coffees in Geneva, and we'll be as right as rain.' I look at him imploringly, but I know he won't go for it.

'Are you going to moan all morning? The flight is less than two hours, I am sure you'll cope...but I'm not sure I will.'

'I'm tired.' I decide to give his ear holes a rest and shut up for the remainder of the journey. We're nearly there anyway. The dawn is just making an appearance, turning the sky from an inky black to a murky blue. I can see the silhouette of the huge dark building against the emerging blue over yonder.

Aubrey wants to go to departures straight away, get through security, and relax with a coffee. Fine by me. He's carrying what looks like a thin briefcase, can't fit much in there; must be a fan of travelling light too. I tell him he looks perfectly businessman like, give him his passport, and inform him his boarding pass is on my phone. Aubrey has no fear of technology, but his expression implies he expects me to take care of that. I give my passport and phone to the security guy and explain the booking is for both of us. He studies my phone for a while, looks at both of our passports, and we're through. Aubrey was watching closely, 'That was easy enough,' and we queue to put our bags through the scanner. I put my bag in a tray, along with my jacket, belt, and contents of my pockets. I look around and see a stern looking security officer on the other side of the walk-through scanners, staring at me. I start to move forward and he holds up his hand, then points at my boots. I take my boots off and put them in a tray, I remain where I am, so he beckons me forward. I walk through the scanner, and he motions that I should step to the side. I didn't hear any beeping, so I don't know what else he wants. He fetches a handheld scanner and tells me to lift my arms. While he's scanning me, which he's doing incredibly thoroughly, Aubrey just walks through. He strolls though the walk-through scanner and they smilingly wave him along. He could be a veteran terrorist. Why am I getting the personal touch? The security guy is still not happy; he hasn't found anything. Aubrey has his case in his hand, laughing at me. Bastard. Eventually the security guy gives up hope, and waves me through. We find some uncomfortable seats in a bland looking, noisy cafe, and drink coffee. I have a humus and salad wrap for my breakfast; the choice was amazing. We finish and take a wander, to find a quieter spot to sit and wait. We finally get on the fucking plane and find our seats. The air crew go through the usual routine with elegant professionalism. They must have done this a thousand times; how they do it without looking bored is a testament to their training. The crew are warm and friendly when they engage with passengers, but demonstrate that wonderful ability of never making eye contact unless you attract their attention. This lot were truly alert during their training. Aubrey tells me Verb has been recommended a bank by his contact, and he has the address. We don't need an appointment, we simply need to fill out the forms, but we may have to wait to be seen. Great, more fucking waiting. We land, and disembark. I instinctively say thank you to one of the crew as I exit the plane; I didn't speak to her once during the flight, but I reckon she did a good job. We go through passport control, after joining that queue, and as we only have hand luggage we head directly to customs. Once we're through, Aubrey suggests we get a taxi. I stop at the cash point on the way out to get some petty cash for the assignment; and our lads drinking holiday.

'What's the name and address of the hotel?' He's heading for the taxi rank outside.

'*Hotel Pierre, Rue des Roussettes.*' If I try to remember something I can; but if I forget to try, it can be lost forever.

Aubrey approaches a taxi driver, and he stops me in my tracks when he says, '*Nous aimerions aller à l'Hôtel Pierre,*

Rue des Roussettes,' in what can only be described as a French accent.

'*Oui,'* the driver says with zero enthusiasm.

'*Combien coûtera-t-il environ?'* I'm just looking at him; he kept this quiet.

'*Quarante, quarante-cinq?'* He shrugs and raises his eyebrows.

'*D'accord, Hotel Pierre s'il vous plait.'* He motions for me to get in, so I get in the other side of the vehicle.

We're driving away from the airport, joining the flow of metal heading towards the city. I'm not great at French; I recognised enough words there to get the gist, but not enough to join the conversation. 'I didn't know you spoke French.'

'I lived there for a while. In Marseille. I lived with a beautiful woman named Claudette for some years.' He's been around for many years, and he can't tell me about his entire life in one afternoon, but nonetheless, he still says things I don't expect. 'I was curator of a gallery, and we had a nice life for those years.' He stops talking and is looking out of the window. He's lost in thought, thoughts stirred by Claudette in Marseille. I don't want to bring him out of it by asking questions; he'll tell me if he wants to. But I'm fucking dying to find out what happened there. After a while he sighs, looks over to me, and quietly discusses the plan for today. The taxi pulls up outside the hotel, and the driver says, '*Quarante.'*

I pull the money out of my pocket and I'm scanning through it, when Aubrey selects a fifty franc note and gives it to the driver, '*Merci, gardez la monnaie.'*

'*Merci Monsieur, passez une bonne journée,'* he says, finally smiling.

We enter the hotel and I let Aubrey lead the way, he can do the talking. He checks us in and gets our keys, speaking French with graceful ease. The receptionist is giving him some directions, or advice, I don't have a fucking clue, I'm not listening. I'm assuming Aubrey will fill me in with the relevant stuff. Our rooms are next to each other on the fourth floor, so we take the lift. We agree to freshen up and he'll knock on my door in about thirty minutes. I put my bag on the chair, take my boots off and have a shit. I'm lying on the bed when there's a knock on my door. I let him in, and sit down to put my boots on. As discussed, we get in a taxi outside the hotel and go straight to the bank. We wait in yet another fucking queue, and I'd like to pretend it's for an unidentified period of time, but I can't. There's a huge analog clock on the wall telling me exactly how long I've been standing here for. When we get to the counter Aubrey delivers his bombshell to the poor cashier, '*Bon matin…*' he pauses, '*…c'est encore le matin, n'est-ce pas?*'

He turns slowly and looks at the knowing clock, '*Oui, c'est le matin. Nous aimerions ouvrir un compte.*' Our plan is to hit them with the admin involved with opening an account, just before lunch time. Hopefully they'll deal with us quickly, and we won't have to answer too many questions. There's a look that flashes across the cashiers face, but he makes it disappear quickly and replaces it with a friendly smile as he fetches some paperwork. Customer service gone mad that is; I was recently tutted at for asking to be served. He knows he's another sea lion that has to perform for the public, so he gets on with it. There's a brief exchange between the two, and Aubrey takes the paperwork to a table across the room. I don't think I'll be able to help other than getting our documents ready, so that's what I do. When he has a question, he'll ask. He sets about completing the forms, referring a few times to the documents I've placed on the table. I help myself to a coffee while I wait. I assume it's for the customers; it's on the counter there, out in the open. Aubrey takes his time, he wants to be thorough, and I can see the cashier throwing us glances every now and then. 'Done,' he gathers the forms together along with our documents, and stands up. The cashier spots this while he's serving a customer, and we amble over to be next in line. We only wait a few minutes before he's free. Aubrey gives him all the paperwork, and the guy speaks kindly while Aubrey and I listen. I don't know why I'm listening. '*No merci, je vais attendre ici,*' Aubrey informs him, and he nods and begins reading through the forms. He's taking a fantastically long time, and I'm getting concerned.

He cross references the info with our documents, then gets up and disappears with the paperwork. Aubrey drops his voice to a whisper, 'He said he needs to check the forms have been filled in correctly, check our documents, and take some photocopies. He suggested it might be more comfortable for me sitting down while I wait. I said I'd wait here.'

'Are you going to make some groaning noises like your back hurts?' I whisper too.

'I think that might be taking it too far.'

'What if he spots something he doesn't like? I'm getting worried now. I've been too tired all day to feel anything else, but now the fear is setting in.' I hope I don't get a sweat on.

'Don't worry Laszlo; we're two businessmen setting up a business account. If there are any problems with the documentation, we'll apologise and say we will return with the correct version. No fear.'

'He's been gone a long time; I could have photocopied the fucking Domesday Book by now.' I'm raising the volume of my whisper, but keeping it at a whisper; and find that it's a bit rough on the throat. We stand here waiting. 'How many hours have we been waiting today?' I don't bother whispering, it's too dangerous for the health, but I keep my voice low. We wait a bit longer, 'Maybe he's gone for his lunch?'

At that, he returns carrying documents and sits down. He immediately addresses Aubrey, holding up papers, pointing at things on the papers, holding up our documents. Shit has he found something? His expression is unreadable; he's barely moving any muscles other than those controlling his mouth. Aubrey's mainly nodding and agreeing, so he's no fucking help. What's going on? He talks for some time, and then promptly stops. Neither of them flinches. Aubrey asks a question, and the cashier is off again; lots of information coming Aubrey's way. He asks another question and receives another avalanche of info. Then the cashier silently puts all the paperwork in a folder, and hands it to Aubrey, smiling. They exchange pleasantries by the sounds of things, and they say goodbye. I join in, and offer a "*merci*" and an "*au revoir*". We walk out of the bank, and the brightness of the day stuns my eyes. My brain is quite stunned too, and I feel somewhat lightheaded. There's a lot of noise here and people moving about, cars growling at each other, and I'm feeling disorientated. 'Let's grab a drink,' I say too loudly to Aubrey, and we walk off.

Chapter Thirteen

I feel Aubrey pulling on my sleeve, he's spotted a boozer and I was about to wander off. We go inside, it's dark and woody in here, and there are an extraordinary amount of spirit bottles lined up behind the bar. The barman sees us and moves along the bar to greet us. He asks a question; I don't bother waiting for a translation, '*Deux whisky, s'il vous plait,*' I inform him, and hold up two fingers, like he doesn't know how to count in French. He says something else that I don't catch hold of, so Aubrey steps in.

'*Gros, s'il vous plait, et n'importe quelle marque.*' We don't speak while he pours our drinks. I don't have the mental capacity to make small talk now, there's only one thing I want to discuss.

The barman puts our drinks in front of us, and says a couple of sentences. I recognise a few words, and I think he said "*quarante*". I pull out my money and select a fifty; I hand it to him and confidently say, '*Gardez la monnaie.*' I remember that one from this morning. I let him say '*Merci*' and something else I don't catch, before knocking back a swig of whisky. Fuck, that burns. Burns really good. Aubrey and I find a quiet alcove at the back of the pub, and sip our drinks for a moment before speaking. 'Have we opened a bank account? Did that actually happen?'

'Yes, we did it,' he takes another sip.

'The cashier was doing a lot of talking; what was all that about?' I take another sip.

'He was going over the account details, deposit and withdrawal procedures, online access, the usual things. He was a nice chap, very helpful.' We both laugh quite heartily at that. I take a swig and finish my glass. I notice Aubrey's is empty too.

'I'll get another one,' and take both glasses to the bar. When I get back, having given the guy another tip, Aubrey has all the paperwork out of the folder. I'm going to need to get some more money out today. I have a scan over the papers, but as it's all in French, so I don't take much in. It all looks beautifully official, and Aubrey's making some positive sounds, so I sit here smiling.

He sits back, sipping his whisky, smiling at me. 'I will give Verb the account details, and he will pass them on to his contact, who will then make the first payment.'

'How long does all this take?' He's about to reply, when I hurriedly say, 'I'm not planning on a giant spending spree, I just want to see the account balance and know this is all going as planned. We could still get ripped off.'

He nods gently, 'I'll call Verb now; tell him the news, and see if he knows more about the payment.' Aubrey calls Verb while I sit here sipping my whisky. I can hear Aubrey telling him about the bank visit and giving him the account details, but I'm not really listening. I'm thinking about quitting my job and moving somewhere new. What about Rosie? I message her while Aubrey's still on the blower. "Geneva is brilliant so far. Hope you're having a good day". Aubrey's finished talking to Verb, and is tidying the papers away into their folder. He sees I've finished with my phone, 'Verb said he'll pass the account details on today, and get back to us when payment has been made.' He reaches for his glass, but stops when he realises it's empty. I say I'll get them in, but he stops me; 'It's my round, but I need to go to a bank. Let's go for a walk, get some money, and get drunk.'

We hit the outside world again. It's still bright and noisy, and I feel like I've been up for an entire day, but it's not even two o'clock yet. We both get some cash out and wander around the old town until we spot a suitable boozer to carry on drinking. We have a discussion about what we want to drink. There are factors to consider here. If we carry on necking whisky at our current rate, we'll both be hospitalised;

so we decide to get a beer. We agree that we'll need to eat fairly soon, which will break up the drinking; so we decide to get a small whisky as well. He's got me drinking a wheaty beer, and I'm rather enjoying it. The place is fairly empty, just a few people coming and going, and we're chatting and laughing like we don't have a care in the world. I love Aubrey; he's one of the best friends I'll ever have. I suggest we try a stout next, and he agrees. Once that's down the hatch, I suggest trying another boozer, but Aubrey says he'd prefer to get a bite to eat and drop the folder off at the hotel. I suggest a timeout to rest and freshen up, and he looks pleased at the idea. We stop off at a bakery and I have my eye on a salted baked pretzel. I quiz the member of staff about the ingredients of the item; well I get Aubrey to do it for me, and satisfied, I make the purchase. Aubrey opts for a hideous looking jam pastry. It's disgusting, it's turning my stomach, I have to look away to eat my pretzel.

Back at the hotel we agree to meet in an hour. I lie down on the bed, not looking for sleep. I don't turn the television on. No message from Rosie. I go to the bathroom and do another big shit; where's it coming from? Do I want a coffee? No, not really. I go out, find a supermarket, buy a bottle of whisky and head back to the hotel. No message from Rosie. I pour myself a nip and sit in the chair with my feet on the bed. My phone sounds; Rosie. 'Glad you're having a good time. Work is hectic. I want you.' I can feel myself getting aroused. Do I want to spend my time wanking in a hotel room in Geneva? What if I haven't finished when Aubrey knocks on the door? I could shout through the door that I need a bit longer to get ready, but I imagine that conversation would destabilise my mood of arousal, and I'd end up pulling on a rapidly deflating erection. It all sounds unsatisfying, so I decide against it. There's a knock on the door; fuck me, that hour went fast. Just as well I decided not to bash the baldigan. I let him in, put my boots on, and we hit the town. First port of call is a Chinese restaurant going by the name of Le Palais D'Or. It turns out we're both Starvin' Hagler, and we polish off starters and mains each, but I eat most of the side dish of rice. Aubrey pays with his card, and we mosey around the old town looking for a watering hole. We both look quite dapper walking along in the early evening sun. There are plenty of people moving about; they're leaving work, doing some shopping, going for a drink. We spot a boozer and find this one fairly busy. We pay for our drinks, two ales, and find a vacant table near a window. I ask him how things are going with Maureen.

'I'm tired Laszlo; this break came at a great time. It will give me chance to regain some of my strength.'

'Coming at you from all angles is she?'

'She's a wonderful woman, and I'm so happy we reconnected, but I'm going to need to invest in some energy pills.'

'Peanut butter,' I tell him, and he just wrinkles his brow. 'Keep a jar of peanut butter on your bedside table when you two are going for it,' his expression doesn't change when I say that, 'and you get a tasty energy boost that keeps you going. Either that or cocaine. Then you can have a coke-fuck-frenzy and risk permanent damage to your member.'

'Thanks for the advice; how are things going with Rosie?' He's already about half way down his beer; tonight could get a bit messy.

'Good. I mean great…' I'm not sure what to say, '…I like her.' I take a swig; it is slipping down a treat.

'I know you do. It's clear to see when you're together, and when you speak about her.' I look at him square in the eyes, and he carries on, 'Maureen says the same. She said the way you two respond to each other is something she's rarely seen. She said there were audible clicks.' I'm a bit taken aback, and happy, and heading into a tailspin of thoughts when he jolts me again, 'It looks like you've found her.'

'I don't know, it's early days.' I have no idea why I'm trying to be cool. I still don't know what to say. 'I've only known her for ten days.' He's not saying anything, just looking at me. 'Maureen isn't just looking good for her age…' I decide that changing direction is my best strategy for concealing my feelings, '…she's an attractive woman. And I say that with honesty.'

'I know you do. The way you feel about Rosie, have you felt like this with any woman before?' Fuck, he doesn't give up, does he? I look at him like he's being unfair, asking me to reveal my feelings. He laughs, 'I know.' He lets that hang there. 'I know the feel of love when it flows through your internal organs making them tingle, making you feel excited when you think about her, making you miss her when she's not there. I know.' We finish our drinks and head off again, exploring. We find another pub and stay for drinks; stout and whisky. I message Rosie when Aubrey goes to the toilet, "I'm going to shag the shit out of you when I see you". Several drinks later, we realise it's getting late, so we decide to head back to the hotel for a nightcap. Aubrey was pleased I'd got a bottle of whisky in. I haven't got any bifta with me, so I was going to have to get to sleep somehow. We have a nightcap in my room and I ask him if he's heard about the recent murders of Desmond Dancer and Lance Figg. He nods his head.

'And Barry Dancer's in the hospital too,' I tell him. My mood's changed; I'm feeling worried.

'You haven't heard the news then? Barry Dancer died yesterday.' He looks at me solemnly; or is he looking worried too? 'That's three people you've murdered Laszlo.' I'm looking at him anyway, but my look intensifies and I focus on his eyes. His face doesn't move but he's looking sad. Fuck, he thinks I'm responsible; well I am. He thinks I'm a murderer. I'm not a murderer. I know that. I just help murderers by inventing reasons for them to kill people. Weren't they going to murder each other anyway?

I'm actually starting to shit myself a bit now, 'Do you think I'm responsible?' There's hope in my voice; and fear.

He bursts into laughter, 'Of course not, that's the way they live their lives.' He's either scratching his cheek, or wiping a tear away.

'You're a cunt.' He's still smiling at me. 'You know that don't you. I was shitting myself then.'

'Sorry Laszlo, I couldn't resist. You didn't start this gangster row now did you?' He looks at me reassuringly now. 'You simply joined in,' and he's off laughing again.

He finishes his drink and heads to his room looking quite unsteady. I'm quite fucking pissed myself. I pour myself another nightcap and see I have a message from Rosie, it was sent a while ago but I didn't notice. "You'd better". I think about having a wank again, but in my pissed state I could be choking the baldigan for hours with no result. I decide against it. What I do is have four more nightcaps and pass out.

I wake up in a tremendous about of discomfort, and horrible pain. My head is throbbing; I'm scared to touch it, it might be twice its usual size. I scramble my thoughts together; we're in Geneva, we got massively pissed yesterday, and I'm point two of a nanosecond away from death. Maybe not, I'm still here. I try to lift my head; bad idea. Not ready for that yet. I don't give a shit what the time is, I need more sleep, but I'm with Aubrey so I should check out the time. What! My phone says 11:26. Check out is noon. I get out of bed and stagger to the bathroom; the pain in my head is joined with pains in my back, chest, sides, legs. Why do my legs hurt? Did I go running last night? I wouldn't have thought so, I could barely walk. I vaguely recall knocking back the final nightcap, which hurled me into a floundering attempt to get into bed. Maybe I received a few knocks during the tumble. I do a piss that stinks; in fact it offends me. It's bordering on a brown colour; I should drink some water. I can taste my own teeth. There's a knock at the door. Its Aubrey, he doesn't look well, but he's got a different outfit on. I stand here in my boxers, with my hair and face a mess, looking at him in confusion. 'Where did you get the clothes from?' I point at his fresh clothes, in case he thought I was talking to someone else.

'I brought them with me. Can I come in?' I move to the side to let him in and close the door.

'A whole new outfit! How did you fit that in your briefcase?'

'Expert packing; I'll teach you one day. In the meantime, you need to get ready. You have about half an hour; I'll meet you in reception.' I see him wince when he spots the whisky bottle on the table.

'How long have you been up for?'

'Hours; and I feel dreadful.'

He leaves the room and I shower and dress. I notice my shirt stinks when I put it on. Stale sweat and stale alcohol. Looks like I spilled some down me by the smell of it. I stuff my dirty boxers and socks in my bag, and check I have all my personal possessions. I look under the bed and in drawers I didn't use. Passport, bank card, money, phone, charger, toiletries; check. I grab the whisky bottle and shove that in my bag too, let's go. I put on my boots and jacket, which also smells unpleasant, and meet Aubrey in the reception.

'You have the same clothes on as yesterday. Did you not bring a change of clothing?'

'I stepped into some fresh boxers and socks, but the rest of my clothes are a bit ripe.'

'You smell like a never-been-washed bar towel.'

'Thank you; can we go?' We check out, and hit the streets. We're both struggling so we don't walk far before we enter a cafe. My head is pounding and the inside of my face feels dirty. My internal organs are battling it out to see which one can die first; it can't be any fun in there. It feels like a layer of grime is cloaking each of my organs, squeezing them, replacing them. I could have a thousand showers and still feel dirty. Aubrey orders a herbal tea, and I go for a coffee. Neither of us orders any food. I get about half way down the coffee and start to feel even more unwell. Coffee sickness. Oh no, not coffee sickness. My stomach feels like a washing machine full of shit. It's on full cycle now and the bigger logs are fragmenting into smaller pieces. It's like a poo soup in there now. I have a feeling that's how it's going to come out too. I should have had a herbal tea. I look around for the sign for the toilets. In the corner. I stroll over unsteadily and enter the toilet, leaving the chatter of the cafe behind me. I'm having a terrible time of it. My bowels are screaming in pain, like some rude person is sticking a screwdriver up my arsehole, but nothing's coming out. I sit here for some time, pushing, sweating, not pushing, sweating. After a while, content that's all I'm getting out for now, I wash up and check my reflection in the mirror. I look like shit. Some areas of my face have started to regain tautness of skin, while other areas are still enjoying the properties of elasticity. I look like Potato. I return to Aubrey and announce I have the shits.

'Thanks for the update. Do you feel fit enough to go sightseeing?' I shake my head, but we hit the streets again anyway. We walk to Lake Geneva, and the view of the lake and mountains is breath-taking. We find an empty bench and park ourselves. That was about a fifteen-minute walk and we're shattered. We're happy to recuperate in such fine surroundings, and we chat aimlessly for a while. It's a warm afternoon; there are clouds moving across the sun, but while their transit is fairly laboured, the sun is bursting through the gaps at regular intervals. I ask him what else he has in his briefcase. 'Yesterday's Y-fronts; do you want to see them?' I decline, but my intrigue has been ignited. I *will* find out what lies within. I could just ask him again.

'What else?'

'All the account paperwork…'

I'm still intrigued as to what else is in there, but I instinctively jump in, 'What? In with your dirty undies? I hope you don't have them draped over the documents.'

'Would it matter?'

'No. Are you hungry? I could find a bakery. I think one of those bready pretzel things might help. I'm not sure what else my stomach could tolerate right now.'

'Good idea, I'll have one of those too.'

I find a bakery easily enough, and try to avert my eyes from all the sweets, cakes and pastries, for fear of puking on the shop floor. I join the queue, I'm trying to look for the pretzels, but I can't see them, my eyes fall onto some doughnut type shapes, I feel ill, stop looking at them, I've started sweating, I'm nearly at the front of the queue now, I see some yellow custard type substance on a pastry, my breathing is speeding up, my stomach is folding over on itself, I feel like retching, I'm at the front of the queue and the

185

cashier is asking me something. I must look like a junkie; sweating one out. The dapper clothing is for my day in court no doubt. Must speak to the cashier. In French. I can't think of any French words. Parapluie! No, that's no fucking use. Sweat is accumulating on my face now. I know. '*Je voudrais...deux pretzels...s'il vous plait.*' Oh fuck, she's talking to me. Let me look in the cabinet and scan the items on sale, without spraying the nice woman with the contents of my stomach. I spot the pretzels and my fear turns to elation. '*Oui, oui,*' jumps out enthusiastically as I point at the fuckers. I have to get out of here before I'm violently ill. She bags up two pretzels without letting on that my sweating is disturbing her. I like her, she's well mannered. I pay for the cunts, and get out of there, right into a breeze that feels fucking fantastic. It rushes over me as if it's in a hurry, but it keeps coming and it chills the sweat on my skin. I can almost hear it whooshing through my ears, cooling my brain a little. I return to Aubrey and ease myself down onto the bench.

'What have you been doing?' He looks concerned, 'You look awful.'

'I feel worse.' I take a pretzel out of the bag, and hand him the bag. 'I had a terrible time in the bakery. Gruesome sugary monsters were looking at me, they wanted me to eat them, so they could eat me.' We both break a chunk of bread off and get to work on the chewing. I only put a small piece in, but my jaw is fucking aching by the end. That piece was maybe a thirtieth of the original formation; this is going to be hard work. We chat, chew, and try and convince ourselves that we feel better. The view of the lake and mountains is captivating, but we decide to take a wander. We're cultural fellows so we decide to spend the remainder of the afternoon visiting a few interesting galleries and museums. In truth, these places not only house works of beauty and wonder, but also have comfortable seats, clean toilets, and a cafe. We spend a nice afternoon wandering, sitting, and enjoying some beautiful works of art and pieces of history. But if I do one more horrific hangover shit, I'm going to need medical treatment. Sightseeing with a giant hangover is taking its toll, so we agree to park ourselves in a restaurant and try to eat something.

We agree on Indian food for dinner, and after looking at a few, opt for Salon Indien. The food is good, and we manage to eat most of it, but it's taking ages. We're eating slowly, giving ourselves chance to process small morsels. We both drink water during the meal; there's not even a mention of booze. We go for a walk after eating, and feeling energised, I suggest a drink. Aubrey doesn't hesitate, but reminds me we have a flight to catch in a few hours. I reassure him by saying, 'Yeah, yeah,' and ordering two beers. We're tired and can't be bothered to walk around trying different boozers; we're comfortable here, so we have a slow relaxing couple of beers. I remember the bottle of whisky. I ask the bartender for two glasses of water by saying, '*Je voudrais deux eau, s'il vous plait,*' which I know isn't right, but she kindly brings me what I asked for, without a hint of intolerance at my imperfection. I neck one glass of water, and ask Aubrey if he wants the other one or should I get rid of it. He says he'll have some water too, and takes a sip. 'Don't fucking sip it,' I reach into my bag and slyly show him the bottle. He takes to demolishing his glass of water. He can't throw back his head and chug it down. I imagine that would exert his swallowing muscles too extensively, and tenderness in the oesophagus would no doubt bother him. Aubrey sips and swigs; his chugging days are long gone. So are mine. So he sips at the glass, in what seems like a vigorous manner, but the volume of liquid doesn't appear to be decreasing. What's he doing? Rotating the water between his mouth and the glass at speed? Maybe he's rinsing before he swallows it. That's weird. I stop watching him; I don't know why I was anyway. He finishes his water and I deftly pour us a healthy measure of whisky each without being detected.

When Aubrey excuses himself to go to the toilet, I message Rosie. "Got hammered last night. I might die today. I enjoyed our time together". I leave my phone on the table. Aubrey returns and we're chatting when my phone sounds. He stops. 'Aren't you going to read your message? It might be Rosie.' My phone sounds again, and he raises his eyebrows. Before I have chance to say anything, he gets his phone out and I've lost him.

I check my phone, it is Rosie, thank fuck. "Are you pickling yourself to save on embalming fluid?" I see the second message is from Rosie too, "Don't die, you smell nice".

I message back, "Not today, I don't, I smell like someone's festival flannel". "How's your day, beautiful?"

I ask Aubrey if he wants another drink, but he suggests it would be more prudent to go to the airport. We grab our bags and jump in a taxi. I pull out the bottle of whisky, there's not much left, Aubrey declines so I finish it off as we close in on the airport. I take a final swig and drain the bottle. I tilt my head back and tip the bottle over my open mouth, trying to coax a few more drops to trickle out. I lick the rim of the bottle to get every available drop; its times like these I wish I had a lizard tongue so I could clean the inside of the bottle. I admit to him that I feel a lot better now, and he nods his appreciation. We arrive and pay the driver; I chuck the empty into the recycling, and we go through to departures. The airport is a drag as usual. We're about to board the plane, so I turn my phone to flight mode. I see I have a message from Rosie, 'Work is busy again. Can't wait to smell the flannel'. I pocket my phone and follow Aubrey aboard. We edge along the aisle at a fantastically slow speed looking for our seats. People are painfully taking an eternity to get things out of their bags, put their bags away, and finally fucking sitting down. The woman in front of Aubrey is blocking the aisle with her arse while she sorts through her bag. Why doesn't she move into the seat area to do that, and get her arse out of the way? The guy in front of her is blocking the aisle by standing there repeatedly trying to force his bag into a gap in the overhead compartment, that clearly isn't big enough. He's getting more frustrated with each shove of his bag. He's screwing up his face and shoving harder; when's he going to stop? He stops and puts his bag down; now he's trying to shove the bags in the compartment further apart, but they're not budging. So what does he do?

He picks up his bag and carries on where he left off, trying to shove his bag into that too-small-gap. Arse-woman has finally sorted her bag out and fucked off out the way, so Aubrey and I get to move forward a metre. Now we're standing by shovey-man, great.

Shovey-man sees Aubrey watching him and says, 'It won't go in.' He looks agitated, but surprisingly steps into his seat area so we can pass. I assume he went back to work on his shoving project. Aubrey and I find our seats, buckle up, relax, and flop into the first available position. When we're in the air, I order two ridiculously overpriced miniature whiskies; they are doubles at least. I wake up and we're taxing on the runway. I look over at Aubrey with blurry eyes and it looks like he's just woken up too. I recall Aubrey and I had finished our drinks and were chatting away. We must have both fallen asleep. Fucking brilliant, I feel like shit and I ache almost everywhere, but I'm glad I missed most of the flight.

We walk to the taxi rank outside, it's late and there's a chill in the air. We're both knackered and just want to get home. We drop Aubrey off first. He reminds me there's a funeral tomorrow afternoon, so he'll see me then. The drive back to mine is nauseating; I feel depleted and achey. I need sleep. I pay the driver; I must think I'm still in Switzerland because I tell him to keep the change. I get in my flat and throw my bag on the sofa. I pour a nightcap and skin up a bifta; I know I'm not going to get a decent amount of sleep, so I've already decided I'm going to be late for work tomorrow. I'm not missing anything important, and Henry and Nicholas won't mind. I finish the bifta and head off to bed, via the pisser. I put on the lamp and see Rosie has made the bed. She adds touches here and there that other people don't do. Maybe I'm guilty of elevating her everyday acts into wonderful gestures because I'm attracted to her so much. Maybe she's just a thoughtful person. I undress, get into bed and pull the duvet over me. Fucking hell, that is amazing! Clean sheets! They smell and feel so fresh. Fucking hell Rosie, nice one. I'd like to think she did it solely to put a smile on my face, but she probably couldn't take the smell anymore either. I reach for my phone, 'Thank you for the clean sheets. Can't wait to make them dirty again'.

Chapter Fourteen

I wake up, shit, shower, coffee, toast, work. I woke up fairly early, so I stick to my usual routine; I should be at work by nine thirty. If ever I'm running hideously late, I drop the toast, and have the coffee and shit at work. That's called having a flexible approach to life. I walk to work and receive a message from Rosie, "Me too. Do you want to meet tonight?"

I message back, "Yeah, I'll message you later." I find Henry in the office and apologise for being late, even though he probably hasn't noticed. I tell him I'll make the time up; he smiles and tells me I already have. He goes back to what he was doing, so I make a coffee and go to my office.

My phone rings, its Aubrey. 'Hello.'

'Hello Laszlo, I have some news. Can you talk?'

'Yeah, yeah, I've been doing it since I was a nipper. I was talking to you yesterday you fool.'

'Shut up. Verb says payment has been made.' Silencio. Not a peep from either of us. 'Are you still there?'

'Yeah. That's great.' I'm feeling excited, on edge, nervous. I want to see a bank balance with all those lovely zeros. I want to see it's real. 'What happens next?'

'Can you come to mine after work? We can have a look at the balance.'

'Yeah, no problem.' My mind is racing faster than Lewis Hamilton on heat.

'Good, see you later.' And he's gone.

My heart's going boom, boom; but I fear it will go kaboom any second now. The money's rolling in; well, the first payment has landed. Thoughts! I need some. I drink my coffee and make a plan for the morning's work; hopefully the concentration required will stop me thinking about the payment. First, I attend to the latest instalment in the never-ending chain of paperwork that circulates around the globe. Like the currents and winds that shape the landscape of our planet, so the paper currents and administration winds shape the landscape of our lives. Administration *is* wind. Excuse me, I just administrated.

Second, I wash the hearse. Third, I have a wash. Fourth, I go to Hudson's and buy a Mediterranean wrap for lunch. I always thought the woman working there was hot, but I didn't think so today. I'm in my shed eating when there's a knock. 'Come in,' I can't be bothered to stand up. The door opens; it's Aubrey. I'm sitting in the armchair, so he sits in the other chair that's still here.

'I mentioned the word retirement recently.' He looks at me as I'm chomping on the wrap, chewing like a demented camel because some lettuce has become attached to my upper left molars. 'I'm going to talk to Henry today about officially retiring my position here.' He's looking at me like he's not happy; I thought he'd be delighted to retire to Florida, or wherever he chooses.

'Gu fhor yhoo,' I shift the stubborn lettuce and compose myself, 'you deserve it. I plan on doing the very same.' I'm grinning like a demented camel that's just got rid of some stubborn lettuce from its molars. Aubrey's not smiling. There's another knock on the door; currently the most popular door on the premises. 'Come in,' I shout convincingly. It's Nicholas.

He greets us both warmly, 'Can you be ready in thirty minutes gentlemen?' He's formal on funeral days, and it suits him. We both agree and he leaves contented. Aubrey leaves to get changed, so I skin up a bifta and go somewhere else. Funerals are a doddle when the process becomes familiar, and listening to people crying gets easier with practice; but some mourners are heart-breaking. It depends what mood I'm in, and a bifta helps take the edge off the devastating sorrow I encounter. It's Climbey Clive today, the man who had too many drinks and forgot his limitations. I meet Aubrey at the hearse, and we drive to the crematorium. We unload the body at the rear entrance and wheel him to the chapel. As we're leaving the chapel, the family are arriving. We nod respectfully to those that look as us, and move slowly across the reception to the rear of the building. I see one woman is the centre of attention; she must be his wife. There's a boy and a girl standing close to her, both teenagers; must be his kids. It's clear they've already been crying. I don't think they'll be getting pissed tonight and climbing walls; one final life lesson from the old man. We get out of here before the wailing starts.

On the drive back, Aubrey mentions retirement again, but again he doesn't look best pleased with the notion. There's something he's not telling me. I could push him for it, but that's not my style and he wouldn't appreciate it. He'll tell me when he wants to. I decide to keep it light and ask him when he plans on retiring. 'Next month probably, I need to talk to Henry later,' he definitely answered my question, but he's not his usual chatty self.

'Are you and Maureen planning on spending more time together?'

'Yes, it's great being back together.' It feels like he's going to say more, but he doesn't.

So I ask. 'Are you two planning on moving to Florida together?'

He shoots me a look, and fixes me with a friendly but curious expression. He looks back to the road. We don't speak for the remainder of the journey. I'm thinking about what I'm going to do with my share of the money; and what is it that he hasn't told me? We get back and agree that I'll go to his house after work, and he heads off to talk to Henry. I spend the rest of the afternoon in the prep room working on a new arrival Nicholas collected while we were away. Fifteen year old boy; multiple stab wounds. What a wonderful world we live in. I finish late, lock up, and walk to Aubrey's.

We chat for a bit before firing up his laptop and getting out the Swiss paperwork. Aubrey's translating the documents, but the website is in English, so this should be a piece of piss. We activate our online account by inputting the account numbers from the Swiss papers, and creating a password. I suggest a variation on Maureen's name, and Aubrey likes it. It doesn't take a tremendous amount of time and here we are; both of us staring at the screen, at the balance. What a beautiful number. Exactly as agreed. We peel our eyes away from the screen to look at each other's expressions of amazement and excitement, then back at the screen again. Zero means nothing, but when you get some together like this, and stick a higher number in front of them, it means a lot more. Aubrey fetches us a drink each, while I carry on looking at the screen to make sure we didn't just have a joint hallucination. Though I could now be having a solo one while he's out the room. He returns and we discuss the money, and the plan for future payments. He tells me that subsequent payments will be approximately monthly, and on different dates. We don't want it to look like a direct debit, so it will be differing amounts on different dates. The next payment is of a smaller amount in three weeks. Fucking hell, I can hardly believe this. I ask him how his chat went with Henry.

'I finish at Partridges next month.' He looks saddened; he's good friends with Henry and Nicholas. Quitting work and moving to Florida should mean he won't see them again. You never know, but it's doubtful.

'I know you'll miss the place, and the lads, but your retirement looks pretty rosy from here.' We look at each other, look around the room, drink our drinks, look at each other again. 'Are you moving to Florida with Maureen?'

'That's the plan. Laszlo…it is easy for me to leave Partridges because I'm old, and retirement is the natural progression. If the Figgs ever decided to reinvestigate Partridges for their missing parcel, my absence would not arouse suspicion.' He stops. I don't know if he's thinking, or giving me time to think.

'Of course,' I say smiling, 'They were probably wondering how you were still…' I suddenly realise what he means, 'What do you mean?' I'm not smiling anymore.

'It may arouse suspicion if you suddenly left town.'

'A, how would they know I'd left town, and B, how would they find me?'

'Don't be naive,' he says quite quickly, then thoughtfully asks, 'would you want to risk it?' We look at each other for a moment and I silently shake my head. We sit contemplating the situation, until he breaks the silence. 'One idea is that you continue working at Partridges for a while, until things blow over. Once the situation has cooled down, you can casually leave Stumpton.'

'Do you have any other ideas?'

'You could quit your job and leave Stumpton…and take your chances.' He doesn't look happy. I have the feeling he and Maureen, and maybe even Verb, have discussed this, and he doesn't like the conclusion either. But he knows it's for the best, otherwise he wouldn't have mentioned it.

'How long is a while?'

'I don't know. Until it blows over. Six months?' I shoot him a look that I hope conveys my utter dismay at that fucking suggestion. 'Maybe more,' and he shrugs, fucking shrugs!

'What? Fuck off, six months, maybe more! It's all right for you sunshine, fucking off to Florida with the lovely Maureen, while I'm living in the same city as the Figgs for the next six months.' At least we're both smiling now.

'It's up to you Laszlo, I can only offer advice. I want you to avoid suspicion, I would prefer it if you stayed alive, and we remained friends for many years.' We're both still smiling at each other, and he takes a timeout to look at his hands before carrying on. 'You are a dear friend, one of the best, and I feel things are going to get better for us.'

I sigh, 'Okay you old cunt, I'll stay at work until this shit blows over. Enjoy Florida.' We both laugh, 'I suppose the good thing is, I'll be able to spend more time with Rosie; see how that works out. I feel like I don't want to miss this opportunity. It was looking like this thing with the diamonds, and shit loads of money, was going to get in the way.'

'Will you tell her?'

'I feel like I want to, but the wisest thing would be to wait until I'm in the clear before I tell her. For her safety it's best she doesn't know. And it will give us the chance to get to know each other properly, without me being rich hanging over us.'

'I agree.'

'Thanks.'

He knocks back the last of his whisky, 'Do you want another?' I nod and he goes off to the kitchen. I have a little think while he's gone, and I reckon I've got a good idea. He returns with the bottle and pours us another.

'I'm nervous about receiving a transfer of a large sum of money into my bank account in Stumpton. This might sound paranoid, but what if the Figgs know someone who works in the bank? I don't want to attract their attention. And the same goes for you and Maureen too. You should open up a bank account in Florida before you transfer any money; hopefully the Figgs don't have associates there too. In the meantime you can make purchases using the credit card. Verb should be in the clear to transfer money to, the Figgs don't know about him.' I don't let him speak, I'm on a roll. 'If I buy a few nice things, maybe expensive things; I'll draw attention to myself. So I don't need much money right now. So as well as using my continued employment at Partridges as a cover for my new found wealth; a lack of purchases will also indicate my shitty financial situation has continued unimpeded. For the few months I remain in Stumpton, I can maybe have some petty cash so I can buy a better brand of whisky.'

He's thinking about it, and I let him get on with it. I haven't finished yet; my good idea is coming up. But I'll let him digest that nugget first. 'SIX months,' he says soberly. Then cracks up.

'You're fucking enjoying this aren't you?' I give him a peeved look, 'You'd better send me a postcard.'

'You can come and visit.' He knocks back another drink; we are celebrating after all.

'I will.' I pour us another drink and press on, 'As I don't need my share for another SIX months, there's no point it sitting in the account doing nothing. You three share it out, so you can set yourselves up quicker. You can spend what you like overseas and the Figgs won't know. When I'm in the clear and leave Stumpton, maybe I'll have a bigger share of the next payment, to set myself up, and it'll even itself out. What do you fucking think of THAT?' I take a smiling swig of my drink; celebrating that one.

He takes his sweet time in answering, and I'm about to ask him again, when he decides to chirp in. 'That is a wonderful idea. Are you sure?' I nod. 'Thank you. You're taking this tremendously well, Laszlo.' I shrug. 'It is a generous offer and I know Maureen and Verb will be thankful too. That reminds me, Verb is planning to invest in a property in Amsterdam. Which will be handy for visiting the Dam.' I nod and drink my whisky. That will be handy indeed. 'Maureen and I will put our properties on the market, she wants to sell fast and never come back, so she's going to offer it for less than the asking price. I might do the same, but for me there's no rush. We'll have sufficient funds to invest in a property in Florida. We've already looked at a few online.'

We finish our drinks and I leave him to make calls to Maureen and Verb, to let them know the payment has landed. I walk home and message Rosie, asking if she wants to come round. It starts to rain, and I'm not even at the end of the street before it starts bucketing it down. The rain is hungry, it's biting my face. It's like thousands of miniature barracudas streaking through the damp atmosphere, heading straight for me. They bite my skin before bouncing off; only to be replaced by more of the fishy fuckers. I'm being battered, and I'm getting soaked. I get home and undress; I dry my hair and find fresh clothes. I'm putting my wet clothes in the washing machine, when my buzzer sounds. It's Rosie; I buzz her in. She comes through the front door soaked to the skin; her hair plastered to her skull. I suggest she takes her clothes off and hang them up to dry, which is a helpful suggestion. I then extend my current mood of helpfulness by assisting her with the removal of her clothes. What a nice chap I am. She dries her hair with the towel I'd thrown on the floor, and I hang her clothes up. I can't keep my eyes off her. Her body is fucking amazing.

'As I'm currently in the buff, do you fancy a catch-up fuck?' She gives me a slow twirl, and I start getting hard. She runs into the bedroom and I chase after her. One hearty fuck later, we're lying on the bed chatting, 'How was Geneva?'

'Great. We got tremendously pissed and did some sightseeing with giant hangovers. I had the shits all day, and I think Aubrey was in the same boat, but he didn't talk about each one after.' Suddenly her stomach growls in a few different pitches. Almost like syllables.

'I'm hungry too, shall we order a takeaway?' We remember I don't have any food in, and make our choices. I phone the order through, and the guy tells me it will be at least an hour. I grab us some peanut butter from the kitchen, and we engage in another fantastic fuck. She wants me to come on her, and I'm only too happy to oblige; until she uses my fresh T-shirt to wipe up my muck. We're having a wash when the buzzer sounds. I inform the delivery guy I'm coming down, and take the long way around the garden to remain undercover. The delivery guy is soaked, so I give him a decent tip. Back in the flat Rosie has an assortment of crockery ready on the kitchen table, and we attack the food cartons with enthusiasm, pouring their contents onto plates and dishes. We share vegetable samosas, sag aloo, vegetable masala, mushroom rice and garlic naan. We eat hungrily, nothing is left.

We have a smoke and a glass of wine on the sofa with The Gotan Project playing in the background. 'What are your plans for the weekend?' I pass her the bifta, and exhale.

'I said I'd go out for drinks tomorrow with some people from work. Do you want to come?'

'Maybe, I might catch up with Eddie.'

'We're going down The Waxing Gibbons, ask him to come.'

'I'll put it to him.' She's only got my T-shirt on, not the mucky one; she got a clean one from the drawer. I had to do the same. I've only got six T-shirts; I'll have to do another fucking wash soon. She's sitting with her feet on the sofa, knees up, facing me, exposing herself as we chat. 'What are your plans for next week?' I ask her.

'I haven't got any as such, why?' She passes me the bifta.

'It's just that we've seen a lot of each other since Anton's party…and I was wondering if you thought continuing that was a good idea.'

'What? What the fuck was that? Ask me properly.'

'Dear Rosie, would you like to officially enter into a relationship with me, one that has no predetermined end date?'

'That's better,' she says in a school mistress way, 'Yes, I would.' Her expression changes, she's going for that naughty look now, 'Am I your girlfriend now?' She's teasing me and I love it. 'Will you introduce me to people as your girlfriend?'

'I won't be introducing you to anyone.'

'Why?' She should be an actor, she going for hurt now, and she's good.

'Because you're embarrassing.' I'm pretty convincing too, at least for this play.

She smiles and asks, 'Is this embarrassing?' and starts touching her pussy and easing in fingers. She carries on for a while, moaning, then takes the bifta out of my hand with her wet fingers, takes a drag, throws it in the ashtray, and straddles me. She lets me loose, and slides down me. Sometime later, I come so hard I can see into outer space. I'm travelling through space. I'm travelling so fast I'm flying past celestial bodies at a great speed, but seeing them in minute detail. My legs give way and I flop onto the sofa; the jolt brings me back to the confines of my flat. I think Rosie died; she also flopped on the sofa and hasn't moved since.

'Are you dead?' I ask with a voice expressing no interest, as I'm skinning up.

'Yeah, what will you do with my body?' she still hasn't moved.

'Just leave you there. I might sit you up and put a glass in your hand. I can come home and tell you about my day.' I light the bifta, and reach for the bottle of wine. I refill our glasses, and she sits up and gives me a kiss. 'I have an idea.'

I'm on a fucking roll with ideas today, and here's another cracker. 'How about we take a trip to Amsterdam in the near future? I have a friend who is about to invest in a property there, and we could pay him a visit when he's there. You'd like him; he's a cool guy.'

'Sounds great. Let's do it.'

'Rosie?' She looks at me, waiting. 'Have you ever considered living overseas?'

'Yeah, that could be good. I think every time I've travelled, I said I wanted to live there. One of my friends moved to Barcelona last year too, so it's something that's been on my mind. What about you?'

'Yeah, I've been thinking about it. I'm not mad about staying in Stumpton for the rest of my life.'

'Me neither,' she kisses me gently and takes a swig of wine.

'We should go on several holidays, suss out some nice places to live.'

'Sounds good to me. I'll think of some places we could go.'